I0702323

Conversations With My Darling

A NOVEL BY

Marquita Antoine

ISBN: Paperback 979-8-9887397-0-8
ISBN: Hardback 979-8-9887397-1-5
ISBN: E-Book 979-8-9887397-2-2

Library of Congress Control Number: 2023916428
Published: Lakeland, FL

To my Mama.
Your love was found in your consistency.
Your love was found in passing on your love for God.
Thank you.

Acknowledgments

There are not many words that can express the depth of gratitude and hesitancy one experiences as he or she releases their heart to the world.

The Lord birthed a vision within me in this novel and it could not have been realized without the many prayers and encouraging words of a select few that I chose to share the vision with. Thank you all for partnering with me on this journey.

Friendship is invaluable and something I didn't think I would experience on a grand scale initially. Thank you to the four women closest to me that have been privy to the insecurities and doubts along this road to publication. Let's just say you know who you are.

Amanda Diaz, editor, and my "fridge" friend, although you are within the aforementioned four, I must say the Lord gifted you to me. I admire your dedication and the excellency in which you do all things, including friendship. You are one of a kind. A million thanks for your efforts in making this book a reality.

My husband, my king, there is not enough space within this page to lavish my gratitude and love upon you. "You had me at hello" and it's been the best decision I've made. Thank you for your steadied support and sacrifices.

Lastly, my children. Each hug and encouraging, "Mama, you got this," truly helped carry me along. I love you beyond words and pray you learn even more about me through my writings.

"Let this be recorded for future generations so that people not yet born will praise the Lord."

– Ps 102:18

"Emma! Emma!" Mama sure could scream for a lady of few words.

Sometimes I wondered if there was another person hidden within her.

"Yes ma'am?"

Southern manners were nonnegotiable in my home. The word "ma'am" took on different meanings depending on how it was used. I found myself reciting it when I was unsure how to respond, when I had a question or as a simple acknowledgement that I had heard what Mama had just spoken.

Sometimes a man would say ma'am to greet a woman, wish her well, or to lock eyes with her for a moment longer as he held the door open for her.

Mama had warned, "Emma. Never look a man in the eyes for more than two seconds. It's rude, invites trouble and makes you look like you don't come from a good home."

I swear she made up some of the silliest rules just to make my life miserable.

"Emma Rose Griggs!!"

I knew by the tone in Mama's voice, that coming down the stairs slowly was not an option. Plus, she had now added my middle name into the equation, cementing her displeasure.

"Yes ma'am. Yes ma'am, here I am. I'm sorry, I was just—"

"Emma, don't make me call you so many times."

Mama looked irritated and out of sorts as she gripped an opened white envelope.

"I'm sorry Mama. I got distracted."

I shifted my stance slightly, annoyed that I had to admit that my attention was drawn away yet again. She had always urged me to be aware. Apparently being distracted could cause me to miss out on what was right in front of me—whatever that was supposed to mean.

I tried to salvage our interaction by impressing her, hoping the impatience on her face would wash away. "Mama I was trying to remember the key passage of scripture from yesterday's sermon. I really enjoyed it."

"Uh huh."

She wasn't moved, knowing that it was Psalms 23, a passage I had memorized a long time ago. It was worth a shot though, because I hated it when she looked at me with disappointment in her eyes. I didn't want to let her down, but I felt as if I did so often.

Although I didn't know much about her, I had learned to know Mama as a God-fearing woman whose standards were rooted in what the Bible had to say. Being regarded as a good Christian woman in our church congregation's eyes involved teaching Sunday School once a month, yet she managed to do it every week. Besides that, she was always packing up food to send off to our neighbors— Mrs. Hennagen in particular.

It baffled me because we could easily be classified as poor ourselves. We didn't have enough to share what little we did have. In those moments, it was as if Mama could read my mind.

"I just can't not help someone who needs something, Emma Rose. That would be selfish. God will work it out for us. He always has and always will."

"Mother Griggs" was what most people called her at church. I wasn't sure how she had earned the title "Mother" as opposed to "Sister" because most other women at church were addressed as "Sister something or another." In my opinion, she wasn't even old enough to be counted as a Church Mother. Mrs. Hennagen, who was near ancient, had lived long enough to deserve the title, but Mama wasn't even fifty yet.

Plus, she was my mama, no one else's. I didn't like the feeling that other people were staking a claim on her. It was bad enough I had to share her with my cousin Maddie. We hardly ever saw eye to eye on anything. I think that's why Mama had always made reading the Bible a priority for Maddie and me. She wanted us to be able to connect to the characters and understand that they were human just like us. She probably hoped we'd figure out a way to work through our differences, but the only problem was that I couldn't determine if the stories were meant to guide and encourage me or to place fear in my heart and reinforce how a "proper" person should behave in God's eyes.

After all that was always high on Mama's list: *proper* behavior, which did not come easily for me. I mean it was hard enough to keep up with the list of rules Mama managed to enforce based on her beliefs in God let alone those heaped on by school, family and "becoming a woman." Proper behavior just sounded convoluted. Maybe I was like one of those defective manufactured items that needed to be recalled.

A forced whistle rang out from the tea kettle on the stove, snatching me from my thoughts, while simultaneously rescuing me from Mama's reprimand. She dropped the white envelope onto the table and hurried to remove the black pot from the stove.

Mama loved a good herbal tea. In her eyes, it could cure just about anything. Anything, except Daddy's condition.

"Mama, did you need me?" I stood in anticipation of why she had summoned me in the first place.

"Oh yes. I need you to go and drop something off to Mrs. Hennagen for me, but make sure you take Maddie with you."

"Mama, I'm almost eighteen. I can manage alone."

I decided against an accompanying eye roll, thinking how much I would actually like to make it to my birthday this year.

It wasn't just the fact that I was almost an adult and Mama still didn't trust me to walk alone two blocks up the street that bothered me. It was also that she would make me bring Maddie along and Maddie, simply put, just drove me crazy.

She was Aunt Joleen's daughter and Aunt Joleen wasn't, well…she wasn't exactly like Mama. She had wound up pregnant at a young age and was unmarried when Maddie was born, making her the rebel of the family. Luckily, she was so beautiful that having a child didn't keep her from having prospective boyfriends. Too many in my opinion.

Her latest boyfriend, Paul, decided at some point that he no longer wanted to be with a woman with a kid because out of nowhere, in the middle of the night, here comes Maddie, with a pillowcase full of belongings on our doorstep.

I remembered that night so vividly. Mama had been left standing on the front porch with her housecoat and bonnet on shouting, "Joleen! Joleen! You can't keep doing this!" as Aunt Joleen's car disappeared into the darkness.

Maddie was left looking at me and Mama with the gaze of an abandoned doe. I think we were all in shock as we stood there in the dusk as if Aunt Joleen would suddenly have a pang of conscience, walk back up the road after having told Paul where he could go and scoop Maddie up into her arms. But no, that didn't happen, and we eventually headed back indoors, leaving the hope of Aunt Joleen's return in the night.

It wasn't Maddie's living with us that drove me crazy or the fact that I had to share a room and essentials with her. It didn't even bother me that she was little Miss Sunshine at school. What absolutely infuriated me was the fact that although she had every right in the world to be angry and disgruntled, nothing seemed to upset her. She never cried, complained, or even rolled her eyes like every other normal living teenager. She was always optimistic.

I wanted to shout in her face sometimes, "Don't you care?! Aren't you furious? Cry! Throw something!!"

But nope, Maddie was the most collected and gorgeous girl I knew. She reminded me of the quintessential young woman from movies that was described as unaware of how beautiful she was.

She had the perfect hazelnut complexion, light brown eyes, soft facial features and most cooperative hair. Her body was proportionate and she was the not-too-short that it makes you feel awkward and not-too-tall that you tower over your peers kind of height. And although Maddie never wore form fitting clothing (besides Mama would never have that anyways) it was hard to miss her appealing body shape—long legs, curvaceous areas, toned arms, and an elongated neck that accented her slightly deepened cheek bones.

Any boy that I had known to meet her found her desirable and every girl at Peachtree High acknowledged her beauty. She was either oblivious to it all or she just didn't care, but either way, it annoyed me. Her perfect-ness and ability to move forward without a care in the world made my flaws stick out even more.

"Uh huh, almost eighteen and still getting distracted."

Mama crossed her arms, her irritation at my runaway thoughts had returned.

"But Mama, Maddie is only one month older than me and I'm not incapable of walking on my own…" My voice trailed off as I mumbled the last few words.

Mama cut her eyes toward me as a final warning.

"Emma Rose, you better watch that mouth of yours. God says to not be disobedient to your parents. Besides you 'never miss your water til your well runs dry.' You're gonna miss me when I'm gone one day."

"Oh Mama!"

I couldn't count how many times I had heard that from her. As I had gotten older, we didn't talk as much but that saying probably took up at least forty percent of the words she aimed toward me.

"You will find out one day. My mama died when I was a young girl and I'd never talk back to her the way you do me. Now go get Maddie. I want to get this to Mrs. Hennagen before it gets cold."

Mama grimaced as she picked the white envelope up once more before sitting down at the table. I wanted to know what was inside of it but dared not ask since I had already gotten on her bad side.

Patience was something that I needed to develop a bit more of, but I knew when to let things go and this was one of those times. If she had wanted me to know what was written on the letter she'd have told me. Plus, Mama didn't tend to let on about what she was thinking or feeling most of the time anyhow.

It was the recognizable expression she wore that made me nervous. Her furrowed eyebrows carried a sense of heaviness like the days right before Daddy had died, almost four years ago. I couldn't understand it then but now I knew he had met the definition of the term "functioning" alcoholic.

Mama had always said it was the war that had actually killed him; that he was never the same when he had come back home. She believed that no boy should have had to go off and fight in a war, see such horrible things and then be expected to return to a country that didn't understand what he had been through nor had the resources to truly help him.

I pushed the thought out of my mind as I hurried up the steps to get Maddie. That was one memory I didn't care to dwell on.

"Is everything okay Emma Rose?" Maddie must have felt the tension of my footsteps.

I hated being called Emma Rose but her and Mama had adopted it long ago so I had to accept it. Additionally, when Maddie spoke my name, it was in an annoyingly chipper voice such as that of if hummingbirds could speak. Sure, it was my given name, but you didn't hear me going around calling them by their middle names. Mama would lose it if I ever tried such a stunt.

It was understood that legacy was important in our family. The expectation was to name your child after an aunt or grandmother. So, I suppose I could be thankful that Mama didn't do further damage by placing Emma Louise or Emma Gertrude on my birth certificate. Aunt Rose was probably the best pick out of all my great aunts. There was Rose, Louise, Gertrude, better known as Gerdy and Mahelda. Maybe it wasn't Mama's goal to set out to embarrass me and she had just picked the best option from what was available. However, mentioning my entire name so regularly wasn't necessary.

Mama's birth name was Ruthie after her maternal grandmother and Aunt Joleen was named after her paternal one. Maddie was named on a whim, however. Supposedly her middle name, Lyn, was inspired from Aunt Joleen's love of a boutique store in town called

Georgia Lyn. I heard that Big Mama, Mama's grandmother, had a lot to say about that.

"Emma Rose?"

Maddie was now standing in the doorway of the bathroom since I hadn't responded to her the first time.

"Everything okay?"

"Yeah. Mama wants us to go drop a plate off at Mrs. Hennagen's."

"Okay, let me grab a jacket." Maddie bounced into the room without any questions.

Whenever Mama asked her to do something, she jumped straight to it without any extra thought. I wanted to ask her what she was doing in the bathroom. Wasn't it important? Aren't you annoyed you have to stop just because Mama said so? It would do no good though. Maddie would only respond with some irritating positive adage such as: "Now Emma Rose, it does no good trying to change what you have no control over."

If that was her response today, she would be right because there was no getting out of whatever it was that Mama wanted done in this precise moment. I just wished Maddie would at least become cross or something. Anything to let on that she really was a human teenager and not some preprogrammed friendly robot.

"All ready," Maddie reappeared dressed in her favorite jacket.

It was faded red denim with lots of wear but passed as trendy at school. Other people only saw a gorgeous girl that made anything, such as that old jacket look fancy. But I knew the story behind it.

When Maddie was dropped off on our doorstep, she had almost no belongings with her. She was wearing a ratty t-shirt, shorts, sandals and was holding a dirty pillowcase with a couple of things inside. I guess Aunt Joleen was maternal enough to realize that the chilliness of the night required a jacket, so she had placed her own over nine-year-old Maddie's back.

She could have kept that too big jacket as far as I was concerned. It couldn't protect Maddie from all the other coldness she would experience awaiting her mom's return. But Maddie loved that thing and wore it anytime Mama would allow. She would try to wear it in the summers too, but Mama forbade it for fear she'd have a heat stroke. It had always been baggy on her, but she didn't care how she looked while wearing it. Now that she was older, she had grown into it, and it fit perfectly.

The jacket, itself, though, had become a part of Maddie's identity. She was almost a different person when she wasn't allowed to wear it. What Mama didn't know is that was the one area that Maddie did disobey her in. Towards the end of the school year when summer was approaching, Maddie would still carry it to school in her backpack.

"Okay, let's go." Maddie readjusted her collar once more as she headed down the steps.

I followed behind her taking notice that Mama had now moved to the front sitting area and was drinking her tea as she looked out the window. Her eyes were full of concern yet blank simultaneously. She sat gazing out the screen door, no doubt observing the beautiful fall day. The sun was beginning to set and the array of colors within the clouds complimented the leaves that had begun changing hues.

Mama would often sit in the front room so she could see her flower garden. It held hydrangeas, roses and small bushes that didn't bring forth any flowers at all. What I loved about that room was that it gave a direct view of our porch and the swing that hung at the east side of it. "Missums" is what I called her.

The porch swing is where I'd retreat when Mama got in one of her moods or when I needed to escape Maddie's awful humming and sashaying around. I'd come out and sit on Missums for hours. Honestly, that swing was like my next best friend. It knew all my secrets. I'd sit on it with one leg perched up, head tilted back and close my eyes as the wind blew through my curls.

My curls resembled that of a loose afro. The front and back part of my hair was especially loosely textured, but the middle was a bit tighter coiled. When Mama would help me grease my scalp, she'd get to the middle and exclaim, "Oh my! Who's in there?!"

We would laugh because neither of us had a clue as to why the middle of my hair was coarser than the rest. It never formed a round afro, nor did it hang loose enough towards my back like Maddie's.

Her curls were loose and reached her shoulder blades. Some girls called her hair *Wet and Wavy* like the weave, only Maddie's was natural.

I tended to gently tie my hair up to form a poof but whenever I'd take a seat upon Missums, I'd have the urge to release the ponytail and let my hair behave wildly. I didn't know if it was an act of defiance against Mama's desires for me to be presentable at all times or an act of freedom on my behalf, but it made me happy nonetheless.

"Maddie, carry this gently, it has a few eggs on top and I don't want them to break."

Mama handed her a bag for Mrs. Hennagen and then looked over towards me.

"Emma Rose don't be dazing off while y'all are gone. Pay attention. You need to be aware of your surroundings, you hear me?"

"Yes ma'am."

"Okay girls hurry up and go so you can get back."

I thought of how the exchange that had just occurred was typical. Mama spoke to Maddie lovingly as she entrusted her with what was important. For me, just a stern warning: dry and matter of fact.

I followed Maddie out the front door, and we began heading towards Mrs. Hennagen's house.

Chapter One

Mrs. Hennagen opened the front door of her small home. She didn't have a large porch like we did but had just enough space for us to step up and knock. A white metal awning shaded our heads while we waited. We had learned to anticipate a wait due to her age. She didn't move very fast.

A small garden sat beneath the front window with a few yellow azaleas growing next to her "Stokes Dwarf" shrubs. Another door was situated along the side of her house where a white faded wooden banister and four steps led the way into the secondary access. The door opened directly into Mrs. Hennagan's kitchen, but we only entered that way if she shouted for us to do so.

"Hello girls," Mrs. Hennagen smiled expectantly.

"Good evening." We replied, almost in unison.

A whiff of sweet potato pie hit my nose as soon as the door opened. Mama had mentioned how great a baker Mrs. Hennagen had been before she had to "slow down." The smell was intoxicating, especially as we approached the kitchen.

Her home had a small sitting room right off the doorway but after about ten steps you were practically in the kitchen.

"It smells amazing in here." Maddie allowed herself to be overcome by the pie.

I must admit that was one of the only perks of having to bring things over to Mrs. Hennagen. She always had some desert or fresh bread to enjoy.

"You can just sit that bag over on the table for me, Madison." Maddie carefully placed the bag on the kitchen table and smiled at Mrs. Hennagen.

"Aunt Ruthie says there are some eggs in there for you. I'd be happy to put them away for you if you'd like."

An unspoken rule was *never*, unless given specific permission, go into someone else's bag. We usually never knew what was inside of the plastic bags, aside from food that Mama had us bring to Mrs. Hennagen. Unless, however, we had seen Mama pack the bag with something specific.

"Thank you, Madison. I'll get those now." Mrs. Hennagen reached over and opened the bag, retrieving the eggs.

Her dark brown hands were full of wrinkles. Her fingers were thin and sometimes shook even when she wasn't moving them. Her fingernails were cut short and she still wore her wedding ring even though her husband, Pastor Hennagen, our previous church pastor, had passed on a little after Daddy died.

The church had always looked in on Mrs. Hennagen to make sure she had everything she needed. Mama made it her personal mission to make certain she was doing well since we lived on the same street. Our living close by somehow increased the expectation that we needed to be available for Mrs. Hennagen.

"The church can't do everything alone, Emma. It's our job to help." Mama frequently reminded me.

"Well Darling, how are you doing? You're quiet as usual." Mrs. Hennagen particularly liked calling me Darling for some reason.

I guess either I or my name was unmemorable for her. I couldn't figure out for the life of me why she could remember Madison but not Emma—a two syllable name.

"I'm well, ma'am," I responded, trying not to sound annoyed.

"Looks like the weather is coolin' now. Fall is finally here. You girls ready for it to cool off?"

When Mrs. Hennagen tried making conversation, the weather was always her go to. There was hardly anything an elderly lady and teen girls had in common, let alone were able to talk about without some sort of awkward silence.

"Yes ma'am. Fall is the best time of year. The absolute best." Maddie beamed, unbothered. If she were outside, she would probably be twirling as she said it.

"Mmm hmm, I've always been fond of the fall too."

Mrs. Hennagen agreed before looking towards me hoping for a response.

I gave a slight smile as I shifted my stance, thinking how I wished we could just drop the bag off and go. I'd much rather be at home right now. Tomorrow was the last day of school before fall break and I had to give my final answer to my teacher about what senior assignment I had chosen.

At Peachtree High, when you were a senior, you had to participate in a final senior assignment. If you were in an extracurricular activity such as the debate club, chess club, theater, or sports, you were allowed to use the meets and games towards fulfilling the assignment. However, I was not into any of those things and students like myself, who could live without the joys of extracurricular activities, had to fulfill a much different assignment. The options were pretty slim: (1) Create your own approved after school activity with three participants or more; (2) complete a speech and present it in front of a teaching panel on the benefits of education and how you will plan to leave your mark on the world after graduation; or (3) volunteer at a government funded center for 60 hours and write a short paper of what was learned during the experience.

In Byron, we were short on government funded centers so that pretty much meant volunteering at the public library, courthouse, city food bank or going to the neighboring city and volunteering at the juvenile detention center. All of these were a huge no for me so I had no clue as to what I could choose.

"I know you all have school tomorrow so I'll let y'all get home, but can you help me out by taking your mama some of this sweet potato pie? And if you really wanna help me out, will you take a slice for yourself too?"

"Yes ma'am!" Maddie and I both exclaimed, agreeing on something for the first time that evening.

****

Peachtree High wasn't the most eye appealing building. It was a one story, all-red brick building with huge black letters that read "Peachtree High" on the front roof. There was a little marquee that sat in the grass adjacent to the front sidewalk and the only time I cared what was written on it was when it reminded us of our holiday breaks.

One more day until fall break, I thought to myself to help motivate me in getting on with the day.

It wasn't what I learned in school that irked me. The learning itself was fine, and sort-of expected. It was the extra shenanigans that teenage boys and girls brought to the environment that I could do with less of.

The first morning bell rang as I walked through the doors and headed to my locker. I had seven minutes for my passing period so I walked quickly.

"See ya later, Emma Rose." Maddie cheerfully went off toward her class.

I sputtered a bye under my breath.

"Hey Emma."

Terry waved at me as I grabbed my precalculus book and shut my locker. I could count on him to be there every morning to greet me and walk with me to pre-calc.

"Hey Terry, ready?"

"Yeah, I'm always ready. It's you that's always late, remember?"

"Whatever." I laughed, knowing he was right.

"Seriously, Emma, hurry up we are going to be late...again." Terry shouted back at me as he increased his pace towards Mrs. Lee's classroom.

He was thinner than the average boy for his age and always complained about how he needed to get his weight up to at least 175 pounds.

"Anybody who is 6 '1 must be at least 175 pounds, Emma. Otherwise, it just looks as if they are starving."

I could hear his voice inside my head and giggled knowing that he would never make it. His parents were just as skinny. But I'd never burst his bubble and would continue to let him dream.

He always wore his shirt tucked into his pants and God forbid if he forgot his belt. On the rare occasion he did forget to wear one, our day would be ruined because he'd be so obsessed with not having one on. Today, his beloved belt was intact, his khaki pants were neatly ironed, and his glasses sat in place over his ears.

He turned back to look at me as the tardy bell rang. His perfectly round brown face was filled with concern as he made sure I was behind him and had made it into the classroom on time. His expression relaxed once he realized we had made it. I couldn't make out if he was more worried that I'd be late, and he would have to endure pre-calc alone while I went to the office for a tardy pass, or if he was just being protective.

We were best friends and I suppose that's what best friends did even if one friend was a boy and the other a girl. We had become accustomed to each other's presence. If either one of us were missing, it made the other uneasy. Yep, completely normal, I told myself.

"Good morning class," Mrs. Lee began her usual teacher spill.

"Today we are going to pick up where we left off yesterday: functions."

The class groaned. Most teachers gave you a free class before any holiday breaks, but not Mrs. Lee. She was determined to kill any sense of joy we had today. I suppose crushing kids' dreams was one of her goals in life.

Mrs. Lee laughed as she began writing on the board. "Come on everyone. Turn to page 172 in your textbooks. You have plenty of time to goof off during your break."

I tried to concentrate on the domains, ranges and rules Mrs. Lee was going over, but I just couldn't. I still hadn't decided on what my end-of-year project would be. Plus, I tried to look for the white envelope last night that Mama was fiddling with but couldn't find it. Normally I wouldn't dare touch her things, but I needed to know what was inside of it. I had bigger concerns than how the elements of set A paired relationally to the elements of set B. At least, I think that's what Mrs. Lee was saying. Besides, I could do precalculus in my sleep. Math had always come easily for me. I looked down at the options on the sheet in front of me:

It is the time of year in which your Class of 1993 Peachtree senior student must select an End-of-Year Project. Your student will be expected to work diligently toward this task and will likely need your support fulfilling this project. The options are: (1) Participate in an approved extracurricular program that has some competition level meets; (2) Organize an approved extracurricular program with three or more members; (3) Prepare a 15-minute speech with a visual aid on how his or her education has helped shape his or her beliefs thus far and how it will aid him or her in future endeavors. Your student will need to be able to recite this speech in front of the school faculty and volunteers. The speech must be approved beforehand, and your student must be prepared for feedback and questions during this 15-minute timeframe; or (4) Pick an approved site to volunteer for 60 hours during the remainder of the school year.

All hours must be logged and signed off by the site director as well as an essay written by the student recounting his or her experiences and how it has helped them grow as an individual.

Ugh. I sighed heavily as I laid my head down on my desk before looking toward Terry who I knew would be staring at me. That boy noticed any and everything that I did.

He mouthed the words, "Pay attention."

Sometimes he just didn't get the weight I felt. Out of all the people in my life, he was the closest to me but remained clueless on how stressed I was. He was either unaware or thought I was being dramatic and refused to acknowledge it.

The bell rang but I sat glued in my seat because there was no use trying to sneak by Mrs. Lee. She had warned me that today was the last day I could turn in my option sheet. She also had kindly informed me that I was the only student to have yet returned my project form.

She smiled at me patiently as she neared my desk. "So? Got something for me?"

I didn't respond.

"Terry, you can head to your other class, sir," Mrs. Lee said matter-of-factly as he stood frozen by his own desk, waiting for me.

"Yes ma'am."

Terry dropped his head and exited the classroom. He'd likely be standing by the door until I came out. He would never leave me behind—unless of course it meant him being late. Add that to the list of things that Terry hated: no belt and being late.

"Mrs. Lee," I began to form my excuse.

"Let me stop you right there, Miss Emma. If you're gonna give me an excuse, save it. We have talked about this. You are a very smart girl and I know you don't apply yourself like you could. Imagine the things that you could do if you truly believed in yourself."

Mrs. Lee loved to remind me of how I lived beneath my "potential." I knew she was only trying to be helpful and that's what teachers do, but man, I didn't know what she expected of me. I wasn't some sort of Einstein or great mastermind. I was just me and honestly, even that was confusing and a little under and overwhelming.

"So, what did you choose? Remember, I told you that if you can't decide, then I'd be forced to decide for you. Is that what you want?"

"No ma'am. It's just that I don't prefer any of these options."

"Is that right? So, what would you prefer?"

She stared at me as she pulled up a chair. "Don't worry about being late to your next class; I'll write you a pass."

Terry had for sure figured out he'd be late if he waited on me.

"That's the thing. I really hate all these Mrs. Lee. I don't understand why we must do such a project anyhow. We finally made it to our senior year and instead of being celebrated, we are being punished by having to do some major project that isn't realistic!"

My voice had raised due to the feelings swelling within me.

Mrs. Lee didn't seem bothered.

"Realistic? Tell me what is realistic, Emma."

"I don't know but it's not this." I slouched in my chair melodramatically knowing I was defeated.

"Hmm. Well, if you can't tell me what it is then how can you tell me what it isn't? What's really bothering you about this project, Emma?"

"It's everything. Y'all are forcing us to be someone we are not. What if I don't wanna be in a club or play a sport. So what? Then I have to form my own club. Well, that's too much to ask of any teenager who barely has any idea of what she wants.

"And if that doesn't work, then we have the option to say a speech. Not a 5-minute *reasonable* speech, but a 15-minute speech. That's hardly reasonable? I don't want to be a public speaker.

"Oh, and my favorite— we can volunteer at some horrible site where we honestly won't learn anything. We'll just check a box to get it over with and give up any free hours of our time doing something pointless just to check that box. Mrs. Lee, seriously, just to fulfill some dumb requirement that should never be there in the first place. What do y'all want from us?!"

The words flew out of my mouth and there was no taking them back.

I expected to be sent to the principal's office for being disrespectful but when I looked at Mrs. Lee, her soft smile remained.

"Wow, you are passionate about your beliefs there, Miss Emma."

We sat looking at each other for what seemed like minutes. She was doing it again. She had me stuck in a place that forced me to think about our interchange and take in what had just happened.

"Emma, I hear a lot of strengths in your argument. I don't agree with them, but I'll tell you one thing, I've been teaching high school students for five years now and very few can articulate their beliefs with such passion the way you have just done. Not only that, but the concepts you are challenging are precisely why I think this project will be great for you. But we are still in the same spot we were when we began. I'm not asking you to be a hundred percent on board with the options you were given, but I am asking you to pick something that you think you can do.

"Life is like that a lot of times, Emma. Just because you don't agree with something completely or just because it's not your way, doesn't mean you give up on it altogether. And it sure doesn't mean you huff about it but aren't willing to do something to bring about a change you are more comfortable with.

"Better yet, if you feel this way, how many others may also but not know how to express it?"

I stared at her as she spoke, willing myself beyond the room, not wanting to be a participant in this conversation.

"So, what do we do now Emma?"

Mrs. Lee's expression was now like that of my mother's.

"I don't know, you pick." I turned my eyes toward the door, still frustrated.

"Well, let's see. You clearly don't want to be a participant in any organized activity or sport so maybe not that one. Not much for public speaking so I'd advise against the third option. And we sure don't want you going to a site to just "check a box," do we?"

"Fine. I'll volunteer. I just want to get this over with."

I scribbled my name and marked the fourth checkbox. And with as much attitude as I could muster, I left the paper on the desk, refused to look at Mrs. Lee and walked out the door.

Chapter Two

I preferred sitting toward the middle of the bus because most of the loud and obnoxious kids sat in the rear. The one's up front normally were the kids who liked to be alone or feared the kids in the back. They sat up front, thinking that being close to the bus driver would make them safe. I figured if I sat somewhere in the middle, it was a sort of happy-medium.

I didn't identify with the unruly kids but also didn't want to be associated with the ones in the front. One thing I could count on though is that wherever I sat, Maddie would be close. She would have loved to sit right next to me, but I preferred to have my own seat if I could get away with it unless the bus was full, and then I would allow Terry to perch beside me.

Thankfully, it was a one person to a seat kind of day. I desperately needed time alone to process. After the encounter with Mrs. Lee this morning, I couldn't find a sense of focus and had no desire or energy to concentrate on anything else.

Mrs. Lee was the only teacher I knew that that couldn't grasp the concept of how kids operated. No other teacher had dared have us complete schoolwork today. Instead, the remainder of the school day consisted of free periods and movies that went unwatched while the students carried on with side conversations and random outbursts of laughter. Engaging in the usual teen chit-chat during free time did not interest me. I preferred writing instead.

As much as I wished I could be one of those girls who could doodle and draw beautiful illustrations, I was not gifted in that area. But words, they flowed. I could write to no end. I tended to capture whatever stimulated my senses in the moment. If the room was cold, I could easily characterize or narrate an adventure involving a winter breeze or snow-capped mountains that I'd never actually been to.

If I heard someone make a joke, it was easy to imagine a comedian's tale. I didn't need much to motivate my writing because the thoughts that seized my mind were frequent and endless. Mama would get on to me about "daydreaming," but what she didn't understand was that I didn't really daydream as much as my mind was just stuck in thought.

Perfect! I took notice that the sixth row back was open.

I relaxed into the bus seat, allowing my things to occupy the remainder of it. I couldn't wait to go home and swing on Missums, let my hair loose, and let my thoughts flow as the wind blew on my toes.

"You gonna tell me what happened or what?" Terry huffed, stealing my chance at peace, as he sat noisily behind me.

"Ooh what's going on?" Maddie chimed in eagerly, plopping into the seat across from me.

"She had to stay behind with Mrs. Lee to pick her senior project. Then the rest of the day she's been acting all crazy and attitudinal." Terry liked to say I was being "attitudinal" when he couldn't pinpoint my mood.

I rolled my eyes and pulled out my headphones and Walkman.

"Oh no, you don't!" Maddie moved my backpack from the seat and sat next to me.

"Move, Maddie!" I shouted.

"Nope. Not until you tell us what you came up with. Come on Emma Rose, tell us every tiny detail. Don't leave one thing out." Maddie was relentless, looking over at me like a kindergartner awaiting her teacher to read a book to the class.

I stared at her with my best glare, hoping she would take the hint and let it go.

"Emma, you know your crazy faces don't work on me. Spit it out! Besides, I'm not moving seats until you tell us."

She reminded me of a puppy that no matter how you treated it, in a matter of minutes, it was still wagging its tail, showing an incomprehensible devotion.

"Fine. But move seats first."

Maddie hopped back to her seat, plopped her face in her hands and waited in anticipation.

"I really don't see what the big deal is guys."

Terry peered over the seat. "Mrs. Lee wasn't the only one waiting to find out which one you would pick, you know. I mean, I'm your best friend and you haven't told me squat."

Seriously, these two made me want to pull my hair out.

"Well, there's not much to tell. Mrs. Lee ended up choosing for me because I told her I didn't understand the point of having to do it anyway. It's all just some dumb thing they make us do to make them feel like they've impacted our lives in some way."

"Yep, I see why she chose for you," Terry remarked sarcastically before leaning back in his seat, popping open a skittles bag and shaking his head in disappointment.

"I don't think it's dumb," Maddie chirped.

Of course she wouldn't. She was like little Miss Peachtree herself. Every teacher loved her, and every student adored her. I was surprised she wasn't a cheerleader because the girl was as bubbly as a coke. Being captain of a cheerleader squad would just seal the deal. I wondered if she would have been if we could afford it, but Maddie would never ask Mama for a cent, especially not for her own personal use. I think she considered being raised by Mama more than enough and something she'd always be indebted to her for.

"Well Maddie, everyone's not you, ya know? We don't all have to just go with the flow and accept everything people expect of us. It's burdensome if you think about it."

"A burden," Maddie laughed. "Oh, hush Emma, it's no burden. It's just something you gotta work at. Hard work pays off, you know."

Sometimes I wanted to just choke the niceties out of her. "Thought you wanted to hear every detail, Maddie. Do you want my opinion or not?!"

"Emma, calm down. We just wanted to know what you chose."

Terry sensed my aggravation and had returned to his perched position on the back of my seat. His breath was saturated with fruitiness after stuffing the entire pack of skittles into his mouth.

Turning around toward him, I examined the worry on his face. Anytime I'd get worked up about something, he would become stressed and begin hovering like a concerned pet. Honestly, I wasn't sure why I was so riled up. I guess it just really bothered me when people told me what I should do, be or how I should feel, especially when I didn't even know the answers to those things.

"Fine. In the end, I asked her to pick for me because I found it all unnecessary. Of course, she started going on and on and I couldn't take it anymore, so I ended up choosing to volunteer, which was what she wanted me to do anyway. Happy?"

I refused to look in Maddie's direction because I was still aggravated at her. However, Terry, I could never stay upset with him even when I really tried. Like the time he was supposed to meet me by the lake for my birthday and he forgotten and took a nap instead. I was so mad at him but the moment I saw him the anger had faded and I was just glad he was near.

"Hmm…Emma Rose Griggs volunteering somewhere. Never thought I'd see the day." Terry laughed in jest.

Yeah, I guess he was right, I thought.

I leaned against the window of the bus and turned my Walkman back on as I tried to silence everything around me in an attempt to salvage the bus ride home.

****

Our front yard wasn't big at all considering the size of some of our neighbors' yards. The grass extended from around the porch steps to the road ahead. Although it wasn't huge, it still required us to have our neighbor come and mow it for us because Mama always said that it wasn't proper for a woman to have to mow a lawn the size of ours.

Also, making eye contact with boys for prolonged periods of time, talking when grown folks were talking, interrupting pastors with questions in the middle of Sunday School, talking with your mouth full, chewing gum in the presence of a man, wearing pants to church, wearing dresses above the knee and drinking out of the jug were not okay. Pretty much, it just wasn't *proper* to do anything if you were a woman.

"Hi girls!" our neighbor Joe hollered out.

He had stopped his lawnmower when he saw me and Maddie approaching the house from the bus stop. Thankfully, it wasn't too far from our house because I wasn't up for a long walk today. I felt exhausted.

"Hi Mr. Joe!" We both called back.

"Let your mama know I'll cut y'all's yard next will ya."

"Yes sir."

I rested on our car sitting in the driveway as if taking the next few steps into the house was the equivalent of walking a mile. The 1980 Buick Skylark was brown with burnt orange cloth seats and the back passenger door had a small dent in it. There was a cassette player built in, but Mama forbade us from playing anything but gospel music. If it wasn't Mahelia Jackson, Shirley Caesar or the Winans, chances were, we weren't listening to it in the car.

I looked over at Mr. Joe, wondering why he had asked me to let Mama know he was gonna cut the yard since he always made it a point to keep up the yard for us anyhow.

He was a retired Vietnam veteran like my dad was, only he didn't seem to have the condition Daddy had acquired. With Daddy no longer around to cut the grass for us, I think Joe volunteered out of pity for Mama and us girls. However, he did always seem excited anytime he would come over and the only reason I could imagine a man being so happy about cutting someone else's yard would be because he was sweet on the woman he was cutting it for. I'd never suggested it to Mama though. She would only get upset and tell me to watch my mouth if I had.

Mama appeared in the front door as if she could hear my thoughts.

"Emma, get in the house child."

As I approached the steps, she leaned out while holding the screen door open.

"Hi there Joe."

He gave a quick smile and wave in return.

"I was just telling Emma, I'd be over to cut your yard in a bit."

"That's nice of you Joe. Thank you. I'll make sure to send you something out to drink."

Joe smiled and nodded before turning his mower back on.

Whack!!—- The front door slammed as I entered.

Mama turned quickly, looking back at me in a snappy fashion.

"I'm sorry Mama. It just closes so fast sometimes."

Mama said something softly as she continued into the kitchen.

"Why don't you tell me about your day Emma."

She sat at the small round table near the back kitchen window.

One thing I knew for sure was that when Mama asked me to tell her about something in detail, chances were she already had most of the information. She just wanted to see what my side of the story was.

"Well Mama—"

"Aunt Ruthie, is it okay if I use your hairbrush?" Maddie all but skipped in, interrupting me as she fiddled with her ponytail.

"You sure can Maddie. Your hair looks just fine though. It's so pretty, why don't you just let it be?"

"I just want to wash it and detangle before it gets too late is all."

"Okay go right ahead. It's on my sink counter."

"Thanks Aunt Ruthie."

Mama smiled and began looking out the back window.

"Mama—"

Remembering I was standing there, she looked over at me. "Emma Rose, why are you still standing there? Don't you have something to do?"

"Yes ma'am. I thought you wanted to know about—"

Riiinnnnggg—the phone rang, cutting our fizzled conversation even shorter.

"Hello. Yes, this is Ruthie Griggs."

Mama cut her eyes at me to let me know it was a private conversation, so I carried my backpack up to my room and put it away neatly in the closet. She would have a fit if she came up to the room and saw things flung around and not in their rightful place.

I wondered what was going on. She had clearly wanted to talk to me about something but then had forgotten all about it when little Miss Sparkles came bouncing into the room.

I changed out of my school clothes and threw on a t-shirt and jean shorts before heading back downstairs. Hopefully Mama was off of the phone by now.

"Emma Rose, can you help me untangle this section," Maddie peeked out of the bathroom looking distressed by her freshly washed and now tangled hair.

"Maddie, do it yourself. Don't you have Mama's boar brush anyhow?"

She peeked out once more, this time with glistening eyes. "Please Emma," her voice quivered.

Her face boasted defeat as I entered the bathroom, and her voice no longer had a merriment tone. She appeared sorrowful so I took the brush from her hand, slowly beginning at the bottom of her hair, working my way to the top, being careful to not snag or pull. Her usual level of happiness had not returned to her face as I finished detangling her hair.

"All done." I cleared my throat and put the brush on the counter. I was great at quick witted responses but not so much at empathetic ones.

"Thanks Emma." Maddie's voice trailed as she looked away from me and the mirror.

I wondered what she was thinking but I didn't have enough room in my mind to take on anyone else's issues right now. Besides, Maddie never remained sad. Surely, she would bounce right back in a few minutes.

I heard the bathroom door close as I headed toward the steps. I wanted to desperately go outdoors and sit on Missums and tell her all about my day. No one understood me like Missums. She had no expectations of me, and she sure didn't interrupt me or forget we were having a conversation like Mama had done earlier.

When I got downstairs, I looked through the window to see if Joe had finished cutting our grass but he was still at it. Mama would never allow me to be in the front yard alone with Joe or any other male for that matter unless it was Terry so I'd just have to wait.

I felt angry suddenly. I didn't want to sit and wait to be able to go outdoors. It wasn't as if I was one of those girls who wanted extraordinary things out of life. I didn't ask for much but in this moment, the thing I wanted most was out of reach. I had learned to not want things badly because it's not like it would matter anyway. Case in point, the front porch swing.

I sighed and turned toward the kitchen to see Mama moving about. She looked disorganized and confused which weren't normal traits of hers. What was happening? My anger turned into irritation as I considered the possibility that I was being left out of the loop on something.

Ugh, forget it. I headed towards the back door. I'd just have to settle for sitting in the backyard.

Mama didn't attempt to stop me or say a word as I headed out back. Normally, she'd give me some speech about not dazing off and being aware of my surroundings any time I headed out the door, but not this time. She allowed me to pass without so much as eye contact.

I sat on the steps and looked at our overgrown backyard. Joe didn't bother cutting it much, only every couple of months or so. We hardly spent time out back so I understood where he was coming from. Cutting both his and our front yards was enough as is. There was no need keeping up with a yard that no one bothered to visit.

I enjoyed the fact that the air was cooling but the humidity remained which made me want to jump in the shower. As the wind touched my legs, I felt a sense of relief however. There were no worries about papers, final projects, peers at school, cousins, Mama or church. It was just me and the wind…me and my thoughts. I imagined God was around somewhere too but probably had nothing to say. Sitting on Missums would be much better but this would have to do for now. I allowed the cool air to welcome me as I relaxed back onto the steps. Just when I began to settle, I heard Mama pick up the phone.

"Well, have you heard anything back yet... anything at all?" Mama's voice was hurried.

I jolted back upright and peered through the window in time to see her hang the phone up and put her face in her hands. She let out an extended exhale and then reached inside her housecoat, removing something that looked white. She tilted her head back and closed her eyes and began mouthing inaudible words. They couldn't be heard through the back door at least.

Mama was never one to talk about what was bothering her although she was a woman who was never easily troubled in the first place. If something bad came along, she'd just say it was God's will. She would say that He had it all in control. And that was the end of that. There was no more discussion needed—or at least not on her end.

My attention shifted once I heard the lawnmower stop. Joe was finally done with the yard!

Yes— Missums here I come.

"Emma Rose, come on in here." Mama opened the back door, squashing my plans.

"But Mama I was—"

"Don't 'but Mama' me girl, come on in this house like I said."

"Yes ma'am." I sulked through the door.

"I need you to run this meatloaf over to Mrs. Hennagen. It should've been over there half an hour ago. Lord knows I got too much on my mind these days. Here, take this."

Mama handed me a dinner plate wrapped in foil. I stared at her waiting for her to finish, expecting her usual spill on safety and awareness.

"Is there something the matter with your ears? I need you to get that over there now Emma Rose."

Mama now had her left hand on her hip making her aggravation apparent.

I knew better than to test the little bit of tolerance she had left. Mama was not a short petite woman but looked like the lady on the Aunt Jemima syrup bottle, only with no apron and no smile.

"Yes ma'am. I'm going now."

I tried to contain the grin that was creeping up as I practically ran out of the door. She had never allowed me to go anywhere outside the house alone. I hurried down the steps past Missums before she could realize she had sent me off alone… and in shorts at that.

I kicked at the dirt as I walked down the street and watched as the sun began to set. I did not know God in a personal way like Mama did but boy did I appreciate when he painted the sky. I felt a sense of stillness when I saw the way the light and shadows played off one another behind the clouds. My favorite was the candy cotton skies— dark and light pink wrapped in and out of the clouds with a faint bit of the sun peering through. It was in those moments that I felt like maybe, just maybe He did see me and maybe even liked me. It was as if he was looking down at me affectionately.

I didn't know how to explain it but maybe things would be okay one day. Not today. Things were still all scrambled up and nothing felt in its proper place. I practically yelled at a teacher, Maddie was uncharacteristically holding back tears and Mama had been roaming around aimlessly and making allowances she never would on a normal day.

I held my head back as the wind blew again, taking in the sensation upon my skin. The moment was cut short however when I realized I had arrived at Mrs. Hennagan's home.

Ugh. I may have gotten the privilege of coming out alone today, but I sure didn't win the prize of having to engage in small talk with a lady who I could never relate to. Despite that, I knew I still had to be polite, mind my manners and pretend to care about the weather, recipes, and engage in "back when I was young" banter.

I took a deep breath and allowed it to release slowly as I noticed Mrs. Hennagen was out in the front yard tending to her flower garden.

Here we go.

Pretending to be friendly and acting like the world was okay was just not on my agenda right now. I guess I could pull it together and be "on" for a little while. I did it all the time for school, Mama and everyone else...smile and act like everything was okay. Well maybe I wasn't "on" for Mrs. Lee today—not even a little bit. Even I had limits I suppose.

"Good evening, Darling!" Mrs. Hennagen's voice shook just a little bit as she called out.

Ugh! Darling—Here we go with that nonsense again. Just Emma.

Emma was such an easy name to remember. Plus, it would have really helped me out if she could have just tried to articulate my name for once, especially on a day like today.

"Well now, not much for words again I see?" Mrs. Hennagen looked from her flowers to me and back down again.

"Sorry Mrs. Hennagen. *I wasn't sorry.* How are you today?" I forced a slight smile.

"I'm well. Looks like your mama done went and cooked up something good again."

By this time, she had dusted off her gardening gloves a couple of times and turned to face me fully.

"Yes ma'am, it's meatloaf."

"Well let's get that inside. Actually, do me a favor will ya Darling? Run it in for me. It would take me forever just to get in there and come back out. I wanna finish talking with my flowers."

"Talking to… Oh yes ma'am," I minded my words and did what Mrs. Hennagen asked.

When I came back out, Mrs. Hennagen, sure enough, was bent over speaking to the flowers in her garden. I suppose she would be headed off to someone's nursing home sooner than later.

"It may look a little strange, me out here talking to something that you may think doesn't matter huh?" She chuckled softly as if she knew exactly what I was thinking.

"I've been talking to flowers ever since I was a little girl. My mama always told me that if you talk to your flowers, they'd grow quicker and stand up taller."

Mrs. Hennagen continued to look down at her azaleas.

"If I was younger, I'd have a huge flower garden so everyone who came by could marvel at their beauty. Lord knows I have more time on my hands now that my love has gone to be with the Lord. We all miss his voice, don't we," she asked the yellow flowers beneath her.

She then turned and looked at me without standing. The setting sun caught her face in such a way that her brown skin radiated and her deep brown eyes sparkled. Every wrinkle on her face seemed to shimmy with a glow. I don't know if I'd ever seen something or someone with such peace. I couldn't help but to be moved to a smile.

"Hmm." Mrs. Hennagen stood up straight and cocked her head to the side. "You feeling alright child?"

My smile faded quickly and I snapped back into the moment, "Yes ma'am, nothing's wrong Mrs. Hennagen."

"Oh, I thought maybe you felt unwell for a second. Something looked wrong with your face."

I was never one to be able to hide my facial expressions and it made me a bad liar. My words could say one thing but my face always told the truth.

"Oh," I squinted.

"Yeah, it was the weirdest thing, there for a sec—-your mouth did this weird little motion. It smiled."

Mrs. Hennagen stared at me.

I stared back.

We both broke out into laughter. By the time we had stopped laughing, Mrs. Hennagen had to sit in her yard chair to keep from toppling over.

"I didn't know you had jokes, Mrs. Hennagen."

"Yeah baby, well there's a lot you don't know about me," she said through her laughter as it slowed.

✳✳✳✳

As I headed back to the house, I wondered what else I could possibly not know about Mrs. Hennagen. I knew that she was married to Pastor H before he passed away and that she would always sit on the first pew on the left side of the church. She rarely said "amen" in church or shouted when the sermon started to get good. She'd just sit there poised. I couldn't imagine there was much else to her story besides being born, growing up, getting married to Pastor H and now being alone. It seemed mundane to me; like something I'd never want to do. But I couldn't shake the peace and joy she always had. Especially, since she had no kids and "her love" had died. It just made no sense. When Daddy died, I felt numb for days on end. There was no peace and certainly no joy. I was still waiting for both to return.

"Emma Rose, you okay?" Mama was standing on the porch.

I guess she had finally realized she had sent me to Mrs. Hennagen's house alone.

"Yes ma'am. I'm just fine. Mrs. Hennagen told me to tell you thank you for the hot plate."

Mama shook her head in acknowledgement.

"Emma, come sit on the swing next to me. We need to talk about your day."

It looked like I'd finally get to sit on Missums but if Mama wanted to talk, I couldn't imagine the time being enjoyable.

"What's this I hear about you smart mouthing a teacher at school today, Emma?"

I hung my head, "Oh that." I could feel Mama's eyes on my face.

"Mama, I'm sorry. I just don't understand why some teachers gotta be all in your face trying to force things."

"In your face… Let me tell you something, I'm gonna be in your face if you are ever disrespectful, do you hear me?!"

"Yes ma'am."

"Now tell me what made you lose your mind and feel bold enough to act that way?"

"Mama she was pressuring me about my senior project and going on and on about my potential and how important I could be—"

"And, what's the problem? I haven't heard a problem yet. You've been knowing about this project. I'll tell you what the problem is Emma. Ever since your daddy died, you turned into this child that would rather sit around and daydream all day. Well guess what baby? I miss your daddy too. I do but he ain't coming back. Now is not the time to be lazy and get lost. Do what you gotta do and push on. God's always gonna be with you, ya hear me?"

Tears began pelting the porch. *Lazy— Lazy—*is that what she thought of me?! I felt like I was about to explode on the inside.

"Gon' pull yourself together. No need crying over it Emma Rose. You just got to do better."

Mama leaned over and hugged me but her hug was the last thing I wanted right now.

"Emma, if I receive another call about your behavior from school, we are gonna have a real problem. Understood?"

I had no words, only more tears. Angry tears. Misunderstood tears. Pointless tears.

Mama waited for my response, nonetheless.

"Yes ma'am. Understood."

Then, she went indoors, without looking back and I was finally alone on Missums like I'd wanted.

Chapter Three

As I laid in my bed that night, my mind kept replaying the word *lazy* over and over. My heart felt dampened and like it would explode all at the same time. The emotion I felt was like a roller coaster that would not let up. It was going to be a long night for sure.

"Emma." Maddie whispered. "You awake?"

I thought to myself, if I weren't awake, I would be soon due to your pestering. I rolled my eyes, tried to lie still, and chose not to answer.

"Emma Rose, you awake?"

"Geesh! What Maddie? If I were asleep, I'd be mad at you for waking me up with the same repetitive question."

I sighed heavily hoping she would pick up on my irritability.

"Do you ever wonder if the stars in the sky are angels?"

Nope, she didn't. She either chose to ignore it or my irritation had flown over her head.

"No Maddie, I don't! I am, however, wondering why you chose to bother me with that question while I was trying to fall asleep."

"Well, Emma Rose, I wonder if they are angels watching over us. But you know, even though they are far away, they're still close. Like they can see you up close even though they are millions of miles away. Kind of like angels with binoculars." Maddie giggled softly.

"Maddie, that sounds just plain stupid. Besides you can't see stars every night, so it doesn't make sense if angels are supposed to always be with us."

I had no clue if stars were angels, but my annoyance wouldn't allow me to give Maddie any grace in the moment.

"Well, that's just it, Emma. What if the days we see the stars the most, are the days that we need to know our angels are with us the most? Like God sent them to us to help us feel better."

I glanced out of the window and noticed that the night sky was filled with bright stars this evening. I didn't know that I believed Maddie's theory, but it sounded comforting on a day like today. Maybe she was on to something.

"Sometimes I wonder if my mama is out there and can see the angels in the sky too. And maybe when she sees them, she thinks of me as well." Maddie's voice softened as she turned over.

I knew better than to respond to that comment. Honestly, I didn't know which was worse: a parent who dies and leaves you, or a parent who is alive and chooses to leave you. I truly couldn't understand why Maddie continued to have false hope that her mom loved her. If Aunt Joleen loved Maddie, she would have never made such a selfish choice to leave her and run off with some man. Yet Maddie remained optimistic, joyful, and willing to forgive and love Aunt Joleen.

My mind couldn't rest as I continued to think of Maddie's situation. Before long, I could hear her soft snore. I looked toward her, wondering how she had fallen asleep so quickly.

Her hair was placed neatly in her bonnet, and it was tucked over her ears. Her beautiful hazelnut skin could still be made out in the faint light of the room. As I examined the stillness of her face, a wave of gladness came over me that she was here safe with Mama and me. If Aunt Jolene could abandon someone so beautiful and positive, it was her loss.

Maddie got on my nerves but I had to admit she was spectacular. I didn't know that I believed there were angels with binoculars looking after us every day though. There were just some things I couldn't reconcile in my head. But one thing I did know, was that when I opened my eyes tomorrow, I'd get to see Terry and start out with a clean slate. He was the constant in my life. I pushed spying angels out of my mind and drifted off into a gentle sleep.

****

"Are you two working?" Mama looked at me sternly as Terry and I set up the tables in the fellowship hall.

"Yes ma'am," we said in unison.

Today we were having a youth luncheon at the church.

Mama was involved in pretty much any occasion or event at the church, which meant so were Maddie and I. Thankfully, Terry's mom was pretty much involved in everything too, so we were able to make almost any event enjoyable.

Terry's mom, Sister Brown, generally oversaw our church's youth events and was the main reason most of the young people showed up. She worked as a social worker and from what Terry had mentioned, was very effective in her role. She was smart, funny, witty and best of all, she didn't come across as judgmental like most older people at church. Although Sister Brown was fun to be around, we all knew when she meant business. She would remind us that there was a time and place for everything.

"Okay gon' sit those tables down without all the cackling. Remember there needs to be eight chairs at each table or else we won't have enough room."

Sister Brown made sure we knew that this time was set aside for work and not play.

Any time Terry and I were together, you could count on a tremendous amount of laughter though. Sometimes nothing was even funny, but we just had that effect on one another.

"Yes ma'am." We attempted to suppress further giggles but of course that made us both want to laugh even more.

"So how much trouble did you get in yesterday when your mama found out how you snapped at Mrs. Lee?"

"I didn't snap. I simply… inserted my opinion." I enjoyed sarcasm especially because I was pretty good at it.

"I just figured since I had *such* potential and was *such* a leader, as she says, that I should be able to bless her with my opinion." I laughed, amused by myself.

"Yeah okay," Terry rolled his eyes. "But how did Mother Griggs take it?"

He knew how much I hated the term "Mother Griggs."

He began using the phrase to get under my skin at first, but sometimes he would use it innocently. Right now, however, he was attempting to bother me, but I refused to give in to the bait.

"Well, let's just say she didn't love the idea that I disrespected someone. I'm sure she thinks I made her look bad in some kind of way and that's the only thing she's really concerned with."

I looked over to see her smiling and leaning in intently as she talked to another one of the ladies of the church.

"I swear sometimes she only cares about how my actions will affect people's perception of her."

"Oh, come on, Emma. You know your mama loves you. She's just trying to make sure you turn out alright. Although...I don't know if she'll have much luck with that." Terry joked as he straightened a chair at one of the tables.

"Hey! Whatever! I'm fantastic." I punched him in the arm, not believing the last piece of what I'd said.

"So, are you giving one of the short speeches today?" he asked.

"Nope." There was no way I was going to get up and speak in front of anyone.

"Well, my mother politely signed me up for one."

He seemed annoyed by his mother's actions, but you'd think he'd be used to being in the spotlight by now. It was safe to assume that Sister Brown would volunteer him for any slots that were not filled willingly by other kids.

"Umm and you thought she wouldn't? I mean seriously, Terry, you always speak at these things. You either read a scripture, sing a song, or give some kind of encouraging word. Honestly, I'd be more surprised if you weren't speaking."

"Yeah, you're right. It *is* kind of my thing, huh?"

"'It is kinda my thing, huh?'" I mimicked his display of overconfidence. "Of course, it's your thing, Goof-head. No need to brag."

"Hey Emma."

Sister Brown walked over towards us after the tables were set up properly.

"Hi, Sister Brown."

"My son was telling me that you all planned to be up to no good over the break."

I looked over at Terry and back at Sister Brown, "Ma'am?"

Sister Brown laughed. "Don't worry Emma, I'm just talking about y'all hanging out over break is all."

"Mom, you're not as funny as you think you are. Please stop." He rarely found Sister Brown as amusing as the rest of us did.

"Sure, I am Teddy, you're just not cool enough to know it." She flipped her hair and walked off with a satisfied smirk.

"Yeah, *Teddy*, you're just not cool enough—"

"Don't call me Teddy, Emma Rose," Terry snapped back.

"Fine."

Terry hated being called "Teddy" as much as I hated being called "Emma Rose".

Fairly soon, the fellowship hall was full of youth chattering as they began to pour in and find their seats.

"Okay everyone, settle down and find your seats now," our youth pastor Brian began to speak.

Pastor Brian was in his early twenties and preferred to only be addressed as Brian. He said anything beyond that made him feel old.

"Tonight, we have the privilege of hosting our 4th quarter youth luncheon thanks to all the hard work by the ladies here at the church. Come on, let's give them a big thank you."

Mama and the other ladies smiled and nodded in response to our applause.

Brian continued, "Now you all know that we have quite a few seniors graduating in May, so we have invited them to lead this luncheon out for us. I'm going to have Terry come up and lead us out in prayer, followed by a quick introduction. Everyone please stand for prayer as he comes up."

We stood as Terry headed to the front of the room. He oozed of confidence whenever he would speak in front of crowds. Despite his thin frame and glasses, he had plenty of self-esteem and poise in these situations. I always feared that people were staring at my imperfections so there was no way I'd ever be willing to put them on display by standing before so many people.

Terry would joke, "Of course they're staring at you and definitely pointing out your imperfections, like that little dot right there." He'd point at a spot on my face, and we would both laugh as if he'd never made that joke before.

I observed him as he began speaking. I particularly liked his outfit today. He looked relaxed. As opposed to the usual pressed collared shirt tucked into khaki pants, today Terry was wearing blue jeans and a Calvin Klein T-shirt. He loved that brand and raved about how soft their cotton was.

"Bow your heads and close your eyes everyone."

After he had finished praying, he invited everyone to take their seat before continuing.

"I wanted to encourage you all with something today. I was thinking about how many of us have things going on in our lives right now. For instance, school is crazy right now alone, right? There is a lot of pressure about which things we should choose to do and which things we should avoid. We aren't taken seriously all the time by adults although we are very close to being classified as adults ourselves. It's a confusing time in most of our lives…"

Terry continued speaking and most of us tried to pay attention to what he was saying but a speech is a speech whether it's coming from a friend or not. They were just hard to get through. However, encouragement that came from another youth typically made me feel better than anything most adults would say these days. Plus, I admired how Terry could stand in front of any person at any time and remain composed and articulate. He rarely let anything get to him except for that time I was mad at him for missing my birthday. He nearly cried while trying to explain what had made him miss my important day. He told me in so many words that nothing else mattered as much as I did—except for his mother, I'm sure. That was a given.

But now, as he stood up front encouraging everyone, all I could see was his strength. I'd always envied his positive outlook. He lived with his mom and dad, but his dad was hardly home. His dad traveled often and bought plenty of gifts to make up for his time away from home. Terry would say that sometimes when his dad said he was working, he really wasn't. He said that he's just learned to live without a father; at least, without any expectation of one. I had asked if he would rather have more time with his dad instead of all the gifts. He looked away from me, then up at the sky and said, "Emma, ya know, I don't know him enough to know if I'd like to spend time with him."

I couldn't imagine having my dad around and not knowing him or wanting to spend time with him. My dad was one-of a-kind I suppose. But Terry was just the resilient type. Any time I was "attitudinal," he would try to cheer me up with some sort of optimism. I wasn't quite sure why I hated Maddie's positivity but envied Terry's. Hopefulness was something that didn't come easy for someone like me. I had learned that if there was any good in my life, it would eventually end. God would ultimately take it away, almost as if I didn't deserve to have good things around. So, when Mrs. Lee would bring up things like potential and leadership, I would think that those sorts of things shouldn't be directed at me but at someone like Terry... or someone like Maddie… anyone else who could see the glass half-full.

"So how about it, everyone? How about we choose to take it one day at a time and trust that God knows what's best for us?"

Everyone applauded as Terry ended his speech and returned to sit next to me.

"Good job, Goof-head."

"Thanks."

"That was a nice speech there," a shaky, familiar voice broke in.

I looked over to see Mrs. Hennagen's face as she lavished her praise on Terry. I wasn't surprised she was in attendance since she was often present for events at the church. Pastor H was especially fond of the youth events when he was alive and would frequently maintain that the youth were the future, and it was the church's responsibility to guide us so that we could take over one day.

"Hi, my Darling." Mrs. Hennagen looked my way.

"Good morning, Mrs. Hennagen."

After exchanging smiles, she headed off to her seat before the next speaker made her way up to the front.

"You know she talks to her flowers," I whispered to Terry.

"So wait, she's a flower whisperer?" Terry gasped and laughed.

"Oh hush," I laughed. "I'm just saying it's weird is all."

"Well maybe she thinks you're weird, *'my Darling.'*"

Terry and I giggled.

Shhhhh! Mama said while cutting her eyes at me and Terry.

"Yes ma'am."

As Terry and I finished our croissants and tuna sandwiches, Brian approached us with his usual smile.

"Hey, you two."

"Hi, Brian," we both replied.

"So, what's new in your world?"

 Brian invited himself to the seat directly across from us.

"Nothing much." Terry responded first per usual.

It was easy to talk to Brian since he was close in age. He didn't feel so much like an adult. Plus, he was unmarried and could keep up with our slang, making him pretty much our peer; a peer with a little bit more experience in life. He didn't press and was okay with short responses.

Another reason I liked him was because his feedback didn't consist of only the Bible or *"What Would Jesus Do?"* He understood us, which was probably why he had chosen to be our youth pastor.

"What about you, madame?"

I shrugged, "Nothing new over here either."

"Okay, how does it feel to be in your senior year this year? Any big plans?"

Terry quickly chimed in. He could speak for hours on that topic. He had big dreams of going to Clemson University for marketing or mechanical engineering. He was one of the smartest people I knew but didn't act like he was better for it. He was confident and intelligent but easy to be around.

"Okay, wow, I hear ya. Sounds like a great plan, Terry. How about you, Emma?"

Brian turned back to me not willing to let me off the hook that easily.

"I don't know yet Brian. Honestly, I don't know how we are expected to be grown-ups all of a sudden and make such hard decisions, you know?"

"Sounds like you've put some thought into that answer," Brian laughed. "Seriously though, Emma, it is definitely a difficult thing to be expected to know what to do when you've never had to do something before. Terry's speech was encouraging in that area though: 'one day at a time and trust God will help you.'"

"Yep, you're right," I smiled hesitantly hoping that would end the conversation.

"I know that it feels impossible to know anything more than what you're going to wear the next day, or how much you need to study to pass a certain class. But the truth is, it really is best to take it one day at a time. No one should expect you to have it all figured out. You will make some mistakes as you go, learn from them, and keep going. Things can get messy, but the beautiful thing is that in the mess, God promises to be with you to guide you."

"Wow Brian, you went all pastor-y on me," I laughed.

"Yeah, but it happens to be true, for me back then, when I was in your same shoes, and today, when I still don't have it all figured out."

"Like why you still root for those sorry Cleveland Browns," Terry teased.

"Well, some of us are loyal—more than I can say to you and your bandwagon antics," Brian jarred back.

They continued back and forth with football for a bit while I considered what Brian had just said.

How can God allow messy things to turn out beautiful?

I didn't know if I believed that. The "one day at a time" thing I got but the rest I wasn't buying. It was just all so confusing.

"You okay?" Terry asked.

"Yeah, I'm fine. I just need to go to the restroom."

Brian had moved on to another table and was no doubt asking them the same questions.

I locked eyes with Maddie as I headed to the restroom. She had awakened in her usual good mood this morning and seemed to still be in one. She was sitting next to Annette and Shyla, also seniors, and her best friends. Brian was right about several of us graduating next May. I hadn't really paid much attention before.

"Well, hi there," Mrs. Hennagen smiled as I walked into the corridor heading to the bathroom.

"Hi." My answer came out fast and was short.

"Well, what's wrong my Darling?"

Leave it to Mrs. Hennagen to feel as if she had the right to impose. It was obvious that I wasn't in much of a talking mood, but she wanted to push and be nosy anyway.

"I'm fine."

"That little smile from the other day is missing," Mrs. Hennagen said playfully.

"Yep. Long gone," I responded shortly once more.

Sheesh! Get the point lady. I don't want to talk to anyone right now. Just go away,

"Well, I can see that you aren't okay. But hey if you don't wanna talk Emma then that's fine by me. No one's gonna force you."

She pushed past and walked along the corridor, leaving me with her sharpness.

I stood there for a second trying to process what had just happened. Forget the fact that she had been short with me in return, but she had also called me by my name. She had called me Emma. Out of all the times for her to finally remember my name, it was now. Seriously?!

"But you know what, you can't stay angry all your life. It won't get you far." She half yelled from down the hall as she exited out of the side door.

Angry?!

Seriously, what did Mrs. Hennagen, an old lady with no clue about life in my shoes, know about my feelings? How could she tell me I was angry? I was not *angry*. I was not *lazy*. I wanted to run after her and yell that she didn't know what she was talking about. Plus, why would I want to talk to someone like her anyway? She could never understand.

I rushed into the bathroom and sat rebelliously in the large empty stall. Apparently, it wasn't being mindful of our elders to use the large stall unless the other was taken per Mama. Older people needed the large stall so that they could have more room she would explain as if I cared.

"Oh girl, did you see his shirt though?"

Giggles poured forth as two girls entered the bathroom. The back bathroom was where most of the girls would come, talk, and take some extra time before getting back to church service.

"He looked so fine standing up there."

"Chelsea you are crazy. I don't know what you see in him. He's nothing but skin and bones."

"Yep, my skin and bones," Chelsea giggled some more. "I could see us having really cute babies one day."

What was up with girls these days planning to have babies and getting married? Chelsea was a junior for goodness' sake. Such silliness. And to my point, teenagers have no idea what they want in life.

"Well don't worry, you can have him because I don't want him," the other girl responded.

I couldn't make out the voice of the other girl, probably because she was too busy applying her lip gloss over and over in the mirror. I knew the sound of lips smacking from lip gloss thanks to Maddie, who was obsessed with the stuff, especially the pink sparkly kind. I rolled my eyes in the stall, wishing them to leave sooner than later.

"Well maybe Emma might want him... you know they spend a lot of time together," the other girl continued.

"Tuh! Nope they are only friends. I'm the girl for Terry. The only girl."

Chelsea had the "only friends" part right, I agreed silently.

"Okay, whatever," the other girl said leaving the bathroom.

I could hear them continue to whisper as they headed back toward the luncheon. So much for sitting in the stall with a sense of defiance. I didn't know if I was more annoyed with Brian, Mrs. Hennagen, or the idea that someone thought Terry was cute and husband and daddy material.

Eww! The last part was especially disturbing. The thought of Terry in some kind of romantic relationship was for sure the most bothersome. He wasn't even that kind of guy. He was a boy, but I didn't see him that way. He was my best friend. He was just plain Terry. And to think that I would *want* him as anything other than that was just plain dumb.

Knock! Knock!

"EMMA! ARE YOU IN THERE?" Terry shouted from the hallway.

"Seriously?!" I threw open the stall and opened the bathroom door.

"You've been in there forever Emma, are you okay?"

He met me with the oh so familiar expression he got when he was concerned about me. His eyebrows deepened as he looked attentively at my face, making sure all my features were in their correct position. His brown eyes scrutinized me in a nonjudgmental and pure way.

My anger melted as I looked back at him, knowing that I was safe now that I was near my best friend. I knew that if anything wasn't alright, he'd give his best effort to make it so. When he was especially worried, he'd come in close, just in case I needed to whisper. He was a natural protector and maybe that's why Chelsea saw him as the marrying type.

He wasn't ugly by any means which helped. I secretly loved how his yellow undertones intermingled with his brown complexion and his eyebrows lay neatly in a controlled arch pattern. He had a very thin mustache that you had to be close to notice. His lips were not too full or too pink but the perfect shade for his face. And his chin had a square-round combination that was flawless.

"Emma, seriously, is everything alright?"

"Terry, I'm fine. I just needed to use the restroom."

I pushed past him and the safety he offered, unwilling to give into vulnerability.

"Ohhhhh… so you went to poop."

Terry cocked his head to the side, his face loaded with a full grin.

"Don't be gross!" I turned and punched him in the arm again.

"I mean it's totally fine if you had to drop a hot one really quick."

Ugh!

There he was, the Terry I knew well. The gross boy best friend that knew how to lighten any situation. He was most definitely *not* the marrying, let alone the get-into-a-romantic-relationship with type. He was just a goof-head teenager boy. My goof-head teenager boy.

Chapter Four

Terry was the only boy Mama allowed in our house. Even still, we could only sit alone together downstairs because he wasn't allowed in my room. It seemed a bit contradictory since she permitted us to go to the lake by ourselves pretty frequently. Mama trusted Terry, especially since she had a front row seat to how protective he was when it came to me. She said that it had always been that way since we were little kids.

We grew up together in church and were inseparable. If Terry had been a girl, he'd probably have never left my house. Sister Brown and Mama would have been inundated with sleepover requests night after night. Only once did Mama ever ask me if I "liked" him. I remember dang near spitting my lemonade out at her. I couldn't believe she was seriously asking me such a foolish question. I just didn't see Terry in that way. My mind couldn't fathom him as anything other than my best friend.

"Come on, Emma. We are going to be late," Terry called to me as he rushed outside past Missums.

Although it would serve him well in the future and ensure his success, I did not share Terry's disdain of being late.

"Calm down, I'm coming. It's not like we have any *real* place to be, Goof-head."

"Um, seriously?!"

I knew he would be offended since we were heading to the place that he had idealized since he was in middle school.

"Emma, if you're gonna be a pain today, just stay here."

"Yeah right."

Sister Brown had invited me to go on a road trip with them to Clemson University, Terry's dream school. Clemson hosted a high school senior event every fall break to try to woo students into applying to their university or in Terry's case, to invite future students to tour the campus. It was the only college that he had ever talked about growing up and the only school he'd apply to if his mother didn't make him put in applications to others as backups.

So here I was, headed off to support him although I had no intention of enrolling at Clemson, let alone any other school for that matter. I figured there were other things I could do while making up my mind about the world. I could work somewhere locally and get an apartment and experience adulthood a little bit before making huge decisions on where I fit within the world.

"Good morning, Emma."

Sister Brown smiled as I found my spot in the backseat next to the cooler and random bags she had packed.

"Good morning, Sister Brown!"

"We should be back by 8 or 9 tonight!"

Sister Brown shouted up to Mama who was standing on the front porch with an uneasy look on her face. If it wasn't for her trust in Sister Brown, she wouldn't have let me go on such a road trip. She was overprotective and even had difficulty letting Maddie and I go to school without being worried silly about us when we were out of her sight. It made me wonder if something had happened in her past to make her that way.

Maddie came outdoors and roosted herself next to Mama. She had a huge smile on her face and began waving as we pulled out of the driveway. Suddenly, I felt glad that Mama had Madison. I could count on Maddie to ease some of the worry. She would probably play cards with Mama for a while and spend time sipping tea in the front sitting room as if it was the best time of her life just to ensure

Mama had company. Knowing that Maddie would give her all to take care of Mama helped soothe my own anxiety.

The sun hadn't quite risen, so I set my head back on the headrest in hopes to get a little more sleep before we arrived at Clemson. Sister Brown had begun humming to the gospel album playing in the background while tapping her fingers on the steering wheel to keep the beat. The melody was soothing, encouraging my plan to take a quick nap.

My eyes caught a glance of Mrs. Hennagan's house as we headed off down the street. In the front window, a light shone through the curtain. I wondered why she was up at this time, but I supposed all older folk woke up early. Mrs. Hennagen was the last person I wanted to think about though. The way she had spoken to me at church the other day still bothered me. Sure, I was curt first, but that's how teenagers were wired. She was supposed to be a nice church lady; a pastor's wife full of patience and kindness, but our encounter proved that to be false. Or maybe I was missing something, but I doubted that.

"Emma, have you given any more thought to what your senior assignment will be this year?" Sister Brown turned the music down so she could hear my response.

Terry found the question amusing and let out a chuckle. I narrowed my eyes toward him in the mirror, knowing he'd be looking into it to catch my reaction.

"Get this mom...Emma is going to— "

"Terry, I'm pretty sure she didn't ask you. She asked me. Why don't you mind your business and worry about your own stuff," I snipped.

"Ollhhfff!" Sister Brown laughed. "That's right, I *did* ask Emma not you, Teddy. Mind yo bizness! Is that how y'all say it these days? Not business but *biz-ness* right?!"

Terry and I both glanced at her.

"Mom, just stop. Please don't act like this when we get to Clemson. As a matter of fact, just stay a few steps behind us, okay?"

"What?! It's not my fault you can't handle me being hip."

"See that's it right there, Mom. That! —That! No one says 'hip'. Just stop!"

She gave him a sideways look and they both surrendered into laughter. Terry would give his mom a hard time ever so often, but he secretly loved how she tried to keep up with him as he got older.

I missed laughing with my dad in that way. There was nothing that we couldn't go on and on for hours about. Daddy was full of jokes and Mama used to get onto him for clowning around with me for too long some days. We just enjoyed being near one another. He'd always tell me I was his ray of sunshine; what kept him going. I just wish I could have kept him going a little longer is all.

"Well, Emma, so how about it? Gonna answer my question?" Sister Brown persisted.

"Yes ma'am. I have to speak with Mrs. Lee about it a little more when I get back to school but—"

"You're going to have to do a little bit more than speak," Terry teased. "You're gonna have to— "

"Boy, hush and let her finish telling me… I don't know why she keeps you around with all this interrupting you do."

"I do." Terry sat up tall. "Let me list the reasons why."

I rolled my eyes and sank in my seat. *Here we go.*

"I'm incredibly smart, I keep the time for her because Lord knows she can't be on time to save her life, I'm so funny she can't stand it, I'm pretty charming, and most of all, I'm probably the handsomest thing she's ever laid eyes on."

"Oh, is that it?! Well, I'm glad you cleared that up." Sister Brown was not buying it.

"More like the most annoying, bossy, and big-headed *thing* I've ever seen," I corrected. "You must have confused me with Chelsea."

"Chelsea?"

I smirked in the mirror.

"Yep, you heard me right. Chelsea from church. She has the weirdest crush on you. She was going on and on about how you were this and that... you may as well just marry her because I don't think you'll find anyone else later in life."

"Hmm, Chelsea, huh?" Sister Brown said slowly, taking mental notes.

I didn't have to worry about Sister Brown repeating anything. She was good for confidentiality, that's why so many of us kids felt safe talking to her and coming to any events she put on.

Terry sat in his seat quietly.

"What? No smart mouthed comebacks, Goof-head?"

"It appears I can't have a serious conversation with your kind," Terry said in his sarcastic, bougie voice.

Anytime Terry wanted to get out of a conversation or if I'd won an argument, he'd resort to this overly aristocratic voice and ignore the rest of what we were talking about.

"Yeah, yeah, whatever!"

"But please carry on with what you were saying to my mother," Terry continued to avoid my comment.

"Oh yes, Emma, so what does Mrs. Lee need to give you more information on when you go back to school?

"Well…. I landed myself into volunteering at the juvenile detention center, but I just don't think it's something they should make us do. It's kind of stupid. I mean, you send one kid to volunteer with other kids. It's kind of like the blind leading the blind. I feel like it's something they want us to do to just to say we did, but they didn't put much logic behind it."

"Watch out mother, this one can be quite passionate—" Terry chimed in with that annoying voice once more.

"Hush!" Sister Brown and I said together.

A moment of silence passed before Sister Brown encouraged me to go on, using a now soft and compassionate voice, "Emma, you can continue if you'd like."

"Oh no, thanks, I'm done," I had already begun looking back out of the window, dismissing the thoughts of school from my brain.

"You know, Emma… I hate to admit it, but my knucklehead son is right. You do sound passionate about this whole thing."

"I guess," I mumbled.

"Maybe this is exactly what you should do; go volunteer with other kids who don't have it figured out either. Maybe you will learn why it is that you're so fervent about it all."

"It all?"

"Yes, you seem to have some strong feelings and views about adults, students, and the world around you. We all do. I just think that maybe this can help you understand what those views are exactly and why they are there to begin with."

I felt as if everyone was mocking me when they spoke about how "passionate" I was. I wasn't passionate, I was just voicing my opinion. Passion is something I knew very little about. The closest thing to passion I could relate to was going out and sitting on Missums alone from time to time. None of what Mrs. Lee had said or what Sister Brown had just spoken made much sense to me. They both had made my comments into something deep, but it was just my opinion of the dumb senior assignment I had to complete, not some grand epiphany.

As I closed my eyes against the headrest, I felt the sun beginning to peer through. I turned to see a cotton candy sky. As I marveled at the view, I wondered if God was looking back down in awe of me.

Of course not!

Such a silly thought. I shut my eyes and leaned back into the headrest one more time, determined to get some sleep before arriving at Clemson in the next couple of hours.

****

"Okay Emma, we are here now," Sister Brown called to me from the front seat.

As I awakened, I could feel the sunshine beating down on my forehead. Terry had a huge smile on his face as he looked out the window. His eyes danced as he took in the view.

College students were milling around the Clemson campus. They didn't look very intimidating; well, most of them. I had expected to see young adults of a bigger stature for some reason.

Older people were sprinkled throughout as well but I wasn't sure if they were teachers, students or both. I tried imagining walking around, eating lunch or possibly even staying on campus with people that were so different in age than I was but my mind couldn't settle on such an idea.

Taken in by everything around me, I turned to see a girl wearing a shabby backpack cross the parking lot. She wore long braids extending down her back. Her sunglasses were trendy, and her lips nicely glossed. Earphones sat on her head as the chord disappeared into her backpack, likely plugged into a hidden Walkman or cassette player.

She looked around the parking lot as she crossed and returned her gaze to what was in front of her. She appeared poised and determined, yet tranquil. I wasn't sure what about her captured my attention, but I was fixated on her. She couldn't be much older than myself, yet she was here carefreely navigating the large university.

"Emma, let's go!"

Terry stood at my door waiting for me to make a move to get out of the car. I hadn't realized he had opened the door.

"I'm coming Goof-head. Chill out."

"My orientation starts in fifteen minutes, and I don't want to be late."

"You don't say?"

I looked at him sarcastically as I crawled out of the backseat and grabbed my mini backpack purse.

"Don't worry, I won't make you late today. I know how important this is to you."

"That's more like it." A grin took over Terry's face as he continued examining the school grounds.

"Okay now listen, I'm going to walk a little ways behind y'all and sit in the back with the other *too-cool-to-be understood* parents so go on ahead and know I'll be right behind you if you need me."

Sister Brown knew when to give us kids some space and I loved her for that. Besides her ability to be easy going, although I'd never admit it, she was funny and, kind of cool. If Mama had been here, she would have made me walk side by side with her and would fasten herself to me. Not only that, but she'd make sure to ask a million questions and inform whoever she was talking to everything there was to know about me, beginning with my birth.

"Emma, isn't this great? It feels so far from Byron, ya know?" Terry continued looking around as we entered the Prospective Student Information Center.

"Yeah, I know exactly what you mean. It kind of seems fake… like those movies we watch."

"You mean *surreal*. It feels surreal."

Terry held his head back as he examined the tall beams and the architecture of the high glass ceilings.

"Yeah… surreal, Mister Know-It-All."

"Yes ma'am, Terry Brown." Unbothered by my comment, he confirmed his name during the check-in with the registrar, a younger guy with glasses and a less than enthusiastic face.

"Alrighty, you're checked in. You can find a seat anywhere in the auditorium." The guy spoke without ever making eye contact with Terry.

"And here's your visitor pass as well." He handed me a sticker to put on my shirt. "As long as you are with him, you will be able to access everything."

That sounded right. As long as I was with the smart guy, I'd be able to get through it all.

I followed Terry into the auditorium where refreshments and binders were set out on long tables. He picked up his binder while I grabbed some oatmeal raisin cookies before finding our seats.

"Okay everyone, let's get started. I'd like to welcome you to Clemson—."

The woman up front began her announcements and covered the itinerary for the day. She introduced a panel of students, ranging from freshmen to seniors. Out of the six students, there were two women, one of which was Asian and the other Caucasian. The other four were males, of which, one was Black. One thing, as natural as breathing for me, was scanning the room to see who looked like me. There was a particular comfort in knowing other Black people were around, especially in large rooms. Knowing that there was at least one Black person on the panel made me feel at ease, like I belonged or that I at least had the potential to, like the girl with the braids I had seen in the parking lot.

Terry, on the other hand, who I'm sure had never felt out of place, leaned in with his chin in his hands and his elbows on his knees as he paid close attention to the lady speaking. I could see the sparkle in his eyes as he was drawn into his future. He fit here. He was made for it. Even if I couldn't see myself in an environment like this one, I could absolutely visualize Terry at Clemson and I was genuinely happy for him.

"Pay attention."

He whispered as he leaned close to me without taking his eyes off the woman speaking. It was an art that he had mastered, to be able to sneak in a side conversation without people noticing. When I didn't respond, he glanced over to check on me, likely to see if I had fallen asleep. Once he knew I was fine, he returned his gaze to the student in the front of the room who was now sharing about his experiences on campus.

I began examining Terry's smooth brown skin as he held his focus ahead. Something about how attentive and calm he was settled me. My insecurities began melting away and I knew everything would be okay. Terry just had that sort of presence.

He chuckled with the rest of the audience as the sophomore boy told of how he had overslept one day and been late for a test. It was then that he had realized that his parents weren't joking around about the real world and the consequences that came along with it.

Terry laughed again. By this time, I could no longer make out anything the boy was saying. I was too drawn in by Terry's profile and the pure joy he was experiencing in the moment. Ever since Daddy died, nothing had ever felt so right in the world, yet sitting here and watching Terry enjoy such a simple presentation came closest to the peace I once knew.

A round of applause erupted and I was snatched from my trance just in time to lock eyes with Sister Brown. She stared at me with a half-smile on her face as if she was aware of something that I wasn't.

Had she been watching me ogle her son? And what had she thought when she had seen me?

I quickly turned my eyes from hers and began to fumble with my backpack, pretending to look for anything that could help me escape her silent accusation.

"Ahh Emma! That was pretty amazing, huh?" Terry continued to beam as the other kids filed out of the auditorium.

"Yeah, it was okay I guess." I worked hard to avoid Terry's eyes, still unsure of what had just happened.

"Come on, let's go to the cafe! I can't wait to see more of this place!"

When I didn't get up right away, I could feel him staring down at me with a slight edginess.

"Ok, ok Goof-head." I didn't want to ruin his excitement. I wasn't certain what it was that I had just felt as I looked at him a moment ago, but one thing I knew right now, was that I wanted to finish this day with him at his dream school.

****

"So did you guys enjoy yourselves?" Sister Brown asked as she began driving away from Clemson.

Terry went on about how much he loved the environment, the student body make-up and how he was for sure going to pledge a fraternity when he got settled. It wasn't a matter of *if* but *when* he was accepted, and we all knew it.

"What about you Emma? Think you could see yourself going to college next year?"

Now that I was a senior, people incessantly asked about my college plans. They continually inquired about test taking, scores, extracurricular activities that would look good on college applications, and planning ahead. The thing was though, I had not applied to any schools. As a matter of fact, I had missed the early deadline and now only had until March 1st to submit any late applications. By then, I was told, I would be at the college's mercy on whether they'd accept me so it was best to fill out as many applications as I could and submit them early to ensure a spot.

It was as if going to undergraduate school was the only "acceptable" option in most people's minds. But I had no clue where I belonged or what I wanted to do. It wasn't something that could be forced like many adults believed.

"I don't really see myself that far ahead Sister Brown. I can see Terry someplace like here, but as for me, I don't know if I am the college type."

"Hmm… okay. May I ask what you think the college type is?"

"I don't know, just not me."

I looked down hoping to end the conversation there.

"Well, Emma, maybe that's where you should start. If you know or think you know that you aren't the 'college type,' then try figuring out what type you are."

If I could have walked home to avoid the rest of the talk, I would have gladly chosen the option to do so.

"Yes ma'am." It was the only response I could offer.

"You know, Emma, I don't know what you'd do without me so I'm pretty sure you'll come to Clemson just so I can keep you out of trouble."

Terry smiled back at me, either trying to rescue me from his mom's persistence or hoping for a smart aleck response in return.

"As if I'd follow you anywhere! Besides, I'm the one who keeps you out of trouble, remember?"

"Oh yeah, like that time you picked a fight with Roger Wilson and I had to step in and save you. Or maybe like that time you lost my notes I lent you and then you told Ms. Reyes that she should give me a break because what she was teaching that day wasn't that important anyway. Oooh, or maybe like the many times I have had to get a tardy pass waiting on you in the mornings. You're right, I'm so thankful that you keep me out of trouble."

We all burst into laughter knowing his points were valid. He really was the primary person who kept me on track. I tended to be a bit feisty sometimes, especially when I didn't feel like being "on." Some days I just couldn't muster it, but he accepted me no matter what and whether I was mad at the world with no reason behind it or bouncing off the walls with a weird excitement, I could count on him to be there.

One time, when we were twelve, I rode my bike to the store with Terry and some of his other friends. They were all riding their bikes off a ramp near the neighboring car garage. It wasn't the safest of ramps, but I suppose boys always had some challenge they felt the need to conquer. The group would give Terry a hard time for bringing a girl along with him everywhere, but he always stood up for me and didn't let anyone bother me.

That day they had each taken turns gliding off the ramp. Terry thought it was dumb and refused to even attempt the jump, so his friends teased him to no end. I figured I should rag on him to for being scared so I joined in with the others, badgering him for at least five minutes or so. Terry had looked at me with woundedness in his eyes. He could have cared less if those other boys went on forever, but when the taunting came from me, it stung. To further add to the insult, I figured I'd show him that I wasn't scared to jump the stupid ramp although I was deathly afraid on the inside.

I took my turn heading up the ramp but when I got to the edge, I froze. The whole point was to keep pedaling off as fast as possible to create momentum for the landing, but I hit my bicycle brakes at the end of the ramp and fell onto the concrete below. Before I could get my first "ouch" or tear out, Terry was by my side. He saw how bad I was bleeding and knew I was too upset to walk, so he put me on his back and carried me home. He left both our bikes at the abandoned garage knowing they could be stolen but that didn't matter to him because he knew I needed help. My knees and hands had hurt so badly that I sobbed all the way home.

The pain from my injuries wasn't the main cause of my sadness though. I was embarrassed and ashamed as I remembered the hurt in Terry's eyes when I had joined in on teasing him. Even though I had been a horrible friend and betrayed and sided against him, he was still there to make sure I was okay. I didn't deserve for him to carry me home the way he had done, without one question or snide comment.

After they knew I was fine, Mama and Daddy were livid. They were shouting out "What were we thinking?" and "You could've gotten hurt so much worse!" Terry had stood up and accepted all the blame. He went on about how he should have never let me come along and should have chosen to leave when he saw how reckless the other boys were being.

Daddy had looked at him and told him that he was glad that he had taken responsibility, but it wasn't enough. He told Terry he had to do better next time, especially if I was ever gonna be allowed to go out and play with him again. The thought of not being able to play with him had made me sick. I watched helplessly as he began crying and pleading with Daddy to give him another chance although he had no fault in it all. Daddy told him to go home and they'd talk about it later. Terry looked back at me with a deep sadness as he left the house. All I could do was cry. I couldn't even admit to my parents that it had been all my fault. Terry was the one being responsible, and it was me that had made the poor decision.

The next day Terry came back with a letter in his hand. He had written some sort of apology letter to Daddy and Mama. I never read it but whatever the note said had made Daddy change his mind and let me and Terry continue to play together for the rest of the summer. He never confronted me about my not owning up to what I'd done nor about my teasing him in front of the other boys. He just chose to pick up where we left off and move forward. That was the kind of friend he was. He was loyal and his friendship was one that no one truly warranted.

I sighed as I thought about the idea that he would be leaving next summer. Without Terry, I would be in a heap of trouble. The fact of the matter was that I needed him but would never admit it to his face. He knew it though and that's why he was so protective.

I winced imagining the idea that he would someday move on and leave me behind. While blinking back tears, I tried to push the thought far from my mind.

Chapter Five

I stared down at the foil covered dish as I headed out the front door. Mama was having me take a plate over to Mrs. Hennagen again. Madison had stayed later at school for her photography club so it was up to me to deliver the plate alone. She had chosen to become more involved in extracurricular activities to boost her application to Central Georgia Tech. Most of us from Byron just called it CGTC.

Madison hoped to become a journalist or a social worker one day. She figured that if she worked on her ability to photograph, she would learn how to capture "moments and important events." She said she would develop an "eye" for things. I wished everyone would say what they really meant as opposed to speaking in riddles.

She wasn't like Terry in that she didn't know exactly how she was going to reach her dream job one day, but she had her mind set on starting down the path she thought could get her there. I had to give her credit for that since I remained clueless on what I was meant to do with my future. Everyone's descriptors of me landed in the category of opinionated, lazy, or full of potential, which didn't give me much to go on.

One thing I was sure about, however, was that I'd much rather not deliver food to Mrs. Hennagen right now. It would be just fine if I never had to see her face again especially after how she had talked to me at church the other week. Besides, I wasn't angry. How dare she tell me I was angry. She knew nothing of my life and what it was like to be me.

As I faced Mrs. Hennagen's house, I felt a familiar pang in my stomach. Her front window curtains were drawn and the window itself was pulled up to let fresh air in. A single candle was burning in the living room while she sat reading. I could hear the instrumental music playing all the way from the front yard.

I looked at her sitting there with her reading glasses on her nose as she intently scanned over whatever she was studying. She nodded her head gently to the other side to make out the words on the page better from time to time. There was a certain loveliness to her as the flickering candlelight cast small shadows about her face.

Woof—Woof—Woof— A dog barked in the neighbor's yard causing Mrs. Hennagen to look out the front window.

She caught me standing frozen like some sort of stalker. I glanced back at her but had no desire to move towards her front porch. As she got up to walk towards the door, I stepped closer. What would I say to her? I honestly had nothing very nice to say so I figured I should just hand her the plate and go on about my way. Besides, Mama wouldn't be so understanding if I were to be disrespectful to Mrs. Hennagen.

"Ya gonna stay out there forever?" She leaned on the door with her hand on her hip.

I walked over and extended the plate so she could take it from me.

"Well, I do believe I asked you a question now, didn't I?"

"My Mama wanted you to have this plate."

Some other not so kind words came to mind but I knew better than to say them. If she wanted to play this game, I could play it all day long. She wanted me to acknowledge her and to respond to her, but I wouldn't give her the gratification, especially not after the way she had spoken to me at church.

"Well, that sounds right. Sister Griggs has a good heart."

Mrs. Hennagen didn't call Mama "Mother Griggs" like some of the other church members, probably because she was older than her and had actually earned the title "Mother".

"How about you? Did you want me to have it?"

I looked up at her, annoyed at her need to press me into a conversation.

"Mama asked me to bring it, so I did."

"That's not what I asked. Did you want me to have it too?"

She was really frustrating me at this point.

"I didn't think about it. If Mama asks me to do something, I just do it. So here I am bringing you your food." I wasn't sure how much longer I could keep my tone in check.

"Mmm hmm. Well, you can bring it in and set it on the stove for me."

She held the door open so that I could enter. I walked past her and into the kitchen without saying a word. After setting the plate on the stove, I walked toward the front room to leave.

"You see that… that's exactly what I'm talking about."

She looked at me as she sat back down to read her book, obviously offended by my unwillingness to cave.

My blood was darn near boiling. She was determined to pick a fight just because she was an adult. She wouldn't quit until I said something not-so-nice and then she'd blame me for being disrespectful. But I'd show her. I wouldn't let her get to me. She wouldn't see me crack.

"Well, have a good day." I said through my teeth as I reached for the doorknob.

"Mmm hmm. The question is, can you have one with all that anger built up?" She continued to look down at her book, although I knew she wasn't reading. She was simply attempting to appear as if she wasn't concerned.

That was it! I had had enough! "You know what, I'm not angry!" You don't know me. You know nothing about me!"

My mouth continued to fire off before I could stop it.

"You're supposed to be a pastor's wife—supposed to be a woman of God—but here you are meddling me just because you can."

She continued peering down at her book, unbothered by the words flying out of my mouth. She was ignoring me and that made me even more mad.

"Pastor H cared so much about the youth and here you are antagonizing me just because… so maybe you're the one who's angry… and bitter… and alone."

There, I had said it. That would teach her to mess with me. That would hit her where it hurt.

Mrs. Hennagen finally turned towards me, placing a bookmark in the pages before closing her book.

My hands were shaking as I stared at her, hoping what I'd just said hadn't really come out. I was suddenly full of regret. I shouldn't have gone that far. But it was her fault. She had gotten me to lose my cool and Mama was going to lose her mind once she found out.

"Those are a lot of words for someone who *isn't* angry. As a matter of fact, those are a lot of big heavy words that you must have been holding on to for some time now. Are you done?"

My remorse began to fade. Was she being condescending now? I had already gone off the deep end so may as well speak my full mind at this point.

"No. No, I'm not. Another thing is, I'm not your 'Darling' either. I hate it when you call me that. My name is one of the easiest names to pronounce—*Em-ma*. You purposely call me 'Darling' to irritate me, just because I'm not all friendly and bouncy like Madison and some of the other girls at church. Well, they may be happy all the time but that doesn't mean I have to be."

"Well, you're finally right about one thing. You are definitely not my Darling acting like this."

I had run out of words for her. I finally told her exactly what was on my mind but didn't feel relieved.

"You have no clue why I call you Darling do you?"

I felt numb and exhausted as my heart continued to race. I couldn't muster up any response to her.

"Well, let me tell you something Miss *Em-ma*. I've seen many things and people in my lifetime. I'm 87 years old and you don't become my age without witnessing some stuff. Some of it has been good. Some of it has been bad but one of the things that the good Lord has blessed me with is the ability to see people. I mean truly *see* people.

"People can be a bit like onions. There are so many layers to us. Most of us are born a certain way and then life comes along and adds extra layers to us. No one hardly ever shows their innermost layer because they are scared. We have this flimsy layer that's easily peeled off on the outside. That part, even though it's frail, protects us. It shows a tiny piece of what's underneath but even still, what's underneath is just another layer. It's a hard one and gives off *just* a little aroma.

"Only people who are truly determined to get to the core, will work to get through all the layers. They will work through the aroma. You understand me? Each coat that comes off gives a stronger aroma. It gives a stronger sense of who you are on the inside.

"Now this aroma brings some people to tears. It brings some people to quit and discard you. The strong and persistent will work through it though. They will work until they get to the core."

Mrs. Hennagen leaned in closer to me as she continued.

"Now the core... that core is what's most vulnerable. It's what's most raw about us. It's what we try to hide because we don't understand it. People aren't going to work to get through all those layers if you yourself aren't willing to, Miss Emma. I know your name. As a matter of fact, it's one of my favorites because it has a flower smack dab in the middle of it."

She smiled as she said, "Emma Rose Griggs."

Something about her saying my name made me relax. The tension in my shoulders loosened and my breath slowed in full appreciation of her acknowledgment.

"Yes, that's right. I know your name. I see your outer layer and I know there's way more inside. And I think it's worth going through peeling back some of the hard ones to get to the aroma underneath. You think I don't know you. Let me tell you, I *was* you."

Her eyes pierced mine, not allowing me to look away. Tears welled against my will. I couldn't hold them back and I wasn't sure I wanted to.

"I'm a Black woman who has grown up in some of the toughest times of this world. I've been labeled Negro, Colored, African American and Black... just more layers through the years. I've seen my friends mistreated and I've been mistreated myself. I watched my friends get married, have babies, and wonder what kind of grief the world would stack on their tiny babies' hearts. I sat and prayed for a baby of my own and questioned why I couldn't have my own child being it was one of the only things I'd ever wanted.

"Yes, I had to carry on in harsh conditions: through my parent's tragic death, and recently, watching the love of my life be laid to rest. You think I don't know something about being angry? Or something about being let down? Maybe something about grief? Well, you're wrong about me. But listen, I'm not here to talk about me. I'm here to talk about you. I could call you Emma but that wouldn't be enough. My grandmother used to call me Darling growing up. She said she called me that because I needed to know that I was special… that I was something beautiful and loved. And you, my dear Emma, are something special and something beautiful, whether you want to be or not."

The carpet continued to catch my falling tears. It was as if time had stood still and all I could hear was her voice. Her declaration was holding me in place as it penetrated my heart.

"But you won't know it until you fight past that anger and all of those big emotions you have."

She allowed me to continue crying as I stood like a statue in her living room. I was ripe and exposed, but she was wise enough to know that I had reached my maximum. I couldn't take in anymore. The feelings were overwhelming, and I didn't know what to do with them. She didn't try to console or lull me but chose to give me the space I needed.

So, I cried and stood there. And she watched and waited.

"I don't know how to do it, Mrs. Hennagen. I don't know how to do it. I wake up and I'm so angry, or I'm so sad, or I'm ... I'm... I don't know what I am most days."

"You know, Darling, it's not something you do. It's something you decide. It's a decision you make one moment and then another decision you make the next. Our minds are powerful, my child."

I closed my eyes to try to block any more tears from escaping my eyes. I focused in on the smell of the candle near the window. It was a mix of apple, cinnamon, and vanilla. If I could only just concentrate on the scent, maybe it would take my mind from the feelings inside of myself.

I took a deep breath, noticing a small breeze flow across my legs. I still wasn't sure how God felt about me or if he even considered me as part of his handiwork, but I imagined that he had used the breeze to send me a small hug, all the way from heaven, to help me in the moment.

I opened my eyes to see Mrs. Hennagen standing. She approached me hesitantly and before I could fight it, she wrapped her arms around me. She smelled of cocoa butter and her warmth steadied me. I didn't try to wiggle out from underneath her arms but leaned into them and let my head rest on her shoulder as the tears continued to drop.

****

Mama was moving about in the kitchen when I made it back home. I had taken too long returning so she had called over to Mrs. Hennagen's. She couldn't help being worried all the time. She wouldn't be able to bear if something happened to me, so she held on tightly to try and protect me as much as she could. Mrs. Hennagen had reassured her that I was fine and explained how we had begun talking which caused me to be late coming back home. She didn't mention my explosiveness-turned-meltdown. I'm glad too because it would have sent Mama spiraling.

"Emma, go ahead and wash up so we can eat."

Mama sat at the small square table next to Madison. I had completely forgotten that they would be waiting for me to return so we could eat our own dinner. Mama hated when we missed our chance at meals with one another, so she made us all prioritize them.

"Yes ma'am."

As I turned to head to the bathroom, I noticed a white envelope sitting in the mail container near the refrigerator. Mama's name was written on the front in black ink but it was sealed shut. It was the same handwriting that I had seen on the previous one that she had gripped so tightly. The envelopes were not postmarked so they weren't coming in the mail. Who was giving them to her?

I quickly dried my hands and hurried to the table hoping my puffy eyes would go unnoticed.

"Emma, why don't you say grace for us today? I think that would be best." Mama's matter-of-fact tone was far from a request.

"Yes ma'am."

As I began praying, I didn't close my eyes but examined Mama's face instead. Her eyebrows were tense, further evidence she was burdened. I hoped whatever was troubling her would pass. When she was stressed, that meant we were all stressed. It just sort of spilled over onto us. She thought she did a good job busying herself when she had something on her mind, but the truth was, she was a ticking bomb that only needed one trigger. Something as simple as Madison or myself asking her a question could cause her to go off.

"Amen."

Maddie and Mama opened their eyes and grabbed their utensils.

"How was the photography club today, Madison?" Mama looked over towards her, awaiting her response.

"Oh, Aunt Ruthie, it was actually really fun."

She beamed as she spoke, full of perkiness. Her eyes danced with wonder as she continued.

"I didn't think I'd be any good at it at first but when Mr. Wallace showed us how something as simple as adjusting the light or camera angle can cause a portrait to come out completely different, I was able to really engage. I never realized taking pictures could be so complex. It's really cool to see how things can be manipulated in such a way, ya know?"

Mama gave a small laugh in response to her enthusiasm. Her eyes twinkled as they conversed. Sometimes I wondered if Aunt

Joleen's leaving Maddie here was what Mama needed. They had always connected in a way that Mama and I had never been able to.

And right on cue, as she took a bite of her mashed potatoes, Mama looked over at me. "I wish Emma Rose would find her something to get into."

"Emma Rose, you'll find something. Sometimes, it just takes a little extra time." Madison smiled towards me knowing how I had taken the comment. While Mama's intent may have not been to tear me down, it managed to land a blow anyhow.

"More like a lot of extra time. Everything we have tried so far has amounted to nothing. Emma Rose, you're just too picky. You'd rather sit out on the porch all day or hang out with Terry. You gotta start trying new things or you'll never—"

"I'll try harder."

I cut her off before she could continue to spout off all the things I could improve on. Lately, that seemed to be the gist of most of our meals together. We would begin speaking casually about general things such as the weather, school, or church but it would always end in the things that "Emma" could improve on.

"I sure hope so," Mama said, moving on to her green beans.

I quickly finished my food and headed over to start cleaning the kitchen. I would do anything to escape more judgment from her.

"Madison, what do you want to do for your birthday next month?"

Mama asked the question as if there were many options. She received a small check, once a month, for Daddy since he had died. She worked an office job throughout the week that didn't pay much either. She made too little money to be able to afford anything above essential items for us girls but made too much money to qualify for food stamps or any other type of governmental assistance.

Money was always tight, but we made it through. Maddie and I had low expectations and didn't ask for much because we knew Mama was doing the best she could to pay bills and take care of us all. She was a tough woman whose words could cut deep, but her heart was generous. She'd literally give a stranger the shirt off her back if it was necessary.

"Aunt Ruthie, can I be honest?" Madison's eyes and tone softened.

"I miss my mama. I know people think I should just move on and be done with her, but if she could just send me a birthday card or a phone call, that would be the best birthday ever."

Mama's face tensed up again.

"You can always be honest with me, Madison. One's mama is someone that will always leave a hole if she goes missing or passes away. It's normal to miss and want your mama despite the circumstances. We'll just have to pray about it and leave it up to God."

Maddie looked defeated, which was a rare occurrence.

"Yes ma'am," she said as she looked at the tablecloth.

Mama's mom had died when she was ten years old. She never told us what happened. She would just remind us how important it was to be grateful for our own mothers, even the ones who had abandoned their children, like Aunt Joleen. She said that it didn't matter the mistakes your mama made because mamas are just people who are just as imperfect as the next person. Even if they make a mistake, without them, we wouldn't be here, so thank God for your mama and respect her anyways.

Mama's logic didn't make much sense to me. I didn't see how someone should honor or respect someone who didn't love them enough to stay and take care of them.

"Thank you, Emma Rose." Mama pushed her chair into the table and set her plate down to be washed.

"I'm going to lie down for a while. I have a headache. When you all are done, settle down and get ready for school tomorrow."

"Yes ma'am."

As she walked toward her bedroom door, I longed to hug her but didn't really know how. Maybe she was like me: a girl full of big emotions that didn't know how to change them. Maybe that's why her face looked so tense all the time. And maybe that's why she couldn't connect with me like she did Maddie. Maybe, just maybe she didn't know how because I reminded her too much of herself. Whatever the case, just as Mrs. Hennagen had hugged me and allowed her love to flow through to me, I wish Mama would turn around, come back, and embrace me so I could feel her love flow through too.

Chapter Six

Mrs. Lee stood in front of the room prepared with another speech. I looked around to see which other students were also required to attend the meeting.

"I can't begin to tell you how excited we are to have all of you here today. Volunteering provides an excellent way to elevate your perspective of the world. So often we are enclosed in our own way of life that we forget that there are others who share the world with us who don't necessarily hold our same beliefs, values, and resources. When you take it upon yourself to…"

Mrs. Lee continued her discourse as she walked slowly back and forth near the podium up front. I'd rather be anywhere but here right now. It wouldn't be so bad if Terry was here with me, but he knew which senior project he would choose from the first time the topic was announced unlike myself. Giving speeches came naturally for him so it was a given. He loved the idea of speaking about how education had shaped him as an individual and how he would use it to further his education and help others in the future. I had to endure this alone.

When I had seen Mrs. Hennagen at church last week, she had asked me about school. I mentioned having to volunteer for my senior project and how I had blown up on Mrs. Lee because I didn't understand the purpose behind it. She had given me a knowing look with a smirk as I carried on. I mean, I understood what the school staff and colleges wished to achieve from it. Mrs. Lee was certain that the project could help us "elevate our perspectives" in which we would be challenged in a way that would both semi-prepare us for the road ahead and allow us to explore areas that we may have never considered otherwise. That piece I understood too. I was doubtful that the actual outcome of it all would be as beneficial as they thought it would be, however.

A soon to be eighteen-year-old is literally trapped between the stage of feeling like a carefree child and a frightened young adult that was expected to move into the stage of having everything figured out sooner than later. For example, what career we should choose for the rest of our lives or how to become financially independent when most of us have never had a job, bank account, or even received an allowance. Oh, and my favorite: Don't fall in love and please don't get pregnant because if you do you will lose your only hope of "making something of yourselves."

Giving a speech, joining a club, or volunteering somewhere did not hold the answer to the billions of questions we all still had. If anything, it only added to the queries that were already there. Mrs. Hennagen had chosen to respond to me by reminding me that to unlock any layer of an onion, a decision had to be made. I didn't need to know all the answers today. I needed to only make the *decision* to attend the meeting. And after that, I needed to then *decide* to listen to the instructions. She said each choice had to be purposeful and I needed to understand that, initially, the process of choosing would be difficult. For this reason, I should begin practicing the art of focusing on one *decision* at a time, and eventually the process would become easier.

"If you aren't sure of where you would like to volunteer, there is a list of approved sites on this table along with business cards for you to take. Please don't hesitate to see myself or any of the other senior team members for assistance."

Mrs. Lee smiled as she concluded, no doubt feeling confident in her presentation.

Most of the students headed to the table with the list of approved sites. I assumed that the juvenile detention center would be on the list. It was the only place that I might be able to stand. I didn't want to spend time at a food bank or shelter. I had enough problems of my own and didn't want to have to see other people's. At least at the juvenile detention center, I'd be able to hear stories of what not to do.

Since I didn't know what I wanted to do with my future, it wouldn't be a bad idea to start somewhere I knew I didn't want to end up. I scanned the short list of sites. There weren't many since Byron wasn't a large city and the locations outside of city limits that were within bus range were minimal as well. I looked at the business cards on the table until I found the one I wanted:

PC Juvenile Detention Center, contact Myra Gaines, JDO, BSW

What had I gotten myself into? I second-guessed my choice as I tucked the business card into my blue jeans pocket.

"Hi Emma." Mrs. Lee met me as I was heading for the door.

"Hello."

"How was your break?"

"It was okay." I wished she would skip over all the niceties and get to the point. I wanted to find Terry so we could eat lunch.

"I'm so glad that you had a nice break. Terry said that you all went to Clemson's Prospective Students event. How did you like it?"

"It was fine. I think he would love it there."

"What about you? You think you could see yourself going off to a university like Clemson?"

"You know, Mrs. Lee, I don't know. Right now, I'm trying to figure out how to complete my senior project. I can't handle more than that at this time."

One thought at a time. I would choose to not get aggravated at Mrs. Lee's annoying questions. However, what I really wanted to say was, *"No Mrs. Lee, I can't see myself there. I can't see myself anywhere but away from you right now."*

"That's one approach to take Emma. One step at a time."

She smiled gently at me, but I knew she wanted to say more. I managed to return her smile, hoping to head towards the door once more.

"But you know Emma, I'm rooting for you to surprise yourself… to believe that you can handle anything you set your mind to. And *you* have a great mind."

Mrs. Lee smiled once more before turning toward another senior student perusing the resource tables.

As I exited the door and entered the school corridor, students were rushing back and forth carelessly for the lunch hour. The freshmen and sophomores remained in class while the upperclassmen either exited the building to go to their cars for lunch or into the cafeteria to socialize. Most seniors went off campus for lunch. Terry nor I had cars but there were several restaurants within walking distance we'd frequent.

Mama couldn't afford to give me much lunch money. She gave me my weekly $8.00 to cover the daily school lunch fee but nothing more. Maddie was able to eat free lunch, so she liked to stick around the cafeteria with her friends. Although Mama was technically her guardian, she did not receive any financial support for caring for her, so Maddie qualified for certain reduced and free items that I did not. Mama would give her $4.00 or $5.00 from time to time so she would have some "pocket change" though. I would normally take my weekly lunch allowance and spend it at one of the fast-food chains near the school, although Terry would usually pay extra for me to have more food than I could afford or offer to cover my entire meal.

Sister Brown and his dad tended to give Terry extra money. "May as well use it," Terry would always say. I really hoped his dad would come home and be a better dad at some point because although he acted as if his dad being gone so much never bothered him, I could tell it did. Not having a parent around had an impact on you whether you wanted it to or not.

"Oh, excuse me," one of two giggling girls slightly bumped into me.

"Hi, Terry," the other girl smiled at him, making slow eye contact as she passed.

The second giggling girl was Rochelle Martin, volleyball captain and class secretary. I observed her smile as she flirted very obviously with him. Her mocha skin was smooth with no sign of the usual teenage acne. Her eyebrows had a natural arch and she had full eyelashes. Her eyes were a deep coffee brown and seemed to twinkle as she looked at Terry. She had one small beauty mark next to her nose. She was a very pretty girl, and she knew it. She didn't act conceited though and was actually pretty friendly. She didn't give most guys the time of day either which I respected. That seemed to be a rarity nowadays. Most girls were desperate for affection from the opposite sex, willing to go to all sorts of lengths to gain and keep their attention.

I had overheard many remarks about Rochelle as she passed boys in the hallways and during volleyball games. She apparently had the perfect build to be a setter and was considered "slim-thick" as the guys liked to say. She had a lean athletic build but her thighs and bottom were appealingly toned and rounded. She was also very smart and in most of the advanced placement classes with Terry.

"You know, you really ought to watch out where you're going." Terry flirted back as he maintained the now annoying drawn out eye contact.

"Alright, fine." Rochelle smiled one more time at him before turning back to her friend. They whispered something to one another and began giggling again.

He watched her walk away for a few seconds before he turned back towards me, realizing I was still standing in front of him.

"Hi," I said shortly.

"Oh, hey, Emma." He gave me an awkward half smile as he turned to look over his shoulder one last time.

"It's fine. I can skip lunch and wait with you as you drool over Rochelle. You know, hand you a Kleenex to catch the dribble every so often."

"Wait, what?" He stammered.

"All I'm saying is if you two are gonna act like that, maybe one of you should actually say something meaningful to one another."

I rolled my eyes as I put my backpack down to unlock my locker. I preferred to put it away when we went to lunch as opposed to dragging it around with me. I already had my money and school ID card tucked into my pocket along with the business card for the Juvenile Detention Center.

"Whatever, Emma!"

Terry slammed his locker door and walked ahead of me. It must have dawned on him that he had gone off too far because he slowed his pace while I caught up.

"You know, Emma, I don't like Rochelle like that."

He looked at me with soft eyes before taking his glasses off to clean the lens on his shirt. After wiping them to his liking, he quickly tucked the corner of the shirt back into his pants.

"She's nice and we have a lot in common."

"Uh huh, sure," I said sarcastically. "Like y'all both like each other and neither one of you want to admit it. I'm a girl, Goof-head, or did you forget? I know when girls like a boy."

"Nope, I didn't forget. You're always irritating me and bugging me about silly stuff… like this conversation right now. Not sure why I picked a girl for a best friend."

He quickly dodged my punch, knowing those words would get a reaction from me. I hated it when he emphasized the fact that I was a girl as it related to our friendship. Just because I was a girl didn't mean I was inferior to having a boy for a friend. It made me feel like he had settled for me, and I never wanted to be something or someone anyone settled for.

He laughed as he rushed out the front doors and headed for the school entrance steps.

"Where should we go today for lunch?"

"I don't know, you pick."

I could never decide on lunch. I think it's just one thing girls were always indecisive over: picking food. There were just too many good options to narrow down to one.

Rochelle and one of her friends must have known we hadn't decided on food yet because she walked over.

"Hey, do y'all wanna go get tacos? I can drive."

"Uh, yeah sure," Terry answered before I had a chance to consider the proposal.

"Great!" Rochelle replied with that familiar smile and prolonged eye contact.

"My car is right over there." She pointed at a black sedan parked nearby.

As we walked toward the car, Terry and Rochelle discussed an upcoming assignment in their advanced English class and how they felt like it was "irrelevant."

Rochelle unlocked the car door and made her way into the driver's seat. She motioned for Terry to sit in the front while her friend and I got into the backseat. He either had forgotten or not cared that I had a vote in this matter. He didn't even seem to notice me or realize I was still there as he devoted his attention to Rochelle.

"Oh yes, I think I'll get in without a problem. My GPA is higher than average, I am an active volleyball player, and I submitted two teacher recommendations with my application." Rochelle expressed her confidence in getting into her top college choice.

"Oh man, yeah, you'll get in with no problem. Do you think they'll offer you a scholarship for sports too?"

His face was different. It was serious and showed full interest in the conversation. He looked intrigued by Rochelle and her responses. His shoulders were relaxed and his smile genuine. As she moved her hand to explain whatever she was saying, he shifted his gaze to her hands and back to her face. I watched her speak, her lip gloss accentuating her lips. Her smile shone bright. Her teeth were picture-perfect and held a natural whiteness. It was easy to see how anyone could be drawn to her. She was like a popular girl who was too down to earth to notice her popularity.

I kept replaying Terry's words in my head, *"you know Emma, I don't like Rochelle like that... she's nice and we have a lot in common."*

He really believed that he wasn't attracted to her. Or at least he wanted to convince me of it. His face was intent and his eyes were concerned when he spoke those words to me. It was as if he wanted to protect me... again. But why would he want to protect me from his feelings for Rochelle? There was nothing that I wouldn't support him in, even if that was him having a girlfriend.

"Oh yeah, like that time she gave us our reports back and they were all marked up. Oh man, I was so mad." Terry and Rochelle laughed in the front seat.

She touched his hand amid their amusement. He may have not noticed that it was premeditated, and she used the laughter as a cover up for touching him, but I did. I knew that even if he didn't like her like *that,* she liked him in that way. She liked him how Chelsea from church did. She could see herself being his girlfriend, maybe even getting married and having babies someday. Terry didn't know it yet, but he wanted to be liked by Rochelle in a romantic way.

I looked out the window as my stomach suddenly felt uneasy. I really did mean that I would support Terry in anything but maybe it wouldn't be easy while he was looking at another girl the way he was doing now. Besides, he always had a tender spot for me, and I knew I could get away with almost anything and he'd always be there. He'd always love and protect me. But now, I saw his guard falling for Rochelle and it scared me to have to share him with another girl in any way.

I hoped with all my might that he meant what he had said and that he didn't like Rochelle in a romantic sense, but deep down, I knew that was simply not the truth. The truth was something that I was not prepared for. The truth was something that, even I, didn't want to admit.

"How about here, guys?" Rochelle turned to look towards the backseat where her friend and I were sitting.

We both shrugged. Maybe Rochelle should ask Terry about my inability to pick a restaurant. All I knew was that I was hungry, but the thought of them together had made my stomach sour.

"Okay, so I'll make an executive decision," Rochelle giggled. Suddenly, her laughter began to frustrate me. Not everything, clearly, was that funny. However, Terry laughed with her anyway.

"Well, that's probably the best because Emma is not going to be helpful in this at all. I always end up picking."

I could see Terry dart his eyes at me from my peripheral vision, but I did not feel like looking at him right now. He could spend his time looking at Rochelle for all I cared. That is what I would do. I'd just go with the flow and pretend like it didn't bother me. After all, not caring had always worked for me before.

"You okay, Emma?" I heard Terry's voice drop in tone as Rochelle pulled into a parking spot.

"Yep." I reached for the door handle.

I just needed to get out of the car. I needed to escape the feeling of being trapped inside. I looked up to the sky for a sign from God. Maybe there would be a cotton candy sky or some sort of design in the clouds to make me feel seen; to make my emotions seem relevant. Nope. It was an overcast day. The wind blew softly, and my skin felt sticky from the humidity. The situation was hopeless. The day was doomed.

"Emma Rose." He grabbed my arm lightly and leaned close to my ear knowing I felt vulnerable. Even when I tried to hide it from him, he still knew.

"Hey, it's going to be okay you know? I don't know what's wrong. But I promise I'll be here with you through it."

I listened to his quiet words as he tried to respect my need for privacy. He knew I'd be distraught if the other girls heard them. I stuffed my tears inside as he squeezed my hand. He didn't always use words with such depth but when he did it was because he could sense the massive feelings beginning to suffocate me from within. He attempted to snuff them out through his reassurance.

The first time that he had promised to be with me through hard things was after my dad's funeral. That day was so hard and a bit of a blur. So many people were coming by to hug me and Mama and tell us that they were "there for us." I didn't even have enough strength to lift my head as I sat on the pew in front of my dad's coffin.

Tears had poured from my eyes like rain. My head pounded, the room spun, and I felt as if I would vomit. I had no awareness of what was happening around me other than the fact that the man I loved with all my being was no longer coming home. He wouldn't be there to meet me with that awkward, forced smile when I arrived from school. He would no longer be there to tell me to "Shine bright, Baby Girl! Gods got a plan for you."

Mama was the one who knew the Bible inside out and attended every church gathering. She held an office in the church and tried to live her life the "way a Christian should." Daddy on the other hand, struggled with his drinking. The war took away who he wanted to be, is what he used to always say. He didn't make it to church every week and he cursed more than Mama had liked. He was an imperfect man but his love for me was always apparent. He didn't put any extra pressure on me to be anyone other than myself. He loved me for me.

We would sit out on Missums for a whole afternoon and not say one word to one another but that didn't matter. Being with him was enough. I learned lessons from Mama, but it was Daddy that taught me the most about God. Daddy wrestled with his thoughts all the time and in the end, I think he just gave up. He gave in to them with alcohol.

I always thought that if he could still talk about God's goodness while in such pain and try to remind me that God loved me too, then God must be real. I didn't understand God or why he would take my daddy from me, but I tried to not completely turn from Him because a piece of me felt like if I did that, then I'd have to let go of my dad too.

As I sat at the funeral, nothing made sense and the ache in my heart was indescribable. I didn't even remember where Mama was at that time. Many people put their hands on my shoulder and tried to encourage me, but I didn't want their touch. I didn't want them near. I just wanted one more day with my daddy.

Then I felt the familiar touch of my best friend. He sat next to me in silence. I could sense him by his smell and his presence. I cried without pause and never lifted my head, but he continued sitting next to me without flinching. He had finally leaned over and whispered to me, "I'll be here with you through it."

He didn't apologize. He didn't tell me it would be okay. He didn't remind me that "joy would come in the morning light." He just sat with me and made me that promise that I knew I could trust in. In that moment, his words were enough to remind me to keep breathing through my tears. Although the aching of my heart continued, I had felt it simmer down just a little.

Terry had squeezed my shoulder one last time before he had to leave the room at the funeral home's request. I still had no energy to lift my head and look at him that day, but I knew he had meant what he had said.

But today, as he reminded me that he would be here with me through it, I knew that he had no idea what was actually hurting me. The irony was that he reminded me he'd be with me forever, but I mourned the idea of him leaving me to be with some girl. I dreaded the idea of him loving her more than me someday and most of all I couldn't cope with the idea of him leaving to go to school without me.

A few tears rolled down my cheek as I looked into his eyes. He pulled me in close and gave me a hug. I settled into his chest, feeling the warmth and security it offered. I sensed Rochelle and her friend looking at us, possibly not understanding our connection. At that moment, though, I did not care. Terry didn't seem to care either.

Chapter Seven

"How are you, Darling?"

Mrs. Hennagen smiled at me as she held tightly to her coffee mug. Decorated on it was a little girl wearing an apron and puffy bonnet. She was looking down at a butterfly that sat within her palm and lilac-colored flowers bloomed at her feet. There was a pleasant delight in the little girl's eyes as she looked at the butterfly. Written beneath the picture were the words: "God made all things."

"Good morning, Mrs. Hennagen."

"Well, what's going on with you today, Little One?" She blew her coffee before taking a sip.

"Not much. I was supposed to come by to see if you had any laundry you wanted us to do for you today?"

Mama mentioned that Mrs. Hennagen was having trouble with her washing machine and there was no way she would let an eighty-year-old take her clothes to the wash-a-teria.

Mrs. Hennagen laughed softly, "Oh Lord, bless your mama. She really is an angel. But tell her, I'm alright. I don't go anywhere anyhow except for church so I'm doing fine with my clothes for now. Someone is coming out to fix my washer tomorrow."

"Yes ma'am, I'll let her know."

When I didn't readily run off, like I would have done a few months back, Mrs. Hennagen invited me to come in and join her for a while.

"Yes ma'am, that would be nice. Could I use your phone to let Mama know that I'll be sitting with you for a little bit?"

"Of course, Darling, go ahead. Did you eat breakfast already?"

"No ma'am," I shouted over my shoulder as I began dialing home.

"Okay, well that's good for me, I have some biscuits in the oven and some homemade peach jam. There's no way I can eat it all by myself."

After hanging up the phone, I sat at the table near Mrs. Hennagen, excited about the prospect of warm biscuits and jam.

"So, tell me, what's new Darling? You been practicing what I taught you? One thought at a time?"

"Yes ma'am, I have. The other day I tried it out on my teacher when she wouldn't leave me alone. I decided to try to think good thoughts about her, but I couldn't find any. I just don't know her all that well, so instead, I started by choosing to be nice with each of my responses."

Mrs. Hennagen laughed, knowing I had likely fumbled the attempt.

"I wish I could've been in the room that day. I'm sure your face did not match your words." She continued laughing, "It can be tricky, can't it?"

"Yes ma'am. I don't know if I'm very good at it yet. Like the other day I went to lunch with my friend—"

"Terry?"

"Yes ma'am, and some of his friends. I had some difficult things come to my mind. I tried so hard to think of good thoughts, but I ended up crying anyway."

I looked down at the burgundy tablecloth not sure if I should be embarrassed or not.

"Oh Darling, raise your head up. Choosing good thoughts doesn't mean you'll be free from tears. It only means you try to stay positive despite what's happening around or in you. Sometimes we need tears, ya hear? They're cleansing."

BEEP! BEEP!

The oven timer sounded, cutting Mrs. Hennagen's words short. I could smell that the biscuits were ready before the alarm went off however. She grabbed her oven mitt and pulled the biscuits out, seemingly satisfied with their appearance. The smell in the small kitchen intensified and my stomach growled with anticipation.

Mrs. Hennagen grabbed a glass bowl of peach jam and placed it in the center of the table. Beside it, she laid out a spreading knife along with two white plates. Each one had pink and green flowers bordering them. Finally, she placed the biscuits, which were now nestled in a serving platter, onto the table before taking a seat across from me.

"Pray with me, Darling."

I bowed my head in acknowledgment.

"Lord, thank you for this food set in front of us. Thank you for your mercy and all-knowingness. Thank you for Emma and the plans you have for her. Let this food nourish us. In Jesus' name we do pray."

"Amen."

"Help yourself, Darling."

I eagerly grabbed a biscuit from the platter. It was warm to the touch and smelled divinely of honey and butter.

"The key to our thoughts is ourselves, Emma. We have the power to choose each one. Sure, thoughts pop in and out of our minds but deciding to keep them is up to us. Your current job isn't to think good thoughts about your teacher. Now, you should be kind to her and understand that she is one of God's children, but it isn't up to you to think good things about her for you to have a conversation with her.

"When I told you to take one thought at a time, I meant one thought about *you* at a time. You need to pick: Are you the girl that can't be respectful and willing to hear what other people say? Are you the girl who is helpless and hopeless? Are you the girl who can't handle the task in front of you? Heck, are you the girl who can't take the time out to sit and eat breakfast with a lonely old woman? *You* choose how to respond to each thought.

"You were made for hard things, Darling, and you must make a decision with each thought, to be the girl you think God created you to be. Now that can be tricky. If you think God made you worthless and helpless, then it will get very messy, and your life will go down a bad path. But if you think God made you for a purpose and to be greater than you can imagine, then your life and every interaction you have will be able to be used for hope in this world."

"I don't know, Mrs. Hennagen," I mumbled, avoiding her eyes. "I just don't have that figured out. I'm not settled on what God wants from me or if I can be anyone other than who I am right now."

"Well, that's the thing Darling. He doesn't want you to be anyone other than yourself. But if you think that you are not good enough, then you'll never be comfortable being yourself. A secret?"

I looked up at her. "Yes please."

"Even if you don't believe it about yourself just yet, act like you do anyway. It may feel weird in the beginning, but eventually as you see yourself progress, you'll begin to believe it too. You don't have to be 100% certain when you choose to think positively about yourself. But you do have to give yourself the chance."

She took a bite of her biscuit. "Mmmmm now that's good."

I watched as she closed her eyes and began chewing slowly, enjoying each bite. She had a silly smile on her face as she continued eating. It was as if she had drifted off into an unknown land with her biscuit. I laughed as I imagined her skipping through a field of flowers holding hands with a biscuit.

"What?" She smiled at me as I continued in laughter.

"Are you laughing at me? I've tended to enjoy my food since I was a little girl. My mother said I used to hum when I ate. It drove people crazy."

She fought to hold her mouth shut as laughter began to escape.

"Oh, and Pastor H used to just stare at me when we first met. He teased me and asked if I had any other weird things about me that he should know. He married me anyway."

"That's so funny, Mrs. Hennagen. I would have never thought you were in love with food. I would tease you too if I heard you humming with each bite."

"In love? Hmmm. Maybe, but I think it's more of an appreciation of it. I've learned to control the humming, but I still try to enjoy each bite of my food. I count it as a blessing is all. I think food is a gift from God. Enough about me though; tell me how you ended up in tears the other day."

I had been more willing to talk to Mrs. Hennagen lately, but I wasn't ready to talk to her about everything. There were some things I didn't feel comfortable sharing just yet.

"Oh, I don't really want to talk about that part if that's okay."

"That's totally fine, Darling. How about that senior project you have coming up. How's that going?"

"Well, I left a message for the lady that's supposed to supervise me at the detention center. Mama says she will let me know when she calls back."

"Oh yes, that's right. One of my good friends works over that way. If you hadn't heard back from the lady you called within a few days, let me know and I'll give you Myra's number. She is a great resource. She always has been."

"Myra Gaines?"

"Yep, that's her. Is that who you will be working with?"

"I'm not sure, I just know that her name was written on the business card. How do you know her?"

"Let's just say that she reminds me of you, and we too had to develop our relationship through the years. She's much younger than me but we keep in close contact. I think we understand each other since we have the same name, only she spells hers without the extra A. I spell mine, M-a-y-r-a. I'll make sure to let her know you are trying to reach her if I talk to her this evening. That detention center keeps her busy, but she loves being there and helping those youngsters."

"Okay, thank you, Mrs. Hennagen. I'm supposed to meet her for some sort of interview first. I'm kind of nervous but I'll try to *choose* to think that I don't need to be."

"There you go."

Mrs. Hennagen winked at me as she took another bite of her beloved biscuit.

****

Mama was out front talking to Joe when I got back home.

"Hi Mr. Joe." I waved, noticing Mama checking me over from afar to make sure I was intact.

I didn't call many adults by their first names, but Mr. Joe insisted we call him Joe and not Mr. Richards. As long as we put the word mister in front of his name, Mama was okay with it.

"I'm okay, Mama." I attempted to diffuse her apprehension.

"I'm glad."

Satisfied, she turned to continue talking with Mr. Joe.

"Emma you're just in time. There's a phone call for you." Maddie peeked her head out the front door.

I headed into the kitchen, hoping it wasn't Ms. Gaines. Volunteering at the detention center made my stomach flutter. I still had no idea what I would do there and how I could be useful, not to mention, how being there would be useful to me.

"Hello?"

"Hello, Emma," a friendly, flowery voice said from the other side of the phone. Her voice reminded me of an older and more mature Maddie.

"I'm Myra Gaines, your contact here at JDS. I wanted to set up your interview for next week if possible. Do you have a job or any after school activities that I need to consider?"

"No ma'am." I shifted my feet as my stomach tightened.

"Okay, that's great. Do you think you could be here Monday at 4:30?"

"Yes ma'am."

"Do you have any questions for me at this time, Emma?"

"I was wondering if I would be able to have assistance with a bus pass since my mama will be working during the weekdays that I need to be there."

"Actually, yes. Transportation is something that we provide for students who are accepted into our volunteer program. We will ensure, if you are selected, that you have adequate transportation to and from the detention center. Do you have any other questions?"

"No ma'am."

After saying our good-byes, I turned to find Maddie staring at me with her usual irritating smile.

"Soooooo…" She inched closer.

I shrugged at her, not understanding what she was so interested in. It wasn't as if someone had called to let me know I'd won the lottery.

"She set me up for an interview on Monday. Why are they making us interview to volunteer? That makes no sense especially because I'd rather not be there at all. I would rather not do any of this."

"Well, yep, that sounds like your normal answer. So, what if it is different? Do you really want not completing your project to keep you from graduating? You do know we have to graduate together, right?"

"Ugh, Maddie, don't be annoying right now. I don't want to think about it."

"Fine, since your mama is outside, let's talk about you and Terry eating lunch with Rochelle and her friend yesterday. You two never eat with anyone. What's—"

"Nope, not that either. I don't want to talk about that either, Maddie."

I walked over to the den and grabbed the remote control for the TV.

In true Maddie fashion, she followed me and sat right beside me. I felt her intense eyes peering at me. She'd had that habit since we were smaller. She'd always known that I couldn't stand her staring at me, so I'd eventually cave and tell her what she wanted to know.

"Oh my gosh, Maddie!! What do you want to know? We ate with them. It's not a big deal."

"Yeah, but it's a big deal that you ate with Terry *and* Rochelle." We sat in silence for a few seconds. My quietness, more from replaying the car ride in my mind, while Maddie's silence was in anticipation of my response.

"Rochelle *and* Terry. Rochelle, the girl that likes Terry."

I shot a mean look her way. "What are you talking about?!"

"Oh, come on Emma Rose. You know exactly what I'm talking about. You're telling me that you're okay with Terry eating with Rochelle, whether you are there or not?"

"He didn't give me a choice. He just made the decision for both of us." I snapped, suddenly feeling upset all over again.

"*And* how do you feel about him making that decision?"

"Maddie, drop it! I don't know what it is you think you know but you need to let it go. Seriously, you're beginning to make me mad."

"I wouldn't be making you mad if you didn't know it was true. Quit lying to yourself Emma. You know it's true. Terry—"

"Just shut up, Maddie! Shut up! You sound so stupid right now. I don't care about Rochelle liking Terry or him liking her back. Terry and I are friends and that's it. So what?"

I had begun screaming before I realized it.

"*Uh huh.*"

Maddie sat in the same spot without moving. She wasn't bothered by my anger. She never was.

"What I said was, Rochelle likes Terry. I never said Terry likes Rochelle. Those words never came out of my mouth."

I looked at her, my mind mixed with anger and confusion.

"Well, he does okay. He likes her too, Maddie. You should have seen her flirting with him. He just laughed along and stared at her with that dumb goofy *in love* look."

I hung my head down and fought back tears. "He likes her too," I mumbled.

Maddie let out low laughter.

I looked up at her ready to let her have it. How dare she laugh during this moment. Here I was pouring my heart out and she had the nerve to laugh.

She gave me a gentle look and then began to speak quietly. Compassion filled her words, "Oh, Emma, you can't really believe that. Terry could never like or love another girl the way he does you. He could never truly like Rochelle because of how he feels for you. He loves you. Don't you see that?"

I stared at her not knowing what to say or think. I had moved beyond anger into an unknown feeling. My brain couldn't process what was being said. All I could do was gaze through her.

"Emma, you do know you are a catch, right?"

I continued to look beyond her, now wanting the conversation to end. I felt numb and resistant to everything around me.

Maddie just sat there next to me, hoping to wear me down. Her staring didn't bother me this time though. It was her words that had sent my head into a tailspin. Terry, *like* me? It just wasn't possible. I wasn't like Rochelle.

It wasn't that I didn't think I was pretty. I just didn't have the same kind of drive and energy she had. I wasn't a people person and sure didn't have the bubbly personality she possessed. I wasn't the type of person that loved holding intellectual and deep conversations. I didn't take any advanced high school classes and probably couldn't get many, if any, recommendations from any of the teachers at school.

I wasn't a bad student; I just didn't see the point in trying to excel at school when it was only something that merely needed to be completed. I learned what I could but didn't work hard at trying to learn anything that I felt couldn't assist me later in life. It just wasn't practical to do so. Kids like Rochelle and Terry had plans to go to college and do great things with their lives while I was just trying to make it through the day most of the time. Maddie needed to understand that I was not the type of girl Terry would be attracted to. We were just friends.

I tried to imagine myself being a special girl that a boy like Terry would be interested in, but I couldn't force myself to pretend I was someone I wasn't. I was who I was. Emma, a B-student, daughter of a widowed mother and deceased alcoholic. My story was not the most tragic; God just didn't write anything glamorous into it.

As I continued to think, my mood lightened because the truth was, I never cared if boys liked me or not. I *did* care, however, what

Terry thought of me. I wanted to be a good friend to him. I pushed aside the thought of him seeing me as anything beyond that. Plus, he belonged with someone like Chelsea or Rochelle. He deserved someone of their caliber.

"Emma, please say something," Maddie begged.

I moved away from her, attempting to create some sort of distance.

"You're wrong, Maddie. Terry is just my friend. He made a promise to be my friend forever and that's what he's doing. Now can we please just drop it."

I no longer wanted to watch TV. I just needed to be alone. Mama was still outside talking to Joe so sitting on Missums was out of the question for now. Besides, if I made any endeavor to wander outside, she would accuse me of being nosey. Instead, I headed up to my room and laid on the bed hoping nap would help me forget the mess Maddie had just stuck me in.

Chapter Eight

It was cold in Mrs. Gaines' office. It reminded me of the principal's office at Peachtree, not that I was accustomed to being sent there often. It just had a similar lonely feel to it.

Papers were scattered around her desk and piles of manila folders were stacked atop of the filing cabinets behind it. She was either insanely busy, unorganized or both. There were no posters on the walls, except a faded "Dare to Dream" picture. The advertisement had four teenage children, all different colors, sitting on the stoop of someone's front porch. One was smoking a cigarette, while two others were engaged in conversation. One boy, however, stood apart from the other teens looking up to the sky. If it was meant to be a motivational poster, it wasn't working.

"UumHuuuH!" Mrs. Gaines cleared her throat as she sorted through the papers I was required to bring in: my current transcript, a referral from Mrs. Lee, and an agreement signed by Mama.

Mrs. Gaines' forehead appeared strained as she read through the papers. Her skin had an olive tone to it, and little brown freckles decorated the bridge of her nose and tops of her cheeks. She wore her hair in an unraveling bun. The strands was fine and a few moved about her head wildly anytime she repositioned her head.

Her face was round, matching the rest of her body. She was clothed in a loose flowing floral shirt with grey business casual pants. Her shoes were flat and looked worn. She sported a simple wedding ring but no other jewelry. Her overall demeanor screamed exhaustion.

A red-headed guy who could be no more than twenty-one popped his head into the office uninvited. "Excuse me Myra, I know you're with a candidate, but we need you up front for just one second."

"Okay…" Mrs. Gaines' voice trailed as she stood. She looked over at me, smiled, apologized, and promised to return as quickly as possible.

As she walked past, I could smell the perfume she had selected for the day. It reminded me of a fresh rain scent.

Now that she had left her chair, I could see a picture frame sitting on the back end of her desk. There was not much room for any decorations, let alone all the papers that were spread about the desk, but one little picture frame sat beside her printer.

I moved closer to get a better view. I secretly loved seeing people's families, hearing their stories, and wondering what made them *them*. I always imagined what their lives were like and if I could relate to them or possibly be a friend of theirs.

A little girl smiled at me from the frame. Her eyes glimmered brightly and she had the biggest, snaggle-toothed grin. Behind her was a man who was also smiling. Their similar features undoubtedly identified him as her father. Plus, the joy in her eyes and the richness in which she was laughing, had to come from someone she deeply loved. I imagined him tickling her in hope of assisting the photographer to capture a genuine moment of delight.

The happiness of the portrait overtook me as I sat back in my chair, refusing to unfasten my gaze from the little girl's infectious expression of joy. I began reminiscing on the great times I had with my dad when I was about her age. He used to love going fishing. He said it helped him to clear his mind.

One day, I whined just enough, hoping to finally convince him to take me with him. He gave in, although he tried to resist as long as he could. When we arrived at the lake, we sat on a rickety old boat for a few hours together. We didn't catch one fish, but we laughed and joked, and I listened to him tell stories. Eventually, he began to invite me to fish with him often and we caught plenty of fish together.

I laughed aloud as I recalled the first time he had taught me to clean a fish we had caught. I had squirmed and dang near cried at the sight of the fish alone. It was so slippery and slimy, and I couldn't get over how creepy it felt watching its eye stare up into mine.

As I remembered Daddy's voice and smile, Mrs. Gaines' door opened abruptly snatching me into the reality that he was gone.

"I am so sorry, Emma. Things can get crazy around here." She shot me another smile as she sat in her chair. "Now where were we?"

"You were reviewing my paperwork," I said gently, clearing my throat.

"Yes, yes. I am actually very impressed by your grades Emma. Looks like you have a 2.9 GPA, which doesn't come easy."

I looked back at her quizzically, thinking that a 2.9 GPA wasn't much to be impressed by..

"You look confused. What are you thinking?"

"Oh, just …. well, that's the first time anyone has made my GPA sound like it was something to be proud of."

"Hmm," Mrs. Gaines looked down. "Well, I can say with confidence, as a young woman who grew up in this community, a 2.9 GPA is something worth celebrating. I understand it's not a 4.0, but Ms. Griggs, considering a lot of the barriers the people in this community are faced with, a 2.9 tells me that you're refusing to lie down and die."

"Lie down and die?"

She let out a quick laugh that sounded like a mix between a snort and hiccup. I had never heard someone laugh in such a manner. I hoped she didn't make that noise in front of people often.

"Oh Ms. Griggs, I'm sorry. We have just adopted certain sayings around here. When I say 'lie down and die' I simply mean that whatever obstacles you may have in your life, have not overtaken you. I know many kids who give up. They feel like they can never overcome their circumstances, so they give in and don't fight. In a sense they just lie down and allow themselves to be defeated. Their spirit and will die. The students that come through here with even a

2.0, I celebrate them because that tells me that they are choosing to not yield and succumb to the life dealt to them. And you, Ms. Griggs, strike me as the type of young woman who will not just overcome her obstacles but you, My Dear, will soar."

Soar? Yeah right.

My idea of overcoming was more along the lines of getting out of high school and that was it. I'd get a decent job and work my way up. Mrs. Gaines had it wrong; soaring was not my forte.

"Ms. Griggs, do you believe that? Do you believe that you are meant to soar?" She looked at me with a similar expression as Mrs. H.

It was a direct non-judgmental gaze that I felt could see right through me. It made me uncomfortable. I looked down and cleared my throat, hoping to divert her but when I looked up, she was still focused on me, awaiting my response.

"Well, I think that grownups like to tell us kids that we can be anything we want, or we can change the world, and in your case, we can soar. It puts a lot of pressure on us. We are all just trying to figure it out."

Mrs. Gaines repositioned in her chair. "It is a lot of pressure, Ms. Griggs, but it's not put on by us adults as you say, rather it's put on by you."

I stared at her. *Was this lady crazy?*

"You have a choice." She leaned in closer, staring even deeper into my soul.

"You can have a positive outlook and believe in yourself, *or* you can allow the negative thoughts and obstacles you sense become pressures that dictate how you live life. I say, you are meant to soar. You say, it's just a cop out by adults. What's your role in it, Ms. Griggs? How do you go about figuring it out, as you say?"

She sat back in her chair as if she had just dominated her hand in cards.

She knew Mrs. H alright. They sounded just alike. I was pretty sure she didn't want me to answer the question she had asked aloud, so I didn't respond. I just continued to glare back at her with an intense regret for having chosen to engage in the conversation to begin with. I should have just agreed that I was meant to soar so we could have moved on to some other impersonal, less intrusive topic.

"I'll tell you what though, Ms. Griggs, I admire that you have a voice at your age. You aren't afraid to speak out against things you see as unfair. Keep that up. Don't let anyone deter you from that; even me." She gave me one of those empathetic smiles once more and then turned her eyes back downward to further examine the papers I had brought in.

I began twiddling with my fingers, frustrated by her polite remarks but even more irritated at myself for having made her feel as if I was interested in her perspective. As she continued to read my personal questionnaire sheet, I glanced back over at the smiling girl in the picture. Her happiness was so pure that I couldn't break my gaze away.

"This is Lindsey, my daughter." Mrs. Gaines brought the picture frame closer so I could get a better look.

"She's six and a half. You can't leave off the 'half' or she'll have a fit." Her laugh did not contain the obnoxious snort this time around. *Thank heavens!*

"She's cute… and really happy."

"Yeah, they all start out that way," she joked.

I wasn't going to do this with her. I wasn't going to continue to make small talk with her and pretend like she had the potential to be a friend. I forced a sideways smile and quickly looked toward the door at the back of the room. Maybe she would get the point and move the interview along quicker.

"Ms. Griggs—" She began.

"Can you just call me Emma?" I couldn't take one more "Ms. Griggs."

As expected, she returned my rude interjection with a slight head tilt and warm smile.

"Emma, I have a philosophy in life. I am not owed respect by others if I cannot first come to respect myself. If it bothers you that I call you Ms. Griggs, I'll refrain for now, but I do hope you can come to accept and value what the title 'miss' adds to who you are."

With that, she did a quick half turn in her office chair and rose to a stand.

"Now how about I cut right to the chase… Emma."

She chose to sit in the chair adjacent to me, as if my request to be called Emma somehow was really a plea for her to come closer.

"From the moment I spoke with you on the phone, I had a feeling that you would be the young lady I chose to volunteer here. As a matter of fact, when you walked into my office today, I knew I didn't need to conduct a formal interview because you were the person I would select. You may be wondering why. Well, let's just say, by the end of your time with us here at PJD, you'll know exactly why."

I assumed PJD stood for Peachtree Juvenile Detention, but I refused to ask her to clarify. I just wanted to go home.

"Come with me, Ms. Gr– Emma."

Mrs. Gaines led me out of her office, past the many other cluttered desks, most of which looked unoccupied and as if they were just overflow spaces for tons of paperwork that needed to be filed. Weary smiles were exchanged between her and a few other office staff as we walked by.

A short corridor emerged once we had exited the office area. The ground was a gray and white concrete mixture and the walls blank. White, fluorescent lights settled between the rectangular tiles of the ceiling. Stains and old bugs adorned the dirty slates and flickering lights. There was also a stale smell lingering in the air. At the end of the hallway was a brown door with a small rectangular window covered by a poster or some other object to prevent people from seeing in or out.

"Alright Emma, I want to introduce you to a few people here. Before we enter, this is our STATUS OFFENSE AREA, also known as the SOAR area."

Wait! Had she meant I was meant to soar or meant to S.O.A.R. like these kids? Bad word choice, Gaines!

'Kids in this area are here for offenses such as running away, curfew violations, truancy from school, underage drinking and some are here for what we call continual 'acting out.' They have not necessarily been sentenced to jail, but most of their offenses are against the law due to their age. I believe it's a pivotal time in their life and they commit these minor offenses because of their environment or how they view themselves. Although their violations are typically minor, they can lead to more serious crimes later.

"This is my favorite part of my job because I feel as if I can impact their life in a way that they will consider choosing a better path. We currently have ten kids in the SOAR area, all ranging from the ages of twelve to fifteen. Sometimes we get some older ones but not right now. "

She continued to ramble on as if I wasn't still stuck on the first sentence that had come out of her mouth.

"One of the criteria to be placed in the SOAR area is a violent free background. There are three to four staff members always present with the kids. I'd like you to meet them but don't feel any pressure to engage in conversation unless you want to."

Excuse me, but yes, I feel a lot of pressure!

"I would actually prefer it if you didn't the first time around. I'd like you to just observe. It'll pretty much be an in and out visit today. Any questions?"

Did I have questions? Of course, I had questions! This was supposed to be an interview. I hadn't planned on being thrown into an area with a bunch of juvenile delinquents. Ugh! Today was not going in my favor.

"Not that I can think of," I said with just enough attitude to let her know how displeased I was.

"Okay good. If you think of any while we are inside, try to wait until we leave the room. I don't want any of the kids to think you are whispering about them. We sure don't want to give them the wrong impression, okay?"

The wrong impression! What would happen if they got the wrong impression?

My stomach dropped and I unconsciously took a step backwards. Maybe I should have just joined a club or written a speech. I was good at writing. Besides, I always got an A in English.

"No need to be nervous, Emma. I'll be with you the entire time. I won't let anything happen to you here. Promise."

She met my eyes with another encouraging smile as she badged her way into the door.

"Hey, Mrs. Gaines."

A Black man who had to be in his early twenties welcomed her into the SOAR area.

"Got company today I see." He smirked in my direction, knowing that even though I was playing it cool, I was screaming on the inside.

"I'm Eddie. Most of the kids call me Mr. E. You're welcome to call me either."

He extended his hand to mine. It, along with his face told a story in themselves. His hand was a pecan complexion, his nails were cut short and were clean underneath. Despite the impressive cleanliness of his nails, the skin on his hands was course and the veins along his arms popped out without much exertion. It was clear that he was no stranger to manual labor.

His face had a scar along the side of his ear. It was easily noticed but not necessarily unpleasant to look upon. His goatee was small and unkempt, hinting that he had not gone to a barber to shape it up in quite some time, if at all.

The word *Ambria* was tattooed on the side of his neck. I wondered who she was. Guys typically didn't go and get just any girl's name tattooed on their necks. She had to be special, such as a mother or a daughter. There was one caveat though. It was common for a person to have a name tattooed on their body to commemorate someone's passing. However, it was too early to ask those sorts of questions. Despite my curiosity, I tucked them away for later.

I met his hand with mine and gave him "the nod."

He laughed, aware that I was still trying to play it cool.

"This is Emma." Mrs. Gaines spoke for me. "She's going to be with us for a little while until she graduates."

"Okay cool. What school you at?"

"Peachtree."

"Aight! Well maybe we can get you to stay with us after you graduate if you don't have plans to go far away to college."

He raised his eyebrows as if he had just offered me a deal I couldn't resist.

I cleared my throat and looked away not knowing what to say in return.

Eddie, getting the hint, turned his attention back to Mrs. Gaines. "Making rounds?"

"No, not yet. I'll come back later and complete them. I wanted to introduce Emma to the team that she will be working most closely with." She smiled and waved at a woman who had entered the area from the door in the rear.

"Hey Mrs. Gaines," the woman walked over.

"Emma, this is Lisa. She is another one of our Youth Development Specialists in the SOAR area. We call them YDs for short."

"Seems like y'all call everything something for short around here."

I chose my tone carefully, hoping to shy away from sarcasm although it was warranted. I was still upset with Mrs. Gaines for throwing me into the deep end when I was only here for an interview.

"True," all three of them said simultaneously.

"Emma, we are happy to have you here with us. We are like a little family so we will make sure to take good care of you okay, Hun?"

Aha! She was *that* person. My guess is I'd be every sort of hun, sweetie pie, sugar plum, and dumplin' there was. It made sense though. She had an athletic build and wore her red hair in a ponytail. She was dressed in cargo khaki shorts with a white shirt that read "Good vibes only." The final flag was her white Reebok shoes and mid-calf socks. My guess was that she was that carefree and overly optimistic person that you didn't know whether to hate or appreciate.

"Okay, gotta go Mrs. Gaines. I came out to grab a couple of things, but I told the boys I'd play dominoes with them."

Mrs. Gaines chuckled. "Yeah, you better hurry back. I know how intense those domino matches can be."

"Exactly! Nice to meet you sweetie."

Lisa hurried back to the rear door, swiped her badge and disappeared into the adjoining room.

"That's where everyone else is?" I pointed to the rear door that Lisa had entered.

"Yes ma'am. Wanna go check it out?" Eddie motioned towards the door.

Mrs. Gaines gave me a gentle nudge as she headed towards the room.

I followed behind cautiously. I hadn't taken notice of the window beside the mysterious door before. It was a 12x12 square that allowed us to see into the area before entering.

Eddie badged into the room and after the door clicked, he opened it with a forceful tug. He and Mrs. Gaines entered before me as I continued taking small steps, not convinced I wanted to commit. My mind screamed at me. *Abort! Abort.* It was too late for that though.

There were about ten adolescents in the area, like Mrs. Gaines had said. They didn't look like delinquents however, they just looked like kids I'd see at Peachtree or in passing. Some were sitting at tables working on what appeared to be homework. A few were seated in a space watching television. Others were around a larger table, with dominoes spread about it. They were all selecting their dominoes so none of them noticed or cared about our entrance.

Off to the side, in a chair was a boy, about fourteen, who was reading a book. I couldn't make out what he was reading, however. An overly snuggled teddy bear sat beside him in the chair. His brown skin glistened as if he had poured an entire bottle of baby oil on his legs and arms. He wore a faded t-shirt, jean shorts and some fairly new Nike shoes.

Whatever the book was, he was completely enamored by it and the loud noises in the room didn't seem to bother him.

"Aye yo!" Eddie yelled out.

The individual noise stopped. Pencils quit moving, dominoes were set down, eyes turned from the television and everyone in the room focused on him. They had all looked toward Eddie without a second thought. Everyone except the boy who was reading his book; he continued to read.

"This is Emma! She's going to be hanging out with us for a while. I need y'all to treat her like you treat me. Got it?!"

A mixture of the words, "man, whatever, yeah right, *psshhhtt*," and other unrecognizable words came out of the kids' mouths. Clearly feeling the interruption was unnecessary, they turned back and finished whatever they were doing beforehand.

Lisa offered me a reassuring smile from where she was seated, and Eddie wandered off towards the kids who were watching TV and sat beside them. He leaned in close to them and must have made a joke because the kids began laughing.

"The young man next to Lisa is Bernard and the lady sitting next to the other kids at the other table is Sheila. This is your SOAR team that you will be working with. There is another crew that comes on at night, but we don't anticipate ever having you here late enough for you to meet them."

"Okay." It was the only thing I could think to say.

"Come on, let's get your forms finalized so we can get you home."

She badged us through the door, and I turned to look back at the boy who was reading. He hadn't shifted his position at all, unconcerned with what Eddie wanted to say or uninterested in giving his time to the strange girl that had interrupted their routine.

Either way, I thought about the onion metaphor Mrs. H had used and wondered what the layers of his story were.

Chapter Nine

It was weird seeing Terry walk by me with Rochelle in the hallway at school. He looked my way as he passed but I quickly turned away from his gaze. I knew I had hurt his feelings at church the other day and couldn't describe how I felt other than misplaced. He seemed happy being friends with Rochelle and his eyes lit up when he was around her. Plus, Maddie's insistence on him *liking* me had stirred deeper feelings within me. I just couldn't reconcile any of it. Instead, I decided that he was better off apart from me. I wouldn't have to deal with nagging feelings, and I wouldn't have to subject him to my wishy-washy ways while trying to figure out what was happening inside of me.

"Emma Rose, sometimes I'll never understand you. You can be so darn knuckleheaded." Maddie looked at me impatiently.

Ever since I had snapped at Terry at church and we had been spending less time with one another, she had made it her business to hover. I suppose she thought I needed to be looked after or that I needed a friend. She may have been right though. Terry was my only friend at school before.

It wasn't that I was unpopular or that no one liked me. I just didn't allow myself to get close to people. From my observations, people didn't tend to be trustworthy to begin with. On top of that, if you were to add high school hormones, the desire to "fit in," and fear of missing out on things to the equation, it wasn't safe to regard anyone beyond face value. Most of my high school peers were only interested in looking out for themselves and trying to avoid being labeled as "wack."

High school kids just were not able to be trusted unless you had known them for years and even then, their loyalty could be questioned. Look at me and Terry's relationship for instance. We had known each other forever. He had sat beside me through some of the hardest times of my life, yet I couldn't bring myself to look at him nor be around him right now.

"Maddie, no one's asking you to keep following me around, you know?"

I slammed my locker, suddenly more annoyed than before. I tried to walk off, hoping she wouldn't follow but I knew that there was no chance of that.

"Well, somebody's gotta look after your silly behind." She started behind me until she was walking right next to me again. "I just don't understand why you gotta be mean to Terry just because you don't wanna be honest with yourself. It's quite dumb if you ask me."

"Watch it!" Another senior boy bumped into Maddie as he flew down the hallway.

"Mr. Roberts, no running in the hallway!" The vice principal shouted at him while shaking his head.

He continued to hurry down the hallway as if he had not heard a word the vice principal had said.

"Ugh! Rude!" Maddie scorned as she held her binder closer to her chest.

She drove me crazy most days because of that inextinguishable peppiness and optimism, but deep down, I knew she had my back. We never fully understood each other's ways, but we knew what it was like to be *with* one another. No matter how happy she normally was, I knew her deepest hurts and worries and she knew mine. We knew better than to say them aloud too. There were some days we would just lie across the bed taking in each other's presence.

For instance, Maddie's birthday was coming up soon, near Thanksgiving. She was never very talkative around her birthday, nor did she want to eat much during the holiday. Although she never said anything, I knew she felt helpless and anything but grateful on a day that reminded her that she was another year without her mother. She'd lie the jacket her mother left her in across the bed and either stare at it or snuggle it all morning. Then tears would come later in the bathroom. She thought that I couldn't hear her crying since she was in the restroom, but I could. I sensed when each tear dropped. I would often just sit beside the door and acknowledge her sadness. I'd never tell her that of course. It would make it awkward for her and for me. Instead, I made it my duty to be very nice and try to cheer her up in any way I could.

I didn't show Maddie much attention, not like a good cousin should, but during her birthday and Thanksgiving, I tried to go all out. She usually remained numb and flat faced but I still felt a sense of duty to try. Mama would also attempt to make her feel special during that time, but nothing could truly cheer her up. I hoped that since she would be turning eighteen this year, things would be different this time around.

As she headed into her classroom, she stopped and turned to me, "Emma Rose, you are knuckleheaded and silly, but I still think you are awesome! You should think so too before it's too late."

With that she went into the classroom filled with not-so-eager-to-learn students.

I, on the other hand continued walking towards Mrs. Lee's class, bummed about the pre-calc quiz I had today. I knew the material but I wasn't feeling up for a test right now.

Mrs. Lee met me at the door with her usual smile.

"Good afternoon, Emma."

"Hello." I attempted to walk by.

"May I have a word with you, please?"

Did I have a choice?

I stared at her, waiting for her to speak.

"I noticed that you and Terry haven't been hanging out as much as you normally do. Anything the matter?"

I couldn't believe Mrs. Lee thought it was any of her business to be asking me about Terry or anything in my personal life at all.

"We're okay," I said shortly.

"Well, I'm glad to hear it, but I will say that true friends are very hard to come by, so I hope that whatever is going on, even though you say it's nothing, gets resolved."

The bell rang and I tried to walk away once more.

"Oh, and Emma—"

I turned around with obvious annoyance plastered on my face, "Yes?"

Her eyes were doubtful, and she was not about to let me off the hook that easily.

"Why don't you step outside with me for one moment."

I hesitantly moved into the hallway while she asked the class to review their notes. She also warned them, in a nice manner, to keep their voices down as she went outside.

"Emma, I need to share something with you." She gave me a look that indicated we were in for a conversation that I didn't want to have.

"Okay." I shifted my bag on my shoulder wondering how it was fair for others to be able to review their notes while I was being held up for some sort of one-sided discussion.

"I want to tell you this because I really do think you are a wonderful young lady with a lot of potential."

Oh boy! Here we go.

"Emma, you have a horrible attitude."

Wait What?!

I glared at her filled with rage and hurt. Adults thought they could just say anything because they were older and us kids were supposed to just take it.

"You are such a smart girl and everyone around you who cares for you wants to help you. I can't tell you how many of the teachers here talk about how bright you are but how you are unwilling to try or how bad your attitude is toward them and others. The fact of the matter is that with a bad attitude you will not go very far in life. Relationships are important."

I planted my feet and began to stare at the wall adjacent to Mrs. Lee. I could feel my face turning hot and tears attempting to swell in my eyes.

"The point I'm trying to make is that you cannot continue with a bad attitude, pent up anger and meanness and expect things to be different. You can't expect to be happy and you sure can't expect others to be happy around you and for you to experience success. It's as if you are scared to move beyond it so you stay in this angry rut, pushing everyone away."

At this point, tears had begun to stream down my face as I felt blindsided, or better yet, railroaded by Mrs. Lee. Normally I had something snide and snappy to say in return, but I felt as if a dagger had hit me unexpectedly. I couldn't muster any words.

"Emma, I want the best for you and so do many others. I suspect whatever is going on with Terry can be repaired. I pray that you fix that too because he is the only one that I have seen be with you through thick and thin; him and your cousin. Don't push people away, Emma. You need people."

"Mrs. Lee, I hope you don't think I'm going in your room to take a quiz right now," I managed through my tears. "I didn't ask your opinion in the first place."

"I know you didn't, but as a woman who has been where you are before, I felt it wrong to not speak up. What you do with the information is up to you, but you can never say no one told you."

"Are you done?!" I all but yelled, infuriated that she wouldn't stop talking.

"Actually no. If you choose to stay where you are, it's because you are making a conscious choice to do so. I won't sugarcoat things for you, Emma. You don't need me to. As for not taking your quiz, again that's your choice. I will give you a pass to the bathroom so you can gather your thoughts and I will postpone the quiz until the end of class, however, if you don't take it before the end of the period, I will not give you a chance to make it up."

I didn't wait for a pass. I didn't care if I didn't get a chance to make the quiz up later. I turned around and headed for the bathroom. I had no plans to see Mrs. Lee again today.

Everyone was against me. Everyone.

I hurried down the hallway until I reached the girls bathroom. After throwing my bag on the stall hook, I leaned against the closed door. Tears ran down my face as I continued to replay Mrs. Lee's words in my mind.

Emma, you have a horrible attitude. Don't push people away. Emma, you are horrible!

Although she hadn't actually called me horrible, I knew that was what she meant. I was so horrible that I pushed people away, including Terry. I held onto anger and *meanness. Meanness!* What in the world was that supposed to mean anyway? Mrs. Lee had it all wrong. I wasn't angry. I wasn't mean. I didn't have a horrible attitude. I was alone. No one got that… I was alone. No one could see how lonely I was.

The tears failed to slow as I thought of how Daddy would have been there at home, with his sideways smile, reassuring me when I got there today. He would have told me, "Emma Rose, you are a fighter. Those teachers don't know you like I do. They don't know how tough you are." He would have been on my side and would have made me laugh and given me some sort of snack to make me feel better.

I laughed in between sobs as I remembered the time I had walked into the door and bumped my head. I had been looking back at Terry while joking about something that had happened earlier in the day. The door escaped my attention and I had managed to hit my head so badly that I developed a golf ball sized knot on my forehead. It took almost a week and half for the swelling to go down. I remember anxiously waiting as it changed colors, from black to grey to green, and then finally back to my normal skin tone.

I was so embarrassed that I had missed seeing the door. I wasn't sure if I was more upset that I had hit my head on the door in the first place or if I was just mad at myself for making the mistake of hitting my head.

Mama, of course, reminded me that I needed to pay better attention to where I was going and to quit goofing off. On the other hand, Daddy teased me a little, brought me an oatmeal cream pie and made me laugh. He knew snacks were the way to my heart. He was always on my side and made me feel as if everything would soon be okay.

I thought of how he had pulled me close, continued to pester me a bit and how we had laughed together for half of the night. Every day as the knot grew and changed colors, Daddy jokingly asked me if he could rub it. I couldn't recall a time where he didn't know exactly what I needed to cheer me up.

Unfortunately, Daddy was gone and now it was just me. Mama didn't get me. Terry had forgotten about me and everyone else thought they knew me but really had no clue who I was.

"I think he's going to ask me to the Fall Formal," a familiar voice said as she entered the bathroom.

I silenced my tears and stood as still as possible, hoping my feet wouldn't be noticed underneath the stall.

"I don't think he can dance," the other girl laughed.

"I don't care about that. I just hope he asks me soon is all."

The familiar voice was Rochelle's.

"Well, if you like it, I love it." Her friend continued to laugh and tease.

The girls chattered for a bit, laughing and talking about meaningless things before they exited the restroom.

Ugh! Could it get any worse?

The Fall Formal was right before Thanksgiving break this year. It was the Friday before Maddie's birthday. I was hoping Maddie would think about going to help take her mind off her feelings around her birthday, but that wasn't likely. But it sounded like Terry would be going—with Rochelle. Maybe I should be happy that Terry could date someone like her; someone who defended him and didn't care what her friends thought about him. My stomach still sank at the thought, however.

No matter how hard I tried to reconcile my feelings about Terry and Rochelle, my body couldn't. It didn't believe what I tried to convince my mind of. I let a few more tears fall and then decided I had cried enough. I wouldn't let myself be defeated in this moment. I'd go back to Mrs. Lee's class and act as if her words hadn't bothered me. I'd pretend that she hadn't stirred all sorts of things within me. I would hold my head up high, take my test, and look past her. I would be *on*. After all, I'm used to being *on*.

I opened the stall door, stared at myself in the mirror for a moment. I wasn't sure if I liked who looked back at me, but she was all I had at this time. I took a deep breath, put my shoulders back and forced a fake smile. I wouldn't smile going back into Mrs. Lee's classroom, but I'd at least have a look of being unbothered. She wouldn't see that she had gotten to me. I'd never give her the satisfaction of knowing.

****

"Aunt Ruthie, I just don't want to go." Maddie continued to try to explain to Mama why she wasn't interested in attending the Fall Formal.

"I think it would be good for you is all," Mama tried to make her point plain. "You're not going to be young forever, and you're about to graduate high school. You may as well have some fun."

What Mama wasn't saying was, *"Maddie, you should go so you can forget about your mama this year around your birthday."*

She hated seeing Maddie so sad during her birthday. She would secretly try to call Aunt Joleen up to two weeks before Maddie's birthday in hopes to get her to send her a letter, call her on the phone, or maybe even show up to her daughter's birthday, like a normal parent would but Mama never had any luck.

This year she looked worn out, as if she had given up any hope of getting Aunt Joleen to respond. After all, Maddie was turning eighteen. She would be an adult and legally free to do whatever she wanted, including move on without Joleen or Mama.

"I know, Aunt Ruthie. It's just never been my thing." Maddie spread butter across her roll and took a large bite, hoping to stuff her mouth so Mama would change the conversation.

"Well, I would ask your cousin what she thinks but she's in la la land." She was speaking to Madison but staring at me.

"Mama, I can hear you just fine. I'm not in la la land." I defended myself.

I was simply observing the conversation as I tended to do. She hardly ever said anything to me apart from her criticizing me anyhow. At dinner, it was Maddie and Mama who normally did all the speaking. I figured they never really cared about my input. Maddie would try to include me in the conversation from time to time, but Mama would usually make a sarcastic comment or make it obvious that she didn't feel like my opinion mattered.

"Well, Emma Rose, what do you think?" Maddie looked at me while gripping her fork.

Her eyes begged me to save her from Mama.

I shrugged. "Honestly, I don't care much about school dances either. If you want to go, go. If you don't, don't." I continued to scoop up my peas and eat them.

Mama rolled her eyes. "This is exactly why I didn't ask your opinion."

"Oh, I thought it was because I was in la la land," I muttered.

"I know you better watch your mouth." Mama snapped at me.

I knew when she used that tone, I'd better just say sorry and yes ma'am.

"Yes ma'am. I'm sorry." I looked down, not wanting to see her glare even though my only offense was being honest.

"Aunt Ruthie, have you heard from my mom?" Maddie asked softly, avoiding eye contact with Mama.

Maddie always felt a sense of guilt bringing up Aunt Joleen. She never said she felt guilty, but she didn't have to. Her posture would change. Her voice would soften, her head would lower, and she'd begin fidgeting with her hands. She was currently doing all three. She didn't want Mama to feel bad about taking care of her all these years without her mom's support, only to turn around and ask about her mom as if she was an interested party in her life. Mama was the one stuck with the bills, the sick days, the homework, and the emotions and grief Maddie dealt with, especially around this time of year. Mama was the one who continued to pick up the pieces, yet Maddie yearned for acceptance and comfort from Aunt Joleen.

"No, I haven't Maddie."

The room was silent for a few minutes. Maddie finished her food and took her plate to the sink. As she washed it and put it in the dishrack to dry, she hummed softly. I knew she was fighting back tears though. Then she told us good night and started upstairs.

I finished eating and took my plate to the sink to begin washing it as well. I wanted to offer to put the food away, but Mama's face looked twisted and upset as if she was waiting for me to leave the kitchen. Besides, she liked to clean when she was stressed. She'd put on one of her favorite gospel artists, crank the volume up and tidy up for hours if she could spare the time.

"Good night, Mama," I said softly before exiting the kitchen.

She and I didn't get along the way I'd like but I felt bad for her in times like these. I imagined she wanted to be able to make all of Maddie's pain go away. I know she'd give anything to have Aunt Joleen come back, apologize, and become the mom that Maddie so desperately wanted.

She tried so hard to love Maddie but in moments such as these, I wondered if she felt like it was enough. I wanted to give her a hug and let her know that I loved her, but that just wasn't the type of relationship we had. The irony of it was that that was the kind of relationship that she and Maddie had, but Maddie, the one who typically lavished physical affection upon her, was the one pulling away and becoming the reason she needed a hug in the first place. It normally took at least a month before she was halfway back to her normal self after her birthday.

Mama continued to stare at the wall in front of her and gave me a sort of head nod. As I headed up the steps, I sat down so I could look through the railing at Mama. Just as I suspected, when she thought I had gone, she laid her head on the kitchen table. Her shoulders moved up and down slightly and I could hear very quiet sobs. I'd never seen her full of emotion before. She was always so tough and composed.

After a few moments, she wiped her eyes and got up slowly from the table. She walked toward the kitchen cabinets. I expected her to grab some Tupperware to put the food away. Instead, she reached for the basket that held old mail and coupons in it. She fumbled around until she found what she was looking for, pulling out another white envelope.

The last time I had seen her hold such a letter, she had gripped it and it made her unusually tense. She began reading whatever was tucked inside, tears flowing down her face. After a few moments, she stuck the paper back inside and walked swiftly to the bedroom, leaving the food on the counter and the kitchen lights on. Mama was huge on not wasting electricity so whatever was written in that letter must have been important. The sudden pang I felt in my stomach reinforced my hunch.

I walked down the steps to check and see if she had decided to go to bed. Her door was in fact closed, and she had shut off the lights which meant she was not coming back out for the night. Maddie was upstairs miserable, and Mama was so upset that she didn't care to put the food away nor turn the lights out in the kitchen. The night had been victorious in trouncing our family.

I cleared Mama's plate from the table and washed her dishes. As I put the food away and cleaned the rest of the kitchen, I had a silent conversation with God, hoping He was listening. If He was up there, like Mama believed, He'd better intervene quickly or none of us was gonna make it past Maddie's birthday this year. Maddie and Mama's emotions were clearly wrecked, and I wasn't exactly the person they needed to be around to cheer them up. I had enough problems of my own that no one else cared about. I couldn't be *on* for myself and for them too. God was going to have to show up in a big way.

Rrriiiiinnnnnnggggggggg!

The phone on the kitchen wall startled me. I had no idea who could be calling this late.

"Hello." I picked up the phone not wanting it to continue ringing and bother Maddie or Mama.

"Is Mrs. Griggs home?" An older man's voice sounded from the other side of the line.

"May I ask who's calling?"

Surely, this wasn't someone from the church. They would have had enough manners to not call this late at night. Plus, if it was someone from the church they would have asked for Sister Griggs or Mama Griggs.

"Mr. Williams." He was short.

Mama peered her head out of the room, bonnet intact and she was now wearing her nightrobe. Her face looked spent.

"Who's on the phone, Emma?"

"A Mr. Williams…" I covered the mouth of the phone.

"Oh okay, I'll take that. Go ahead and get to bed now."

Mama watched as I sauntered all the way up the stairs, waiting until I was out of sight and earshot before she began speaking to the mysterious Mr. Williams.

I gave up any hope of hearing Mama's conversation and went to my room. Maddie rolled over to her right side and hushed her tears when she realized I was coming into the room. Although she tried to muffle her cries, the movement in her shoulders gave her sorrow away.

I wish I knew what to say. Maddie was good at trying to cheer me up, but I had no words for her when she needed encouragement. I had nothing to help her feel better at this moment. The only thing I could offer was space.

I slipped into my nightgown and gently laid in the bed. I avoided looking in her direction so she could be alone with her sadness. The problem was that even if I tried to ignore her tears, my body still sensed them. They were overwhelming and before I knew it, I began to let my sorrows fall in the same rhythm as hers.

Chapter Ten

Mr. E glared at me as I sat my backpack down in the SOAR area. I had decided against calling him Eddie. Mr. E had a better ring to it. He had asked me how my day at school was and I had told him it was fine. He stared at me as if he didn't believe a word coming from my mouth.

The truth was my day was far from fine. Maddie had woken with puffy eyes and looked as if she had just gotten over a cold. She had cried all night into her pillow. I couldn't sleep because of the amount of sadness she had emitted. When she was distraught, she didn't speak, which meant I had no one to talk to on the bus and in the hallway at school.

Terry had begun catching rides to school with Rochelle, so I had hardly seen him over the last couple of weeks. At church, he would sit with his mom and avoid me as much as possible. I had officially pushed him away. It was better that way. Afterall in a few months, our paths would part ways anyway. Plus, Rochelle had officially announced that Terry had decided to take her to the Fall Formal on Friday. Terry was never into those sort-of things, but I guess for Rochelle he'd do anything. I guess she was the kind of girl that a boy would do anything for.

I visualized how her hair had bounced along her back in the hallway today. She had been walking to class quickly but at least six people had stopped her to greet her along the way. She didn't seem too busy to respond. Instead, she had acknowledged them and kept that annoying little pep in her step as she strolled along. Every time she turned her head, her braids flipped perfectly, her dimples deepened, and her lip gloss shimmered like a celebrity makeup artist had applied it.

As she had walked past my locker, I heard her discussing the dance. "Terry, I decided on the blue dress so you can get the blue tie."

He had met her comment with a familiar groan while responding, "Fine, I'll get the blue tie," all while playfully smiling at her. I caught a glimpse of their hands touching as he looked back at her once more and then off to class. He had walked right by me as if I didn't exist. He hadn't looked in my direction or acknowledged me in any capacity. It felt as if someone had sucker-punched me. I knew we needed to prepare to go in different directions, but I didn't expect it to hurt this much.

"So, you're gonna try to play me, huh?" Mr. E shook his head and laughed, obviously unsatisfied with my superficial response. "But hey, if you don't wanna talk about it, I'll drop it. Just know you aren't fooling anybody."

He continued to lead the way into the group session that the SOAR kids were about to begin. His demeanor wasn't intense but he had a certain presence to him. I could tell he was street-savvy and genuine. He didn't push into my business, but he let me know, often, that he could see beyond my surface level responses. I didn't know what to make of it honestly. The SOAR kids seemed to really like him, probably because of how real he seemed. He was relatable.

"Just ignore us and pay attention." He told the kids as we walked over to the circle the group had begun to form.

Some kids sat on chairs, some at tables, some on bean bags and some just sat on the floor. Some of them were attentive while others had their heads in their laps. Mr. E said that even when the kids had their heads down or they seemed to be looking away, they were still listening, so it was important to keep speaking even when it seemed as if no one was paying attention.

A couple of weeks ago he had told me, "They're listening, Emma. Trust me, Emma, they are always listening and always watching. Someone is always watching."

He had stared into my eyes as if he was not just speaking about them but also about me.

"I think it's all dumb." One of the boys responded to the SOAR leader. "I mean, if you think about it, what is the point of it all? No one really cares anyway."

The YD had been asking the group to evaluate some of the guidelines of the SOAR program and how they apply to their everyday life. His logic sounded recognizable.

The boy continued, "The judge makes us come here because we are troublemakers. They don't know what to do with us or the problems we face so they throw us in this juvie center. They don't care. It's just a way to make the judge and everyone else feel better. It's all some big dumb process that doesn't ever fix anything."

As he continued to talk, his chest puffed up and his eyes got big. Once he realized he was upsetting himself, he waved his hand away and said, "Man, forget it." He then sat back in his chair looking despaired and annoyed.

As the YD began to address his response, I looked around the circle, feeling a sense of connection to the boy's response. It made sense to me. It was a visceral response to whatever pain and frustration he was feeling. Mr. E nor the other YD seemed affected, however. They just shook their heads and nodded as he spoke, recognizing some truth in the boy's statement as well. Sometimes things didn't have to be true to everyone else for them to be valid and feel true for the person who was expressing him or herself.

As I continued to look around the group, I tried to think of them as more than random kids who were truant or having behavioral issues. I imagined what their home lives may be like. When my eyes fell upon Raymond, I paused. There was something about him that always made me hesitate. From the first day of my orientation to when he had appeared indifferent to those around him, choosing to hold fast to the same teddy bear he was holding today. From every day I'd seen him at SOAR, I couldn't place it, but I felt a pull to him.

I had never spoken to him because I didn't know what to say nor did I feel like he would respond to me anyhow. He had never said one word while I was there. I'm not sure that he ever said a word to anyone. He would usually sit with his earphones atop his head or with his eyes glued to a book. I had asked Mr. E about him. He told me that there was only one true way to find out about Raymond. "Go ask. Go get to know him. Kids like to see consistency. Once they realize you aren't going anywhere, they show you who they really are."

"Okay, that was a great session guys. You can go back to your stations for about an hour before we head into our next activity." The YD dismissed the group that I had zoned out of and the kids dispersed throughout the room.

"So, what did you think about Josh's answer in group?" Mr. E asked me. I knew he was referring to the boy who had spoken about no one caring.

"Well, it's kind of true, I guess."

"You guess….?" Mr. E had no intention of letting me dodge the question he had purposely designed to get me to open up about mine and Josh's similar viewpoints.

"Yeah, I mean a lot of people don't understand the things we have to deal with, especially as kids. They care about us turning out their way. They don't consider some of our obstacles and oftentimes don't give us what we need to be successful in the first place. So, then they try to correct us by trying to reform us in one way or another, like sending kids here. I don't know Josh's home life but I'm sure he has a story. Everyone has some kind of story Mr. E."

He looked at me, as he often did, but this time it was as if his eyes were dancing. It was as if he agreed one hundred percent with my response, or at least appreciated it.

"What?" I asked as he shook his head and smiled at me.

"Not saying a word."

"No, seriously, what?"

He sat his water bottle down on the table and turned his body towards me. "Emma, I believe you already know what. You know a lot more than you let on. I think you're hiding from some things. Instead of accepting them, you run from them and lash out with spicy comments and responses. I won't tell you what you already know. It's up to you to dig it out, wrestle with it if you need to, and then choose if you will use it or not."

He got up and walked away, not allowing me time to process or respond to what he had said. I had no clue what he was referring to. I did not know what he was saying apart from how I lashed out with spicy comments. I did tend to do that, but what was it that I already knew? One thing that I *did* know however was that Mr. E was not going to explain further. He was going to leave me with those words and expect me to figure them out.

I began to look around the room, trying to appear as if I was observing but really, I was still bewildered by Mr. E's words. As I sat pondering, I sensed someone staring at me and turned my eyes to the corner of the room. Sure enough, Raymond, earphones intact, was watching me. Most people would turn their gaze once they realized you had spotted them staring for too long but not Raymond. He dared me to look back into his eyes and say anything to him. He wasn't intimidating though. The problem was, he looked as if he could see through me. Maybe he had heard what Mr. E had said and was trying to figure it out as well. I had no clue, but I couldn't bring myself to say anything to him, only look back in his direction.

"Emma, can I see you for a minute?" Mrs. Gaines' voice interrupted the silent stare between Raymond and I.

"Yes ma'am." I got up and followed her out of the SOAR area.

"How's it going here?"

"I think it's okay."

"Okay good. The YD's seem to think you have a lot of potential and hope to continue working with you. The only thing that I'd like to see more of is you moving from observation to actual interaction with the kids. That may be a difficult step for you, but to make the most of your time here with us, you need to try and get to know these kids and interact with them. Some will be unwilling and that's okay. Part of our jobs is to show up every day whether the kids do or not. When I say show up, I mean mentally as well as physically. Several of our kids will tap out mentally and not want to engage and that's okay. You keep showing up in case one of them decides to one day. That make sense?"

"Yes ma'am, it does. But I'm their same age for the most part and don't feel right saying much to them or trying to give them advice."

Mrs. Gaines laughed gently. "I understand that Emma. I'm not asking for that from you. I'm just asking you to be yourself and be there *with* them. Sometimes no words are needed, your presence is enough." She patted my shoulder softly and gave me her infamous warm smile.

"Do you have any questions for me?"

"No ma'am. I don't think I have any that you could answer."

"Well, you know where to find me if you do, okay?

"Yes ma'am, I do."

She turned and left out of the door. I had gained a lot of respect for Mrs. Gaines. Day after day, she'd come to work with a smile on her face. Her job couldn't be easy, and she didn't have everything she needed to do her job successfully. She worked long hours but I had never heard her become short or terse with anyone around her. She was always willing to help and made you feel as if you were the most important thing to her while you were talking with her.

Her hair was always falling out of a bun or strands were strung wildly as she hurried about the office or in and out the door to go to a visit or meeting. She tended to wear flats, even when she was dressed up in a business outfit. She was always on-the-go, but was always smiling. I could tell she cared and for me, that was enough to earn my respect. I felt similarly about Mr. E, although he showed his care in different ways.

It was just about time for me to catch my bus and head back home, but I knew if I left without saying bye, Mr. E would have another speech to give me tomorrow. I headed back into the SOAR room to announce my departure, expecting Raymond to meet me with his eyes again, but he had his head down in a book and did not look up once as I entered and left the room.

****

"Hey Darling! I'm so happy to see your face." Mrs. Hennagen opened her front door for me.

Mama had asked me to bring over a plate of food for her that evening. Mrs. Hennagen had been sitting in her front room drinking tea and I could smell the herbs as the steam rose from her cup.

"Hi, Mrs. H," I smiled at her and continued through the front room to the kitchen. I normally left her food on the table, or she would ask me to sit it on the stove.

"You can just set that on the stove, Darling. I'll eat it once I'm done with my tea. Why don't you come in here and sit for just a moment and let me know how everything is going with you."

After sitting the food down, I came back into the room like she asked and found a chair next to hers.

"Everything is okay." I looked down at my feet noticing that my heels could use a little bit more lotion on them. Mama would have a fit if she noticed I had left the house with any sort of ash on my legs or feet.

"Tell me more." Mrs. Hennagen sipped her tea slowly.

The steam continued to rise from the cup, the herbs becoming more recognizable. My nose detected peppermint and cinnamon from where I sat.

"There's not much else to tell." I began fidgeting with my shirt.

"Well, I've noticed that you are sitting by yourself at church these days."

That wasn't entirely true. I tended to sit with or right behind Mama's pew while I was at church.

Maddie normally sat with Annette and Shyla at church, and I normally sat with Terry. She was hinting at the fact that I had not been sitting with him lately. I didn't want to talk about him, so I tried to avoid her indirect question.

"I have been sitting with Mama mostly."

She laughed, aware of my attempt to evade her leading statement. I couldn't help but let out a small laugh as well. I wasn't fooling her. I learned that a little bit ago. She was onto me.

"Terry and I aren't… really talking right now."

Just saying those words made me want to cry. My stomach felt knotted, and my breath began to quicken.

"Well, that's too bad. You two have always been joined at the hip. Nothing could ever separate you two. I sure hope you two work out whatever it is soon."

We sat in silence for a minute. She must have known that I could not handle any other questions about Terry at that time, so she moved to a different topic altogether.

"Myra told me that you have been doing a good job over at the detention center. I'm proud of you."

I often forgot that Mrs. Gaines and Mrs. Hennagen checked in with one another regularly.

"Thank you. I'm trying to work up the nerve to speak to the kids there. It just seems so weird that I'm their age and I'm supposed to be a helper."

"Yeah, well that may be the case, Darling, but God has put you there for a reason. You know that nothing's left to chance, right? Just start by being there and ask God for help with the rest. I bet you'll surprise yourself."

I didn't think God cared about the things going on in my life, let alone if he would help me figure out what to do with the kids at SOAR.

"Mrs. Hennagen?" I began slowly, not sure it was a good idea to ask her the question I was about to ask. I couldn't believe that I would even bring it up but there was no turning back.

"Yes, Emma?" She sat up straighter and sat her tea down.

I couldn't look into her eyes when I asked so I stared down into my lap. "Do you really believe in God? Even after Pastor H died?"

There was a still silence for a second, so I looked up to make sure I hadn't offended her too badly. She wasn't. Instead, she had taken a deep breath and was smiling as she glanced at the ceiling and then back down to me.

"Oh Emma, yes, I do. You see, when I met Alfred, I was a young girl. We grew up in church together. We didn't know a lot about God or life. We only knew what we were taught. And what we were taught was that God was real, He loved us, and we should try to obey whatever He asked of us. Well, who even knew what He was asking all the time?"

She laughed at the thought before continuing.

"We fell in love and Alfred had always known that he was meant to be a pastor. God spoke to him differently, you see. I got a front row seat of how God communicated with Alfred and witnessed some miraculous things. Miracles aren't always big showy things. They can be as small as a flower growing in a patch that you never thought it would, or seeing a child who had just badly hurt himself get up and smile as his mother embraces him.

"I got to see a lot of hard things up close and personal too. Pastors are called at all hours of the night for all sorts of things. They see a lot of death and a lot of hurt, which means the pastors' wives see the same. You sort of become a pastor by association once you've married one. I had a front row seat in Alfred going through some difficult seasons as he led our church. His faith never wavered but he carried an extra weight that most people could never understand.

"But you know what? That man kept serving the Lord and knew that his reward would not be on this earth but waiting for him in heaven. So, when my Alfred went to sleep for good, it hurt beyond words. It made me wanna give up on life and follow him into heaven, but I knew that if God hadn't called me home yet, I still had more work to do down here. I found peace in knowing that Alfred was in heaven with God, and he would be waiting for me when I made it there.

"God was a huge part of Alfred's and my life. He was the center. Alfred is up there with Him, but God is still what holds me in place *here*. If I didn't have God and the hope He offers, my life would be in shambles. I wouldn't be able to go on.

"So, to answer your question in a shorter way, *yes*, Emma, I believe in God although Pastor H has died. As a matter of fact, I believe in Him even more now. The Bible says God comforts those who mourn, and He is near to the brokenhearted. It's in hard times that He comes closer to us than ever before. It is in the sorrow and grief that we get to know who He is a bit better."

She waited until my eyes were seared into hers, ensuring she had my full attention. "Lean into the grief Emma, God is there with you."

Tears had already begun rampaging my face as I listened to her recount her and Pastor H's testimony. She spoke the words with such love and fondness. She was truly a beautiful soul and her joy exuded as she shared pieces of herself with me. She had captured my attention. Besides, a calm had entered the room and I was enveloped in it. Although the tears did not stop falling, I was okay with it because something within recognized they were not in vain. They were cleansing something on the inside of me.

And as expected, piercing through the silence and sanctity of the moment, the phone rang in the kitchen. Mama was calling to make sure I had made it safely and was on my way back home.

Chapter Eleven

Mama had somehow convinced Maddie to go to the Fall Formal. I didn't know if she bribed her or not, but I couldn't believe I was standing in the room looking at Maddie in a semi-formal dress.

When she had attempted to convince Mama that she couldn't go to the Fall Formal because she had nothing to wear, Mama had told her not to worry because she'd find her something. Mama must have either gone over to a thrift shop or had one of the deaconesses from church help get Maddie a dress.

The gown she wore was a satin-rose color and had a dull shine to it. On top of the satin rose fabric, a thin shear layer with black lace trimmed the dress. It was a long straight fit with thin black spaghetti straps. Mama had given Maddie a black shawl to cover her shoulders because in Mama's mind, only fast-tailed girls wore their shoulders, stomach or thighs out. As I stared at Maddie, I was drawn to how beautiful she was and now, she was officially eighteen.

Mama had made her favorite cake: strawberry with cream cheese icing. She had also decorated the house with birthday signs we tended to reuse. Keeping with tradition, we sang "Happy Birthday" and prayed together for God to give her wisdom in her years ahead. Mama would normally make the birthday person's favorite meal as a gift to them, along with some money in a card, but Maddie didn't want anything extra this year. She never wanted to be fussed over but this time around, she was adamant.

I continued to stare at my cousin before me. Her physical beauty wasn't what stunned me the most, however. She had always been stunning, whether she wore that beat up jean jacket and sweatpants or if she was dressed up for church. What surprised me the most, in this moment though, was my reflection in the mirror behind her.

I had agreed to go to the Fall Formal as well. I wasn't sure if I'd submitted to my feeling bad for Maddie during her birthday or if it was all the confusing things people like Mrs. Lee, Mrs. Hennagen, and Mr. E had spoken to me over these past weeks that caused me to agree to go. Either way, here I stood.

Maddie had gone on about how she didn't want to go to the dance with a date. She preferred me to go with her so she wouldn't feel alone. I had hesitated when she first asked but saw how fragile she had appeared in the moment. Her perkiness was nowhere to be found. I couldn't handle the pressure, so to make her feel better, I said yes, I'd go. Mama was thrilled of course and must have gone back to the thrift store or the deaconesses to find me a dress as well.

My dress was the opposite of Maddie's. It was a red A-lined fit and came right to my knees. There was no trim or lace on it which was fine by me. The top was V-necked but didn't plunge too far where any cleavage would show. The straps were about 2 inches in width, which meant I didn't have to wear a shawl unless I wanted to. I chose not to of course. I didn't want Maddie and I to appear to be matching in any way tonight. Mama did try to talk me into wearing sheer panty hose, but I was able to convince her that I didn't need them nor a slip.

I stared at myself in the mirror and admired how my hair seemed to be lying down well today. No loose strands popped out of my bun other than the ones in the front that I had let out on purpose. I wore small cubic zirconia earrings and a matching necklace. Neither Maddie nor I wore makeup apart from clear or pink-tinged lip gloss.

She looked back at me, "Thanks for coming with me, Emma Rose."

"I guess I like you a little. Plus, it's your birthday."

She wasn't impressed by my attempt to downplay the situation. She smiled at me, us both understanding that my willingness to go with her on this day meant so much more than whether I liked her or not. I was willing to be there with her in one of her hardest moments. I was prepared to support her when she felt as if her legs would fail.

I knew how much her mother's absence affected her. Aunt Joleen hadn't called her to tell her happy birthday. She wasn't there to help her get ready for her first dance. She wasn't there to tell her how beautiful she looked and how much she loved her. Maddie was left alone to fill in the blanks on her own.

"Girls, come on down. I want to see how you look!" Mama shouted from downstairs.

We both took one more look in the mirror and gathered our purses before heading down to the living room.

Mama stood at the bottom of the steps and looked up at us as if she was one of those men in one of those romance movies who had just seen the love of his life transform into an alluring woman in a ball gown. She covered her mouth with her hand and tears glistened in her eyes.

I couldn't tell if she was taken aback by Maddie and I or just Maddie. I never seemed to impress her on my own, if at all.

As if she was reading my mind, she said, "You girls are just so beautiful. My babies are all grown up."

At that moment I felt proud. I felt pleased to be Mama's daughter and hopeful that maybe I was special after all.

"Okay, let me get a picture." Mama reached for her camera and motioned for us to come closer to one another. She wiped the tears from her eyes so she could see through the lens and told us to say "I'm beautiful" on the count of three.

"One...Two…Three"

"I'm beautiful!!" We both shouted and then giggled.

Before I knew it all three of us were wrapped up in an impromptu hug. Life felt right. I felt a peace similar to when I would go out and sit on Missums. Tonight may not turn out to be so bad after all.

Ding Dong!!

The "dong" was a sort of faded screech. We had gotten used to the weird pitch of our doorbell by now.

As Mama headed to the front door, she let Maddie and I know that our ride had canceled, and she quickly called someone else she knew would be headed to the Fall Formal as well. She looked very proud of herself and went on about how she didn't want us to be worried, so she came up with a quick alternative solution.

My stomach knotted. Mama didn't know too many people that were going to the dance. There were only a couple of people I could imagine that she had numbers to call.

As she opened the door, my heart raced. I was confronted with my current worst fear.

"Well, don't you look absolutely gorgeous!" Sister Brown was standing in the doorway.

"Thank you," Maddie and I replied in unison.

"Oh no, honey, I was talking to my sister here," she said looking at Mama.

Mama and Sister Brown laughed as if it was the best joke they had heard in a long time. I couldn't find anything humorous now that I'd realized I would be riding in the car with Terry. We hadn't spoken in what seemed like forever. Plus, I knew he was going to the formal with Rochelle. It would be bad enough to deal with Terry but to have to see Rochelle and that annoying smile would just drive me off a bridge.

"I mean I guess you two did what you could... you look decent." Sister Brown was determined to sell her joke.

"Why don't I get a picture of all three of you." She motioned for Mama to join us along the staircase.

After snapping the picture, she handed Mama the camera and asked if it was okay for her to take us off Mama's hands.

We followed Sister Brown out the door. Maddie grabbed my hand quickly and squeezed it. She knew this would likely turn out to be one of the hardest nights I had experienced in a long time as well. She gave me a reassuring smile as we headed down the porch steps. It may have been easier if Terry had been seated in the car and I didn't have to look at his face, but he was too much of a gentleman for that.

He stood beside his mom's car with both the front and back doors open. For the first time in weeks, he looked at me. His shoulders were back and his neck elongated. He wore a black tux and blue bowtie. A small blue flower arrangement sat in his left breast pocket. I imagined a matching corsage sat in the front seat for him to give to Rochelle.

His yellow undertones shone through his brown skin despite the sun being set. He wasn't wearing the two things that made him distinct, however. He didn't have a belt, or at least I couldn't see it with the tuxedo jacket buttoned down. He also didn't have on his glasses. His undisguised brown eyes sat staring at me.

My stomach continued to twist as I looked back at him. It bothered me that I couldn't make out what he was thinking. Was he feeling miserable that he had to share a car with me to the dance? Or was he so upset at me that he wasn't thinking anything at all? Worst of all, he could possibly be thinking of Rochelle and practicing what he'd say when he gave her the corsage? After all, he hadn't really done anything to make me upset besides be oblivious to my own silly teen girl issues. They were issues that seemed insignificant and trivial but for some reason in my mind, they were giant, intimidating, and scary to deal with, let alone say aloud, even to Terry.

"Thank you, Terry. You clean up pretty well." Maddie smiled at him as she entered the backseat of the car.

Thank God she knew better than to take the front seat, leaving me alone with Terry in the back.

"Well, I try." He smirked and struck a casual pose, like Stefan Urkelle from the TV show *Family Matters*.

I couldn't find any words so I waved at Mama and eased into the car next to Maddie. Terry shut the door behind me as well as the front passenger door. He waved toward the front porch and walked toward the driver's seat.

What was happening?! No!

He was driving to the dance and Sister Brown was staying behind with Mama.

"Alright ladies, let's do it."

He slowly pulled out of our driveway and signaled to enter the street. He honked the horn as we passed the house and then turned up the R&B music that was playing softly on the radio.

I felt Maddie close her hands around mine. I must have been fidgeting nervously. Then, she asked the question we both knew the answer to. "Are we stopping to pick Rochelle up too?"

Terry looked in the rearview mirror towards me before answering the question. His eyes were nervous and quickly returned to the road. He cleared his throat before finally giving us the answer we already knew.

"Yes."

Even though I suspected what his answer would be as soon as I realized the passenger seat was empty and Sister Brown had stayed behind, hearing him say *"yes"* set my skin afire. I wanted to scream and cry all at once. I wanted to rip up something, anything. Better yet, I wanted to throw something at his head.

My emotions felt like a tornado swirling inside me, and I had no control over the amount of destruction it could potentially bring. What I wouldn't do was cry. I'd never let Terry and Rochelle see the effect this moment was having on me although I suspected he already knew. He always knew.

The car crawled to a stop as Terry pulled in front of Rochelle's house. Maddie and I watched as he took the corsage and walked to the front door. The door opened before he could knock on it and out walked little Miss Perfect.

Her dress was a deep blue color and sleeveless. And she didn't have a shawl covering her shoulders. Her braids were styled in an updo, and her yellow skin radiated in the night. Although I disliked her for possibly inconsequential reasons, she was a gorgeous girl. She smiled and giggled as Terry placed the corsage on her wrist and her mother took pictures of them in the yard.

I stared at him as he seemed to be enjoying himself with Rochelle. He obliged her mother with suave pictures and with the silly poses as well. When he began looking deep into Rochelle's eyes for one of the pictures, I had to look away. Terry wasn't acting; he was genuinely falling for her, and I couldn't take it. He gave no hint of being bothered by our stifled friendship. He had taken what we lacked in our friendship and given it over to Rochelle. He had officially released me, and it was my own fault.

"Hi y'all." Rochelle smiled as she got into the front seat.

No doubt she knew what was happening between Terry and me, but she didn't let on that she had an opinion one way or another. The thing was, she wasn't a girl who liked to start mess, so I didn't have to worry about her secretly spreading our business. She was a genuinely friendly and likeable person. I just couldn't allow myself to do it, not when she was taking away someone so important to me.

"Heyy!"

Maddie's response was much more audible and kind. Mine was more like that of a monotone robot. However, there was no way I was going to appear troubled in front of Rochelle. I could gather enough façade to be polite but as soon as we made it to the dance, I was heading as far as I could in the other direction.

"Oh, and Happy Birthday, Madison." Rochelle looked in Maddie's direction.

"Thanks."

"Oh yeah, that's right!!" Terry chimed in enthusiastically.

He began clearing his throat and we all knew what that meant. He was about to burst into his silly birthday rap song that he recited for anyone's birthday instead of the traditional one.

It's ya birthday- aye aye yo
It's ya birthday-come on let's roll
Stomp ya feet and clap ya hands
Drop it all and do your dance!
Aye aye yo- it's ya birthday
Aye aye yo- it's ya birthday

I held back laughter as Maddie giggled and gave Terry the thumbs down sign. He was a horrible rapper, and he knew it. He didn't mind being silly to make us laugh though.

"Oh, don't act like you don't like my freestyle. As a matter of fact, I'll make sure to save you a birthday dance later." Terry wiggled his eyebrows at Maddie.

"Lord, please no!" She exclaimed with laughter, closing her eyes as if she could imagine the disastrous sight.

I examined the joy she held in the moment and couldn't help but to allow my grin to widen.

I appreciated Terry's awareness of how delicate she was around her birthday. He knew how her mom's absence affected her most during this time of year. He was a pillar in both our lives, only he was closer to me. We caught a glimpse of each other's eyes in the rearview mirror again but this time I didn't look away immediately. I wanted him to know I was thankful for him bringing laughter to Maddie on today.

As he looked away to pay attention to the road, it dawned on me that he wasn't *not* mad at me. Nor was he unbothered by me at this moment. He simply chose to rise above it for Maddie. I had gotten so lost in my feelings that I forgot that she was fighting hard to not be suffocated by her own pain and hurt.

I had tossed her aside to wallow in my own issues, kind of like I had been doing with Terry. He knew that today wasn't about our issues though. He knew it was far more than him taking Rochelle to the dance as well. He understood that despite his and my problems, she still needed both of us today.

Although I couldn't completely let go of the feelings I had over Terry and Rochelle, I could at least table them and ensure that I was there to support Maddie, which was the reason I had agreed to go to the Fall Formal in the first place.

"Thanks for being here with me." Maddie leaned over to me as Terry and Rochelle began to talk quietly in the front seat.

"Of course. And Maddie, thanks for being here with me too." My eyes offered her sincerity.

"I think you should sneak a dance with…" Maddie pointed at the back of Terry's seat to make sure he nor Rochelle overheard her speaking his name. "Seriously, Emma Rose, you should dance with him tonight."

She had to go and ruin the moment by suggesting something so foolish. I hadn't spoken to him in weeks. The eye contact we had in the rearview mirror was more than we had in the past month alone. I was not going to waltz over to him in front of Rochelle and the entire school and ask him to dance with me. It was not going to happen. I planned on babysitting the punch bowl or the wall all night long.

"Well, will you at least dance with me?" She asked softly.

"I'll think about it," I teased, knowing we'd spend the better part of the party dancing with one another.

She socked me in the arm, "You better."

Terry pulled along the sidewalk in front of the school to let us out promising to return once he had parked the car. I didn't really feel like waiting for him only to witness him and his happy date walk into the dance together, but it was clear that Maddie had decided to wait so I stood patiently beside her.

A few parents pulled up to drop their students off at the front of school while we waited for Terry to resurface. A blue car pulled up slowly and another senior boy I recognized, emerged from the tinted window car. The car didn't pull away after the boy exited but, instead, its gear shift into park. Rochelle, Maddie, and I all took a couple of steps back, preparing to run if necessary. I'm sure we had all been given the same "be aware of your surroundings" speech from our parents. We knew it was unusual for a car to stop and park in front of the school, especially when the student had already gone into the building. Besides, if his parent needed to get his attention, he or she would just roll the window down and shout out the window.

As the driver side of the car opened, and we were about to hit a full turn and sprint, I could see Terry quickening his step toward the sidewalk. He had spotted the same thing we had and was going to make sure to get to us as quickly as possible. *Ugh.* He couldn't be bad even if he tried. It was irritating.

"About to run away? Smart girl." The voice coming from the blue car sounded oddly familiar.

I peered toward the car to see if it was really who I thought it was.

"Oh, come on Emma, I'm not *that* black." Mr. E joked as he stood with his door open.

No, he was not a dark-skinned man. His complexion was more of a pecan color and would be considered flawless if it weren't for the prominent tattoo along his neck drawing attention from his face. His smile was wide, and his laugh, obnoxious. There was something commonplace about him, like he was someone everyone in Peachtree knew.

"We were most definitely about to run! I didn't know who you were. As soon as that car door began to open, we were about to be outta here," I laughed.

By this time Terry had joined us on the sidewalk and was standing tall. He was staring at Mr. E trying to size him up and figure out if he was a threat or not. Since Terry and I had not been on speaking terms, he didn't know much about the time I spent at the detention center, let alone about Mr. E.

"What's up, young sir," Mr. E gave Terry a nod acknowledging him.

Terry didn't respond but simply nodded back. His footing didn't shift though. I didn't know if I should be honored or annoyed that he was standing near like a guard dog even though our friendship was on life support. But as I looked at how attentive he was, something felt different. His protective posture was actually attractive. I knew if it ever came down to it, he would fight to keep me safe but seeing how he stood defensively and ready to pounce on Mr. E if he made one wrong move appealed to something else deep within me.

"Dropping your kid off for the dance?"

I turned my attention to Mr. E, knowing full and well he was not old enough to have a high school aged child.

"Oh, full of jokes I see." He responded with another obnoxious laugh. "Nah, I was just dropping off my little cousin. He needed a ride."

"Sheesh, they let anyone drive kids around these days," I smirked.

"Yeah, yeah, yeah, why don't you go on ahead and go inside. Never thought I'd see you in a dress, but you look nice. You look…" He hesitated as he looked at Terry.

"…happy. You look happy."

Terry and I both looked at each other briefly. Mr. E couldn't be implying that I was happy because Terry was near me, could he? He didn't know the half of it. Terry was just being a gentleman. He couldn't help it. His mother had raised him that way and he vowed to be the kind of man he thought his father wasn't.

Mr. E turned to get into his car but then turned one last time toward Terry. "You're doing a good job, young sir. Keep that up."

Terry nodded and Mr. E laughed before getting into his car and driving away.

Terry's distrust remained as he watched Mr. E's car disappear from the stop sign. He just didn't know him is all. I expected him to ask me questions about Mr. E but instead he turned around, walked towards Rochelle and motioned for us all to walk inside.

Maddie stood smiling goofily at me once he had begun walking up the steps with Rochelle.

"What?"

"Nothing," Maddie muttered as she walked ahead of me with her lingering goofy smile.

She spun on her heels and turned towards me, "Nothing at all."

It was obvious that Maddie wanted to highlight that Terry would always be concerned about my welfare. Even if I was being unreasonable toward him, he would always be willing to be there for me. Mr. E even knew it and I hadn't mentioned a word to him about Terry. But the fact remained that Terry was walking through the school doors with Rochelle by his side, not me.

I watched them at the entrance. They had stopped to take their customary picture in front of a balloon arch. He draped his arm around her waist and leaned in. He didn't seem worried about me at that moment. He was happy and with the person he was meant for. The only reason he had stopped near me when Mr. E arrived was because that was the expectation. He was true to who he was. He was cavalier. It had nothing to do with what Maddie and Mr. E thought. Even still, Maddie continued to taunt me with her "I told you so face" as we entered the doorway of the school.

"Okay ladies, let me see a big smile," Jeanie, the yearbook president pointed her camera in our direction.

Maddie and I looked at one another as if we needed each other's permission to comply with the instruction. Instead of smiling, we burst into laughter. Jeanie looked both confused and amused as we giggled away.

She had the right to be confused because there was nothing funny at that time. What Jeannie didn't know was that Maddie and I both understood one fundamental thing: we both had pain deep within us but we also both had each other. Our laughter masked our troubles. It was our pact to make the best out of the evening; to set aside Aunt Joleen, Terry, and any other cares we had for the night. Tonight, we would make the best out of what we had: one another.

Chapter Twelve

It had been a week since the Fall Formal, and I still couldn't bring myself to say anything to Terry. The worst part is that he didn't seem to mind. I felt stupid every time he passed me in the hallway or when he walked into church with Sister Brown. I was in too deep though. There was no way I could go up to him and just apologize. Besides, what would I say? "*Hey! I'm sorry I've been mad at you for weeks for no reason. Would you forgive me and continue being my best friend even though I hurt your feelings? Ugh—*"

"You know, he's not going to play Uno by himself, right?" Mr. E interrupted my thoughts.

Raymond still refused to speak to me but had not so subtly invited me to play Uno with him this past week. I had been updating the group session attendance log when I felt something hit my back. Raymond had thrown a hacky sack at me while sitting across the room with a deck of Uno cards in hand. He just stared at me and expected me to take the hint. Normally, I would have been insulted and shot him a dirty look, but something within me felt as if I deserved that hacky sack to the back. I didn't feel like I deserved anyone's words. So instead, I picked up the colorful round crochet ball and walked towards him concentrating on the feel of the pellets within it. Whatever it was, was comforting as I moved and squeezed it around in my hand.

"Here." I looked down at Raymond who was sitting at the table holding a Draw Four card in his hand.

He reached up and grabbed the hacky sack from me and placed it on the table. For some reason I had expected him to snatch it away from me. Although he was quiet and kept to himself most of the time, he seemed like he could become defensive if anyone intruded on his personal space.

"Why do you come here?" He stared at me while he began dealing cards.

I slowly sat across from him without taking my eyes from his, not certain if he was safe to be around quite yet. Plus, I didn't know how I wanted to respond to his rude question.

"Why did *you* come here?" I shot back. I decided that I didn't like the way he had questioned me. I could try to ignore the hacky sack being thrown at my back, but I didn't deal well with smart remarks. He knew full and well why I was there.

He stopped dealing the cards once we both had seven and sat looking at me like I was an insect on a wall, not necessarily expecting anything great from it. I couldn't make out any emotion in his eyes and he didn't seem amused nor bothered by my response to his question.

After a minute or so, I realized he was not going to make one more move until I had answered his question.

Ugh! I wasn't cut out for this. I had no desire to have a chest beating contest with some kid who I barely knew. I stared back at him and sat back in my chair, letting out an exasperated sigh.

"Seriously?"

He didn't move a muscle but continued to wait. I'm not sure he had even blinked since he had finished dealing the cards.

"Fine, I come here because I have to." I picked up my cards and began sorting them by color.

Raymond collected his as well and we began playing in turn until he slammed a Draw Four card down on the deck. Amused, he leaned in and smiled as I gathered four cards. I wasn't irritated by his move though. I had never seen him happy before so I couldn't help but giggle at his goofy smile.

"Yeah, yeah, you couldn't wait to play that card," I teased.

His lip had begun to curl into a half smile as he continued to look at his hand, figuring out what to play next.

We continued to play for four rounds. He had won two games and so had I. We were ramping up for another when Mr. E. walked over.

"Having fun?" Mr. E looked at me with his eyebrow raised. "I didn't know that was possible."

Raymond snickered but didn't look up from dealing the cards.

"I'll have you know I'm all sorts of fun," I bantered.

"Okay. Well, Miss All-Sorts-of-Fun, you're gonna miss your bus if you don't get going soon."

"Oh man, is it time to go already?" I had completely lost track of the time.

I stood up and grabbed my backpack before leaning down onto the table. I gave Raymond the best serious expression I could muster. "You owe me another game mister. No way I'm letting this end in a tie."

He picked up his earphones and glared back at me. However, his attempt at a serious face could hardly mask the twinge of happiness I saw in his eyes. I smirked at him smugly before turning on my heels.

Mr. E walked with me toward the door, and I could feel him looking at me with that sappy proud face he made when one of the kids in the group had a breakthrough moment.

"Don't say a word." I opened the door without looking towards him because I knew that if my eyes met his, I wouldn't be able to withhold the smile I was desperately working to keep at bay.

"Not-a-word." Mr. E announced the words slowly before closing the door behind me.

I imagined he was looking at me through the window as I walked toward the exit door, feeling like a parent who had just watched their baby take his or her first step.

"Ah! Miss Griggs!" Mrs. Gaines met me warmly as I prepared to exit the building.

"Hi."

I had not seen much of her during my time there. If she was not in her office underneath a pile of papers, she was rushing out the door with her purse and work bag in tow. And if she was not flying out the door, she was in a closed-door meeting.

Today she seemed relaxed. She wore a pastel pink blouse, khaki linen pants and tan colored flats. Her hair flowed freely, and her eyes held an eagerness within them. The freckles on her face danced around her cheeks as she spoke. It was the most peaceful I had ever witnessed her.

"I know you are on your way out, but I was wondering if I could give you a ride home."

"Um—"

"Before you say no, I don't usually offer rides to our youth interns, however, I have not gotten to meet with you regarding your progress here. That's not your fault. It's mine for sure. It's been a bit crazy around here." She laughed as she reflected on her past few days.

"I'd love to chat with you on the way home to make sure everything is going okay for you."

I hesitated once more, thinking of how uncomfortable it would be sitting beside Mrs. Gaines for the next fifteen minutes. Plus, I enjoyed relaxing and winding down on the bus before going home.

"I won't kidnap you," she persisted.

"Okay." It was clear that she wasn't going to let it go.

"Great, let me grab my bags and we will be on our way. It'll be sorta like girl time."

She bounced away to her office as if I had genuinely made her day. After a couple of moments, she reappeared with her bags and car keys in hand.

"After you." She held the door open and motioned for me to lead the way.

****

Mama had stopped waiting at the door in the evenings for me after a few weeks of volunteering at the detention center. Instead, she'd have the front door open with the screen in place. She would either be sitting and having her tea in the front room or scurrying about in the kitchen. Now she had reached a certain level of comfort in which she could carry on with her normal tasks while waiting for me, realizing that I'd eventually come walking through the door unharmed.

I waved Mrs. Gaines off as I approached the porch. Our conversation was nothing like "girl time" as she thought it would be. She inquired about my progression in the SOAR room and asked how she could assist me more. The answers to both of those questions eluded me. I couldn't find a good enough response to them or one I thought she wanted to hear. If I wasn't careful, one answer, could lead to her prying, which was not something I wanted on my agenda.

She seemed genuinely concerned with my experience at the detention center. However, to further convolute things, she gave me unwanted advice on not taking things so seriously right now but trying to find what gives me purpose. She went on about how she had gotten into her current role and how she had always desired to help young people find a "better path."

Although the car ride home was not my idea of girl bonding time, it wasn't as bad as I thought it would be either. It felt as if I was having a conversation with someone who truly found interest in what I had to say whether she agreed with me or not. Plus, watching her become easily distracted at red lights was humorous. She would, without fail, begin gazing out of the window or get lost in people watching, sometimes forgetting to pay attention to when the light had turned green. And then, like she hadn't missed a beat, she'd return to whatever we were discussing.

As I approached the front door, I noticed the screen and front door were both shut. Mama never left the front door shut when Maddie or I weren't home. She was too overprotective for that. She would leave the door open because she wanted us to know we were missed and would always be welcomed home. As a matter of fact, it was her way of acknowledging our absence. Even though she wasn't always good at using her words, her actions were consistent.

I attempted opening the door, but it was locked. The feeling that something wasn't right prompted a panicked knock.

Maddie rushed to open the door.

"Where's Mama?"

"Hello to you too, Emma Rose." Maddie giggled.

"Sorry Maddie, I'm just not used to the door being shut. Where's Mama?

"She's in her room. She's been in there since I've been home."

"And you didn't think that was weird?" I found myself snapping and abruptly pushing past her. "Did you go check on her?"

Maddie rolled her eyes. "Of course, I checked. She didn't want to be bothered."

"Well, what did she say when you checked in on her? Did she respond or just yell at you?"

Mama would never actually yell at Maddie. She had always adored her. She was always gentle with her as if she thought she was one step away from shattering into pieces from the trauma of being left by Aunt Joleen.

"I didn't get a chance to ask her. I knocked and she said, 'Maddie, I'm okay, just resting right now.'"

That was strange. Mama was typically up and about the kitchen or reading her Bible lesson in the front room at this time. She didn't customarily retire to her room before we had.

"Okay, well I'm just going to let her know I'm home."

I began to knock on Mama's bedroom door, willing to be met with her frustration if that's what it took to ensure she was fine. Maddie stood beside me with a look of annoyance and curiosity. Before I finished the cadenced knock, Mama flung the door open.

"You two know I have ears, right? I can hear you all the way in my room."

She stood in the doorway with her black silk bonnet covering her head. She wore a pink and blue housecoat with a zipper in the front. Her house slippers were a deep blue. She had a rule to always keep socks on our feet, especially in the wintertime. If we didn't have them on when we came downstairs in the mornings, she would scold us and send us back up to get socks or slippers. She would say without fail, "You're gonna catch a cold. Put something on your feet."

Right now her face was tired and stressed. Her eyebrows were furrowed and there were clear lines extending down from the corner of her eyes. Her brown skin seemed to be weighed down by invisible anchors.

These past few weeks had seemingly aged Mama. She was hiding something. Something was making her worry but there was no chance she'd be open to talking to us girls about it. "Grown folks business" was just that and Maddie and I knew better than to butt in. Even though Maddie was technically an adult now that she was eighteen, and I was close behind her, we would still be considered little girls for the near future.

Maddie was always considered the "Turkey Baby" since she was born so close to Thanksgiving. Aunt Joleen delivered Maddie six days before Thanksgiving in 1974. And I was referred to as the "Christmas Gift" since I was born on Christmas day. I could hear Mrs. Hennagen's words in my head, "Girl, don't you know you are a gift? It's no coincidence you were born on Christmas."

"Emma Rose, how was your day?" Mama sighed slowly as she patted the top of her head.

"It was good, Mama," I responded, taken aback. Normally she didn't ask about my day. She usually just gave me a satisfactory look once I arrived home safely and asked if I was hungry or needed to get any homework done. Typically, the only time she was interested in the happenings of my day was when she knew something already that she expected me to expound upon.

"Good. Y'all eat those leftovers from yesterday. Quit worrying about me. I'm fine. I'm tired is all."

 She walked past us and headed towards the tea kettle to brew herself some chamomile tea.

Maddie and I looked at one another, not knowing what to say. It was apparent that Mama wasn't herself but since we didn't know how to address the obvious, we ventured off in different directions. Maddie started toward the kitchen to unpack the leftovers from the fridge, and I headed upstairs to take a quick shower. I preferred to wash off after leaving the detention center, especially if I rode the bus there and back. A warm shower allowed a final debrief before returning to my usual thoughts.

I thought of how Mr. E's assertions were right. I had stepped out of my normal territory in the SOAR room and begun interacting with the kids a bit more. It wasn't as uncomfortable to begin conversations nor was it as difficult to hear them talk in group any longer. The first few counseling sessions that I attended with the kids were quiet. He had reassured me that they normally didn't trust outsiders and would have to warm up to my being there. Just like he had predicted, after a few weeks, the kids had become more vulnerable during group meetings despite my presence there.

Initially hearing some of their backstories was challenging. They all had complicated pasts and most of them shared similar pains that I would have never guessed. I avoided eye contact with them as they spoke because it made me feel too exposed. Each week I was there reminded me of a large rubber band unraveling. Something about being at the detention center was changing me.

"Emma, the food is warm!" Maddie shouted from downstairs.

"Okay!" I had been in the shower for at least ten minutes sorting through my thoughts and hadn't realized how much time had passed.

After rushing to get dressed, I headed downstairs to see Maddie sitting at the table with a plate for herself and one for me. She had reheated the meatloaf, mashed potatoes and corn from yesterday, but it looked as if it was fresh out of the oven.

"Thank you, Maddie."

"You're welcome, Emma Rose."

I noticed Mama had retreated again and made a mental note to check on her after dinner.

Maddie began carrying on about Christmas decorations and what we should do to celebrate my birthday this year. She was destined to be an event planner and a great wife to some lucky man someday. She loved to make things sparkle and provide an atmosphere of fun for any festivity you could think of.

At least fifteen minutes had passed with my listening to Maddie's ideas of doing a cookie gift exchange or ugly sweater/white elephant gift swap event for my birthday.

"Let me know what you think, okay?" She was relentless.

"Okay, Maddie," were the only words I could find. I was too worried about Mama plus I never liked celebrating my birthday anyway. It felt weird sharing a birthday with the holiday that commemorated the Savior of the world. There was no way I could live up to such a day.

Once the dishes were put away and the kitchen was cleaned, Maddie went upstairs, and I slowly approached Mama's room. Her door was closed so I knocked softly. When her voice didn't greet me, I peeked in and whispered, "Good night, Mama."

There was no response, tempting me to open the door a bit wider. She was not in her bed or rocking chair which meant she was in her bathroom. The restroom door was shut, and I heard the faint sounds of gospel music and water running. Making the decision to pop my head in to say good night was one thing but interrupting Mama in the shower would for sure rouse her anger. But I couldn't help but wonder if she was okay in the bathroom. I slowly walked over and put my ear to the door, taking notice of her soft synchronized hums. At least she was okay. That was enough for me to be able to leave her room with some sense of peace.

As I walked quietly toward the door, I noticed a white envelope on Mama's nightstand next to her Bible. I knew better than to touch her things but maybe the white envelope was what was keeping her in this somber trance as of late. Before my better sense kicked in, I had picked up the envelope and began opening it. I looked around to make sure I could still hear the music and water running before further committing. The front of the envelope was addressed to Mama. A white letter within the envelope read:

DATE: 11/25/92
CLIENT: RUTHIE GRIGGS
OF INTEREST: JOLEEN ANN HARRISON

STATUS OF PERSON OF INTEREST: URGENT NOTIFICATION AND IN PERSON COMMUNICATION REQUIRED

I tried reading through the letter as quickly as I could, but the water turned off which meant Mama would be coming out soon. I raced to replace the letter in the envelope and to sneak it back near her Bible. With just enough time, I managed to creep out of the room as I heard the bathroom door opening.

What was happening? Was Mama looking for Aunt Joleen and what did it mean that the notification was urgent and required her to speak to someone in person? Mama had received several of these letters by now and she had not mentioned one word about Aunt Joleen to myself or Maddie but there was no way I could ask her now that I had broken her trust by going through her private things.

My heart felt heavy as I imagined Mama trying to find out information on her sister. Mama was a "give it to God and let Him do the rest" kind of a person. If she was seeking Aunt Joleen out, something had to be wrong. Was Mama sick? Was there something going on with Maddie that she needed Aunt Joleen to know about? But why? Aunt Joleen had dropped Maddie on our doorstep like she didn't matter so why would Mama even bother including her in anything? She didn't deserve to know anything about Maddie. Wherever Aunt Joleen was, she needed to stay there. She didn't get to come gallivanting back into our lives.

I laid my head on the pillow and looked over at Maddie who was painting her nails. She was so happy. After her birthday, she had taken a couple of days to sulk and then had gotten her bright smile and peppy personality back. I was glad to see her cheery again so enduring her giddiness hadn't turned into an annoyance yet. Maddie deserved happiness. She was the perfect example of what it meant to "let your little light shine."

Aunt Joleen didn't deserve to be a part of that light after what she had done. Her actions were enough to extinguish anyone's hope but miraculously Maddie's had remained intact. There was no way I was ever going to be okay with allowing her to walk back through those doors. Not now. Not ever.

"Good night, Maddie." I whispered as I turned over to go to sleep.

"Good night, Emma Rose." She smiled back at me with glinting eyes and then began humming *Twinkle Twinkle Little Star* as she continued coating her nails. Before I knew it, her hums had lulled me off to sleep.

Chapter Thirteen

The Christmas decorations that were plastered throughout the school hallways and within the teacher's classrooms reminded me that I could never ignore my birthday, as much as I longed to. I tried to focus on the birth of Christ instead because his birth was worth celebrating, not mine.

Don't get me wrong, I loved opening presents for the holiday but once the focus was shifted to me opening presents that signified my birth, it made me feel as if I was supposed to be something that I never felt I was: special. I was just another Black girl from a single parent home with no idea of what her future had in store. I was not some "gift" that Mrs. Hennagen spoke of.

Besides, if I was such a gift, Daddy would still be here, right? Mama would want to spend at least some of her time talking with me and my world wouldn't feel so inconsequential.

"Okay everyone, enjoy your break!" My teacher shouted as the lunch bell rang.

We still had two more periods before we were dismissed for the day; however, the teachers and the students were mentally checked out already.

I stopped by my locker to put my books away before going to the cafeteria. Inside, I found an unopened yellow envelope with my name written on it. Given its shape, it was definitely a card of some sort. I pondered how it could have been placed in my locker in the first place. The options weren't many being that only two people knew that yellow was my favorite color *and* knew my locker combination.

Seeing the yellow envelope made me grin. The color was so bright… so vibrant… so free, not much like how I had been feeling lately. The front of the card displayed a bouquet of flowers with the words *You Deserve So Much But Here Are Some Flowers*. Written inside were the simple words: *Happy Birthday to the person who deserves the world*. It wasn't signed, making the blank spaces of the card feel larger than the words inscribed within it.

I considered who, out of Terry and Maddie could have left it for me. I lived with Maddie so if she wanted to give it to me, she would have signed it with some long-winded sappy paragraph and given it to me at home along with a homemade cake or cookies. I imagined her sashaying around as she prepared the gift. But no, this card wasn't from Maddie. It had to be from Terry.

I leaned slightly into the locker trying to hide a smile. He always knew how to unlock the happiness within me even when I didn't. My optimism faded though as I remembered that Terry and I hadn't spoken in forever. I had seen him around school and church, but no words passed between us, only a brief meshing of our eyes before one of us chose to look away. I wished he would just come over and initiate a conversation. Then, it would be easier for me to blurt out how silly I'd been and how sorry I was. But instead, each time he silently passed, I felt an intense pang of sadness and loneliness.

I had tried to figure out how to move forward from the mess I caused but I didn't know which step to take. I was in over my head, and I couldn't fathom a way out. Maybe it was my pride. After all, I was Daddy's daughter. I remembered one day how Mama had prepared a large pot of greens with cornbread. Any time she cooked greens it was bound to be a great day. The whole house would exude happiness.

We would sit around, each of us in our own corner. I'd swing freely on Missums, and Maddie would lie in the living room snuggled under a blanket, no matter if it was cold or not. Mama would sit in the kitchen at the table working on puzzles as her music played.

Daddy was normally in the front living room relaxing or playfully kissing Mama. I hated seeing their affection then, but boy did I miss it now.

There was one instance where Mama had a fresh pot of greens going, but Daddy was in one of his moods. He was grouchy and withdrawn and picked at everything such as the door being open too long, the use of the oven causing the electricity bill to be high or how we needed more coasters for the table because the wood was beginning to wear. He even went on about everyone having to listen to gospel music just because Mama did.

Everything, and I do mean everything, was on Daddy's radar that day. Mama was usually the only thing that could calm him. I'd see them retreat for an adult talk and then Daddy would appear better. But not that day. He wouldn't be calmed. He couldn't be pleased. Instead, he griped and complained and refused to listen to Mama's warnings on how the day would be ruined if he didn't stop. Of course, he didn't heed Mama's advice, rather, he exploded into a rage and stomped out the door. There weren't enough greens in the world that could fix the day after that. Mama had apologized to me and Maddie and explained that sometimes pride got in the way of happiness and the ability to say sorry.

"Sorry!" A small freshman boy called after bumping into me. I couldn't make out his face because he was hurrying down the hall.

I tucked the envelope into my backpack. The card didn't matter. Terry had not written any words inside of it, so it was futile. Plus, Sister Brown was the one who had probably made him give it to me in the first place. He couldn't lie about my receiving it because she would, no doubt, ask me at church on Sunday and if she found out he lied about giving it to me, he'd be in trouble. I wondered if she even knew that we weren't on speaking terms. It wouldn't matter if she did know because she was the type of person to still make him give me a card anyway.

As I closed my locker and repositioned my backpack, I realized my appetite was gone. I'd rather forego lunch and just take my exit elsewhere. Plenty of upperclassmen left school grounds for lunch so I wouldn't look suspicious for leaving as well.

As I got close to the entrance however, I remembered Maddie. She would lose her mind with worry if I wasn't on the bus this afternoon. She'd get off the bus looking for me and have a full-on breakdown. She would never quit looking for me if I didn't show up. Her pretty face would be twisted with concern, and she would probably start crying. The last time she thought I had gone missing she was very emotional. Mama had to console her and remind her that I was probably at the lake with Terry. Of course, Mama was right, and I had been with Terry at the lake all afternoon.

There was no way I could leave without telling her. I began looking around the hallways scanning for her face or at least a glimpse of that denim jacket. I searched the corridors to the left and right of me before I found her walking towards me with a gleeful facial expression. She bounced as she walked, and her step quickened as she saw me standing waiting. My stomach dropped and my feet became frozen as she got closer. Maddie wasn't the problem; it was who she was walking with.

"Hey, Emma Rose." Maddie's smile broadened as she planted her feet right in front of me.

She grabbed me and pulled me in for a hug. Her voice was bubbly, and she giggled as she squeezed me. I didn't love to be hugged but I had no energy to fight her. I peered through her arms to make sure I was seeing things clearly. Yep, he was still there looking back at me.

His eyes held a concoction of happiness and sadness. He just stared back at me, not breaking eye contact as I fought back tears. His facial expression remained calm, however.

When Maddie released her grip on me, my eyes retreated to the floor and slowly back up to her face as I tried to think of what to say. The problem was that anything I said aloud would probably loosen the dam holding my tears back, so I chose to remain silent.

"Terry! Maddie! Hey!" Rochelle waved as she walked towards us. She politely smiled at me, "Emma."

I felt like my breath had been stolen. I couldn't get words to leave my mouth, so I simply nodded in her direction. So much for telling Maddie that I was leaving campus. There was no way I was going to mention it in front of Terry and Rochelle. I knew why Maddie had come over to me. I even knew why Rochelle had come over. Rochelle would go anywhere to be near Terry. Those two had become inseparable, kind of like we used to be. What I didn't understand was why Terry had come. I had not called him over, and we had yet to make up so why was he here?

"Emma, I want you to keep an open mind, okay?" Maddie looked serious, causing me to feel unsettled.

"Uh huh."

"We only have two more classes and I'm too excited to start Christmas break to get through those classes." Maddie looked as if she was working very hard to contain a squeal.

Her giddiness gave me hope. Her joyfulness, even now, in something as simple as skipping a class or two before break amused me. Most students had participated in a skip day at least three to four times by now but this had to be her first time. Maddie loved school and was the biggest rule follower I knew. I looked at her intently waiting for her to finish. I expected that huge squeal to return at any point such as a tea kettle that had reached its boiling point, letting out its long-awaited whistle.

"Let's leave and go to the lake." Maddie whispered as she toggled her feet from side to side with elation.

I couldn't help but laugh as I watched her become so delighted over this plan that she had obviously put together herself. Maybe she had placed the card in my locker as a way of kickstarting her proposal. But why didn't she sign it?

Maddie knew I loved to go to the lake, especially around my birthday. It helped to clear my mind and allowed me time to reminisce. Usually, I'd go with Terry and Maddie would tag along. It was nothing special, but the small lake was peaceful, and Terry and I had claimed the lone old wooden bench that was nestled along the path leading to the water. We had carved our initials in it and made up a pretend curse for anyone who tried to take it from us. We were just silly elementary kids at that time and called ourselves making a friendship pact.

The lake itself was surrounded by large trees, making it feel private and set apart from the world. I would sit for hours on that little bench or at the mouth of the water with my feet dangling in the coolness. Terry and I would joke around, sing off key, dance uncontrollably or just sit in silence for a bit. The lake held our confidences and collected our vital moments. It was our safe.

I had begun frequenting the getaway after my father died. Mama had met me at the front door after school one day. Her eyes were puffy, her face exhausted and she still wore her house robe which was uncharacteristic for her in the late afternoon. She had hugged me tightly and told me what I had already suspected based on her appearance. Daddy was gone.

I couldn't express my feelings, so I ran, hoping to escape the truth of what I was just told. Out of breath from racing and nearly hyperventilating, I found myself at the beautiful body of water I had grown accustomed to. I'm not sure how Terry knew but he must have been on his way to my house to visit or Mama may have called Sister Brown because he was right behind me on his bike. We sat there for hours staring at nature. My sight was blurred by tears, but the sound of the lake accompanied by Terry's steady breathing had anchored me.

"Well??!!" Maddie glowered at me, awaiting an answer.

I looked over to see Terry's eyes, also still fixed upon me, and Rochelle staring impatiently with her hand hooked into his arm. I didn't want to go anywhere with them. Well, maybe I'd like to go to the lake with just Terry and Maddie.

A deep cut of sadness lingered from my thoughts of Daddy. I quickly glanced back at Maddie who looked as if she had just won the lottery. I couldn't bring myself to let her down. If Maddie could push past hurt on her birthday, then surely, I could be *on* for her this one time she wanted to skip school.

"How would we get to the lake?" I looked in Rochelle's direction since she seemed unsure about the plan.

"I'll drive. Unless Terry wants to drive my car for us."

Rochelle turned to look up at Terry, but he still had not taken his eyes away from me. Sensing her need to be acknowledged, he returned her gaze and smiled.

Ugh!

A lake trip with the two of them would be more awkward than this moment and there wasn't enough being *on* in the world to make me want to endure it.

"Pllleeeassseeee," Maddie squealed right on cue.

Her delight in this plan made it difficult to back out.

"Fine, but y'all it's kind of cold today." Maybe the chilly weather would change everyone's minds.

"I have some extra blankets in my car. My daddy says I should always carry an extra blanket, fix-a-flat, a flashlight and some water with me at all times. We can stop and get some snacks if y'all want."

Rochelle just had it all together, didn't she?

"Okay, then." I mumbled, almost inaudibly.

Maddie grabbed my arm and cuddled close to me as we followed Terry and Rochelle out the front door.

****

When we got to the lake, there was a breeze coming off the water that made the air colder than expected. Rochelle retrieved the promised blankets from her trunk and we sat in a circle eating random snacks from the corner store.

I loved any kind of Lays potato chip created. While chewing, I crunched loudly into Maddie's ear to annoy her. She hated the sound of people eating or smacking.

"Eww, stop Emma!" She swatted at me.

I continued taunting her as I put another potato chip in my mouth slowly, ready to crunch obnoxiously.

"Don't think about it." She glared her eyes at me.

Terry and Rochelle were both finishing their honey buns. She swooned over Terry while he looked back at her kindly but didn't say much. *And I was worried this would be awkward.* I wondered if she really liked honey buns or if she had just bought one because he had.

Maddie helped ease the awkwardness with her incessant positivity and talking. Meanwhile, Terry and I practiced how quickly we could deviate our gazes from one another.

"I'm trying to convince Emma to let me throw her an actual party this year. We could have a small get together at the house on Christmas Eve and celebrate her actual birthday instead of clumping it in on the same day everyone else in the world opens presents as well." Maddie looked at Terry and Rochelle for help to convince me.

"What do you normally do to celebrate? I never really have parties for my birthday nowadays," Rochelle chimed in.

I shrugged. "We don't ever do anything huge. Plus, I don't like big parties."

"Ummmm. I said *small* get together Emma Rose. I never said big."

"Same thing, Maddie. I don't want it to be a big deal."

"Well, what do you think Terry?" Maddie caught him off guard as he finished stuffing the last of his honey bun into his mouth.

He knew Maddie well enough to know she wouldn't move on until she had his answer, although he chewed exceptionally slow to test her patience.

Maddie set comfortably in her position, ready to wait Terry out.

"Well… I don't know that my opinion matters much."

Good. Terry was smart enough not to butt into—

"But I do think it would be a good idea to have a small shindig for Emma."

So much for Terry being smart enough to mind his own business. First of all, who says shindig? Seriously?!

Leave it up to Goof-head to use a word like *shindig* while trying to speak for me. He knew me the best out of everyone here and how much I would hate the idea of having a party.

He smiled at me, knowing he'd gotten to me. I felt my skin begin to burn with anger as he meddled.

Jerk!

"Well if we do have a party, YOU are not invited!"

Terry pretended to be offended, "Who me? Well, that hurts my feelings, Emma *Rose*."

Ugh!! He was going to do everything in his power to bother me. Now he was using my middle name in mixed company. I surrendered to Maddie because there was no way I'd ever talk her out of calling me by my whole name, but he was just doing it to rile me up.

Satisfied with the results of his passive aggressiveness, he dusted off his jeans and reached down to help Rochelle up before they set out to walk around the lake. I watched them, still infuriated.

"Do you really hate parties that much that you won't let me throw you a small party, Emma Rose?" Maddie's voice was a gentle whisper. "I think your life deserves to be celebrated even if you don't think so."

"Maddie, I just don't—"

"You just don't want a party, I know. It's always what YOU want. It's always what YOU think. Do you ever think about what someone else may want, Emma? You are so stuck in YOU YOU YOU. You don't care if you hurt anyone else's feelings."

Her face had transformed from sadness to anger. "We just love you, Emma. I don't think *you* love you, but we do. You gotta quit pushing us away. You gotta quit being so mean about things."

She scooted close enough for me to smell her shea butter lotion. Our noses now only a couple of inches from touching.

"Emma Rose, sometimes you don't do it for you. You do it for someone else because you love them."

With that she walked away and headed to the opposite side of the lake from Terry and Rochelle, who were now holding hands and pointing at something along the far bank.

As she walked, her hair flowed in the wind, almost dancing. Her denim jacket faded in the distance. She left behind an invisible trail of hurt and disappointment in which I was now held captive. I was left sitting on the blanket at the lake, alone. Just how I wanted it. Or was it? Sadness welled up within me and I chose to let it wash over me. The solitude only nursed my hurts and reminded me of how alone I was and no, it was not how I wanted it.

Chapter Fourteen

I couldn't believe I had gone along with this birthday party. I sat at the kitchen table looking towards the Christmas tree in the living room. There were multicolored lights dancing along the tree and mismatched wrapping paper dressing the boxes underneath. There weren't many presents but Mama always made sure we each had at least two. She often signed us up for the Angel Tree at church to ensure it. We would usually get extra clothes and some money to buy us one present of our choosing.

Our stockings hung near the fireplace, and typically, Mama filled them with candy canes that neither Maddie nor I enjoyed. We didn't have the heart to tell her though. She had always tried to make each Christmas feel as if it was the best one we had ever experienced. Although she made sure we knew that Jesus was the reason for our celebrating the holiday season, she also wanted us to experience the gifts and warmth that came along with it.

Maddie had talked her into a small budget to buy decorations for my party. There were cupcakes and sprinkle designs scattered throughout the living room and kitchen. Maddie had stayed up to make a strawberry cake for me with buttercream icing, my favorite. She knew I would never eat any other type of frosting.

Mama had gotten up early and started a pot of greens. The nostalgia of happiness intermingled with memories of the loss of

Daddy. I had so many emotions building within that I didn't know if I should be glad, angry, sad or maybe all of them simultaneously.

"Emma Rose, it's your birthday! Well kind of…" Maddie giggled as she came in for a long bear hug.

After she had marched away from me at the lake, she had walked home leaving me to watch Rochelle and Terry. It took me a few moments to realize she had gone but when I did, it made me think of how badly I must have hurt her feelings for her to walk home alone without saying a word. When I had returned home, she was sitting on Missums swinging with her head down. Her sadness radiated through the porch, and I couldn't handle seeing her so melancholy.

"Maddie," I whispered, touching her hand softly.

"I don't know how to fix what's in me. It makes me sad too and I don't want others watching me while I try to figure it out."

I had leaned my head over onto her shoulder and she rested her head back on mine in return. We sat on Missums for what seemed like an eternity. Her words from the lake played repeatedly in my mind. I had not wanted to hurt her feelings or anyone's for that matter. Well, maybe Rochelle's. I had prayed to God to help me figure out the right path to take when it seemed so clouded that day.

"Hello!" I heard Mama call out to whoever was at the front door.

"Our first guests are here." Maddie giggled with excitement.

As for me, I took a deep breath and looked upward in a silent plea to God to help me get out of the party.

"Happy Birthday, beautiful girl." Sister Brown hugged me and handed me a card.

Mrs. H gave me a nice firm arm grip and a forehead kiss.

"There's my gift," she said enthusiastically. She further reminded me of how special I was and how thankful she was to be in attendance before Sister Brown helped her navigate her way to the couch. I watched as Sister Brown cut cake for herself and Mrs. H before making further rounds.

A few other people from church arrived with their own well wishes. Shyla and Annette, Maddie's friends, had been invited and once they'd come over to wish me a happy birthday and drop off their gifts, they disappeared into the corner with her for a while.

I personally didn't have many friends, so I didn't expect a large turnout, but Maddie was still quite thrilled.

"Happy Birthday, Emma!" Mama squeezed me so hard that I lost my balance and landed right in her chest.

"Emma, you know I love you, right?"

"Yes ma'am."

"I would do anything for you, and I hope you know that."

It was hard for me to meet her eyes because something deep within me knew her words were true but still had difficulty accepting them.

"Baby, you know you're *my* special gift, right? That's why He gave you to me on Christmas. I don't know what I'd do without you."

Her words caught me off guard. She wasn't usually the sentimental type.

"Mama, what's wrong?" I blurted out.

She laughed. "Something's gotta be wrong because I love you?"

"No, but Mama you got up and made greens. You're hugging me and being mushy and you've been keeping to yourself a lot lately."

She looked back at me both surprised and confused. I didn't know where the boldness had come from, but the words rushed out of my mouth quicker than anticipated, "and I know about those white envelopes, Mama."

"You what?" She took a step backward, the happiness drained from her face.

"Oh Emma." Her eyes left my own and she slowly walked away toward her room.

I stared after her, wondering if I should follow. Her bathroom light popped on, but the rest of her room remained dark. I wondered if she was in there crying, heartbroken by my disappointment. Maybe she was praying or asking God why He had given me as a gift. She probably regretted saying that to me now.

After a few minutes she reemerged. She didn't seem unusually stressed or worried but had the same countenance she normally carried. She refused to meet my eyes though.

What was wrong with me?! I had taken away the only moment in the last few years that I could remember in which Mama was genuinely happy.

After Daddy had died, Mama's joy never fully returned. She spoke to me about God's will and how He would never leave our family and mentioned how He doesn't make mistakes and how He would make sure we were taken care of. She had all those great things to say about God, but some things couldn't be repaired. For instance, Mama had never been the same.

Today she was genuinely happy. Her eyes were full of light, and I saw a glimpse of who she used to be. But I couldn't receive her affirmation. Instead, I had deflected it and turned it into a moment of grief. Maybe that should have been my middle name instead of Rose. *Emma Sadness. Emma Grief. Emma Joy-Stealer.* I was *no* one's gift.

"Emma, I think I hear Missums calling you." Maddie's voice intruded on my self loathing. She grabbed my hand and began walking me towards the front.

"Maddie, I think I hurt—"

Terry was sitting out on Missums. He was looking toward the street and fiddling with his hands, like he normally would when he was nervous or rehearsing something within his mind. I didn't even notice he had come. I thought maybe he had stayed behind at home when Sister Brown walked in earlier without him. Had he been sitting on Missums this whole time?

"Emma, what were you saying? You think you hurt what?"

I couldn't respond to Maddie because I was so mesmerized with Terry. The fact that he was there at all captivated me. I observed how his brown skin began intertwining with the sunset. His profile was nearly perfect, accentuated by the flawless shape of his nose. His lips were full enough to welcome another set to his but not so broad to overpower his remaining facial features. His eyelashes were naturally long with a mild curl. I never understood why boys had impeccable eyelashes while girls had to thicken theirs with mascara.

Not yet aware of my presence, I watched as he repositioned his arm to rest his chin on his fist. His skin was smooth with the slightest amount of hair on his arms. His nails were trimmed and neat, with no sign of dirt underneath. He was a beautiful sight, just as Chelsea had described, only he wasn't just appealing because of his handsome looks, but also because I knew what great qualities he possessed.

I knew things that other girls didn't, like how his heart was abnormally large compared to any other high school boy that I had met and how even when he appeared confident, sometimes he was nervous on the inside. I also knew that he would give his all to make sure I was safe and okay. No other girl was privy to that side of him. It was reserved for me alone.

"Emma?" Maddie tried to gain my attention again but failed.

I calmly pushed the screen door open, almost exploding on the inside when Terry's eyes met mine. He looked like a deer blinded by headlights. Our eyes did not part as I made my way over to Missums to sit next to him. He smelled like Cool Water cologne, a fresh, soothing scent that I found relaxing.

"Hi."

"Hi."

I couldn't think of anything else to say besides, "I'm glad Rochelle isn't here."

Terry erupted in laughter. "Is that so? How do you know I didn't hide her behind the bushes?"

I looked toward the bushes with concern as if it were possible.

He laughed in amusement.

"You were saying something about you being glad I was here without a certain someone." He motioned for me to continue.

"Yeah, I couldn't take any more of you two with those dumb kissy faces."

"Kissy faces?" Terry laughed a little more. "We never had kissy faces."

"Well maybe you didn't, but she *clearly* did." I looked down at the porch appreciating the moonlit stone.

"I think you'd have to have kissed someone to have a kissy face, Emma." Terry's face was now serious.

"Wait, are you telling me that you and Rochelle have never kissed? Aren't y'all boyfriend and girlfriend?"

"Nope. We are still trying to figure out if that is what we want from one another."

"What does that even mean?"

"It means we are going to college soon and we don't know if we really want to take on that kind of commitment for the next few months just to break it off over summer."

I began frantically looking around and underneath the swing. "Oh no!"

"What's wrong? Did you lose something?" He immediately began searching for an unknown item with me.

"Oh, I'm just looking for your briefcase and pocketbook right now," I smirked. "You sound like some old man."

"Shut up, Emma! I can never be serious with you." He smirked back.

"I'm just saying. You got deep really quick."

"You asked."

"So why does she look so in love with you and why do you two always hold hands then?"

"I mean, I *am* lovable." He posed.

"I guess to some people with lower standards," I teased.

We sat for a moment with goofy smiles on our faces appreciating how nice it felt to be near, cutting jokes again. I had missed him so much.

"So…" Terry looked at me with a concerned face.

Uh oh. Here it comes. He wasn't going to let me off the hook that easily.

"So?"

"Gonna tell me what's going on? I mean one moment we were good and then the next, we were sworn enemies. Or at least you were."

I hung my head in embarrassment. There was no way I was going to tell him that I felt insecure about him and Rochelle. I couldn't explain that I feared being left alone and that my best friend in the world would move on without me. I'd be stuck here in Byron forever while he went on to marry Rochelle and have beautiful brown babies.

I was so upset that he had chosen her over me. No one had ever trumped me until she had come along. And he went with her so willingly. Kissy faced or not, he was one step away from abandoning me… like my dad.

"I don't know." Anger replaced my embarrassment.

"Gonna tell me a lie or be big enough to tell me something real?"

"You think you know everything!" I stood up and stared down at him. How dare he tell me what was real.

Terry gently took my hand and guided me back onto Missums. I didn't understand how he could remain so calm when I felt like a volcano was erupting within me. How did he manage to keep his temperament so even and calm?

"I don't know why you are so mad at me?" His demeanor appeared wounded.

"Whatever."

"Emma." Terry's posture didn't change. He continued to hold my hand while looking at me with non-judgmental eyes.

I couldn't hold it in. He had a way of breaking through my façade. "Terry."

Sobs began to come out. Tears fell all over Missums.

 "I can't handle it if you left me too. Please don't leave me."

Instead of using words, he drew me in closer. He tucked me underneath his arm and nestled his chin on my forehead as I rested my ear on his chest. His breath was slow and easy. His warmth was soothing. He need not vocalize how he felt about me. He loved me. It may not have been a romantic love, but it was the kind that lasted forever. It was the kind that nothing and no one could come between.

He sat with me as my tears slowed and my breath returned to normal. How silly I was to feel he would just disappear for good.

Our lives were too etched with one another's memories. We were forever marked by each other.

"Here, you are already beginning to shiver, although I don't know if it's from your pool of tears or the wind." He joked as he placed his jacket over my shoulder. I thought he would release me after but instead he pulled me back in.

"So, you crashed my birthday party and didn't even bring a gift?"

"Well, I did bring you a gift. I just hope you don't hate it."

"What could you possibly have gotten me that I would hate? Wait! You actually did give me a frog one time. Do you remember that? Ugh! I hated that—"

Before I could finish my sentence, Terry's lips pressed softly against my own. His kiss wasn't rushed or urgent. It was sweet and slow. He turned his head slightly to make room for my nose as I adjusted my own. The warmth of his mouth was inviting and made me want to prolong the moment. The way he allowed me to press into his chest while he kept control of our motions increased my desire to be near him. He paused to permit me free expression with his lips before our mouths spontaneously separated.

Once the kiss had ended, he reached up to grab my face in his hands. His eyes told me how much he cared and how he would never be able to describe his love for me. Then he kissed me ever so sweetly again before relaxing back into Missusms and returning me to his chest. He rubbed my shoulder while making sure I was tucked back into his jacket.

"Did you hate it?"

I attempted to hide my smile, but my cheeks exposed it immediately. I tucked my nose into his side to disguise my blushing face. I couldn't answer the question, but he knew. He knew I definitely did *not* hate it.

Chapter Fifteen

"So, what do you think, Emma?" Mr. E made it a point to address me by my first name during the group session in the SOAR room, however, he always referred to me as Ms. Griggs when we were not near the other youth.

"Calling the kids by their first names makes them feel like I care." He had once explained to me when I asked about it.

"When I call them mister or miss in front of their peers, it makes them withdraw a little bit. I want to remind each one of you that you are all significant and have a title. You're either a "sir" or a "ma'am." You're a "mister" or a "miss." There's more to you than just your first name. But being called "mister" or "miss" can also add an extra layer of pressure to be something you feel you're not. In group sessions, there's enough weight already. So, I try to only use the term when I can keep the air light."

Mr. E could have easily been any random guy I had passed in Byron. His pecan skin tone and the tattoos and scars he carried were no anomaly for my hometown. I wanted to ask him about his facial scar, but I couldn't work up the nerve to do it just yet. He would often point to it and say, "Trust me. I've been there" when someone got to rambling on about all he or she was up against in the world.

"*Tuh*, I'm still there." He would sigh in understanding.

I did know about the tattoo, however. He had mentioned how his favorite cousin had been killed in a drive-by shooting when he was in high school. They had lived together for most of their lives, so they were more like siblings. I had never seen him cry before that moment. I observed how the tough man before me had paused to compose himself before continuing with the story.

He spoke passionately about how Ambria's death had caused him to "wake up and realize that life was precious." After he had shed a few more tears and pleaded with the group not to throw away their lives, he took a break from the group to recover. I watched the muscular, seemingly unbreakable man sit with his head down, now appearing fragile. I realized he was merely a man but behind those scars and his hard exterior, he was also a hero. He was a hero because he was willing to show his scars to others to try to keep them from making the same mistakes. He was a hero because he showed up every day to the detention center without judgment, ready to push through the hard walls we had put up. He was an onion peeler for sure.

"So, what do you think Emma?" The words echoed in my head as I stared at Mr. E.

"I think that it makes a lot of sense."

One of the boys had brought up how angry he would become when their classmates would answer questions correctly. He had made the connection that his anger may have been coming from the fact that he felt stupid when he didn't know the answer himself.

"Go on." He motioned.

"Well, I know I have recently gone through something like this. I became angry and was mean to someone I really cared about because of my own fear and insecurities. Thankfully he forgave me and understood but you know not everyone will be so forgiving."

"That's a good point, Emma. Thank you for sharing. We may hurt people when we let our anger turn into negative actions and they may not be willing to let it go. Being forgiven doesn't mean people forget, you know? They may write you off completely. We can't expect everyone else to be okay with our lashing out. That make sense?"

Several of the kids shook their heads in agreement while others looked around. Most of the group had become comfortable with me by this time and only needed to know I'd be consistent and invested. As Mr. E had reminded me frequently, I couldn't just show up expecting their respect, but I had to put "skin in the game." I had to be willing to share pieces of myself too. The topics of the group session could get heavy. I had learned that we all had problems we were working through. It made me feel better knowing that I was not the only one struggling with certain things. Sometimes it was too easy to think that I was the only person going through difficult events.

"You know, I've been mad at my mom for so long." Raymond's voice took me by surprise. Although we had begun playing games with one another during SOAR, he had never contributed verbally within the group setting.

"She gave me my headphones and teddy bear the day she left. I remember her telling me it would all be okay. Well, she lied. Nothing has been okay since she left." He paused and looked around the room, careful not to lock eyes with anyone. He looked like a scared little boy as he began to hold his bear a bit tighter.

"I try to be good for my grandparents because I know they are doing their best. They didn't plan on having to raise me. But I'm so mad all the time. I'm so mad at *her*. It's like when I try to choose to be happy, something reminds me that I wasn't good enough for my mom to stick around. Then I get mad and I just react. And whoever is around catches the brunt of it. It's hard, man."

The room remained quiet for a moment as the impact of his words lingered. Everyone within the circle could identify with some of his pain: a parent leaving, a grandparent picking up the slack, wanting to choose the right path but pain getting in the way; memories that bring you back to dark images, anger being a close companion to help mask all the other emotions you were having, trauma, deeply distressing and disturbing moments. The question was how could we escape it? No one had the answer, not even Mr. E.

"Well, Raymond, you're right. It's hard. It comes down to one day at a time."

"And God." I blurted out.

I felt several eyes on me. It was highly unlikely that these kids had never heard God's name thrown at them to help them get through their issues. Byron was small but it had a lot of churches. I alone had heard God's name millions of times in my short life.

"My daddy…" I swallowed and took a deep breath. *What in the world was I doing?*

"My daddy was an alcoholic. He drank way too much. He was drafted to Vietnam right out of high school and my mama said he never returned the same. He hated the war and the people who had made him go. He was never cruel to me and Mama, but he wrestled with his anger all the time. And he would always tell me that if he didn't have God, he couldn't survive one more day.

"He said that he never knew God in a personal way, but he wished I would learn how to. He said he could always feel God's presence around him trying to guide him through his pain, but he didn't know how to walk through it. He said he wasn't strong enough and that's why he needed to drink. He wanted me to know God because God would help me walk through my own issues one day. Maybe He can help you get through yours too."

Tears fell heavily into my lap as I spoke. I willed them to slow but it was too late. I had opened a door that I vowed to keep locked and it had released a barrage of emotions that couldn't be simply stilled. There was no returning my eyes to the group. They were too heavy to be lifted, anchored into sadness. I had steamrolled myself into an arena of grief by sharing Daddy's words.

"And us!" Mr. E said emphatically, sensing my need for rescue. "Us. Each other. We as people can help each other get through our issues together. That's why it's so important that we learn to talk to one another so we can support each other. Thank you, Emma and Raymond, for sharing."

I could hear people begin to disperse into their area of choosing once the group dismissed. I, however, sat frozen in my chair, staring at my hands. I felt numb.

"Here, you can hang on to this for a second but just give it back before you leave." Raymond sat his bear on my lap and walked away.

The tears had begun to slow but the faucet was now back at full flow as I looked at the worn stuffed animal. There was no doubt that he had held that bear countless nights and cried into it. I'm sure his wishes and pleas to God were vested into its fuzz. He had given me his most valuable and vulnerable possession. I held his heart in my hand, and it reminded me that I was not alone, but it wasn't enough. I squeezed the bear against my chest and let out a silent sob, "God help."

Mr. E. placed his hand on my shoulder and sat with me until Mrs. Gaines entered the room to offer me a ride home. Apparently, no one thought I was in the state of mind to catch the bus home alone. Besides I had lost track of time and awareness of all the others in the room. I was cemented in my sorrow. I didn't remember returning Raymond's bear. I didn't remember leaving the detention center and I sure didn't remember the ride home with Mrs. Gaines. I only remembered my appeal to God.

****

"Darling, won't you have some tea please?"

Mrs. H was looking at me with a concerned expression. She had made some lavender tea and told me to drink it a few minutes ago but I still felt anesthetized. Mrs. Gaines had been so worried about me that she contacted Mama before leaving the detention center. Mama had told her she was on her way out to a meeting and to drop me off with Mrs. H until she returned.

Since Mrs. Gaines and Mrs. H were already acquainted, Mrs. Gaines offered to sit in with us for a while.

"Yes ma'am" I took a sip of the tea, surprised that it was actually quite tasty.

"How are you feeling?" Mrs. H asked, shifting around in her chair to get a closer look at me.

"I feel okay." I managed to look her in the eyes.

"Oh baby." She carefully rose from her chair and made her way to where I was sitting. She embraced me and sighed into my hair. "It's going to be okay, Darling."

"I don't know what happened. I was talking in our group session and then I lost it."

Both Mrs. H and Mrs. Gaines smiled gently at me, hoping I'd continue.

"I was trying to encourage the others by sharing about my daddy and it got to me. Then this kid gave me his bear and I couldn't hold it together."

The tears had begun flowing again. *When would these darn things ever stop running?*

Mrs. Gaines handed me a tissue and patted my back to comfort me. "You know, sweetheart, that means you were being genuine. I can guarantee you made a big connection with those kids today."

"They probably think I'm a big nutcase, "I groaned.

"No Emma, those kids are some of the realest kids you'll meet. Trust me, they can recognize fake from real. You were honest with them today and it's the *real* stuff that makes us emotional. It's the *real* stuff that helps us grow and connects us. You, my dear, have some deep hurt and today you gave others a glimpse into your heart. That doesn't make you crazy. That makes you brave and someone the other kids can't help but to learn to admire."

Mrs. H took a sip of her tea before verbalizing her agreement. "Darling, we are not meant to walk through life alone. Life is messy and it's hard. That's why God sends people to walk alongside us. Even Jesus did not walk alone, and he was God."

"Yes ma'am."

"Your father was an amazing man, Emma."

Oh no! More tears.

"We all have our faults. We all have things that can be too heavy for us to carry alone. I'm so sorry that you have had to deal with loss so early in life, but I'm also grateful that you got to experience the love that he had for you. I have no doubt that his love for you is what kept him around as long as it did. But Emma you can't leave this grief built up inside of you. Grief that is undealt with is dangerous. I don't think you can see who you really are because you are so overtaken by it."

"But how do I deal with it, Mrs. H? How? I don't know how. All I know is that it hurts and I'm so angry…"

"You're doing it, Darling. You are doing it now. You are choosing to talk. Let's start there. Let's focus on that."

"But Mrs. H, why did he do it? Why did he choose to end his life if he loved me so much?" My rage fueled through the blubbering.

Daddy didn't stick around and fight for me. He had given up. I knew he loved me, and I knew he was sad, but he had chosen to leave me and Mama behind as if it would be the same without him. I understood that there were things that he faced that I had not had to, but I could never comprehend why he didn't stay and fight longer. Didn't he know I needed him? Didn't he know I wouldn't know how to recover? Didn't he know that he was my everything?

"Why does my Mama call me a gift if I couldn't even keep Daddy around? If I was such a gift, and so beautiful, and so smart, and all these other things that people say I am, how come it wasn't enough to keep Daddy from leaving? He still wanted to leave."

The room had begun to spin as I spewed the words. My face felt as if one million needles were pricking it and my arms had begun shaking. I felt a loss of control. I was helpless and overwhelmed. Despair had gripped me, and anger clouded my entire being. I was lost within a tornado of feelings that were bound to explode at any given second.

Before I knew it, warm hugs had taken ahold of me. I could sense tears falling alongside mine and two heartbeats pounded within my ears as I tried to settle into the hugs. Both women held on tightly, sharing in my pain and choosing to help me contain the grief that I could not describe. Although I felt broken and as if I was slowly shattering beyond repair, Mrs. Gaines and Mrs. H were there attempting to hold me together.

The smell of lavender and rose scents attempted to soothe me but I wasn't sure it was possible. Even if Mrs. H and Mrs. Gaines held onto me forever, something within me would not be comforted. It defied the moment, choosing to not yield to the peace being offered, feeling as if it wasn't theirs to give.

"Oh baby!"

A new voice broke into the room unapologetically. This voice was different but also the most familiar. It was present from my birth, welcoming me into a new world. It hushed and soothed my cries and was around during every sickness.

This voice was the one that I could count on to meet me at the door each day. The one that disciplined me when I made a mistake but also guided me in the right direction with firmness.

I refused to open my eyes, afraid that if I did, reality would hit harder than it already had. Instead, I focused in on the voice that was currently speaking over me while I took notice of my hair being stroked.

It was the person who had called me a gift before I ruined her evening. It was the woman who although she didn't admit it, I knew was in pain too.

As the tears and my breathing slowed, I realized I was now only in one person's embrace. The recognizable arms of the woman who had never left my side.

"Oh Mama!" I bellowed through my sobs.

Chapter Sixteen

It seemed as if the bell would never ring. Mrs. Lee was currently lecturing on how there was only one more semester left in our high school career and if we put in a lot of effort, we could maintain or improve our grade point average before graduation.

For some reason Mrs. Lee thought it would make a difference if our GPA improved by May, but most colleges had already cut off their deadline for applications by now and were more interested in our SAT scores. I had not done so well on my PSAT last year and was not looking forward to tackling the actual SAT soon. Surprisingly, though, at the end of the first semester, my GPA had come up to a 3.05, but now I was on Mrs. Lee's radar even more. I suppose she felt as if she had a role in the improvement and wanted to see how much more she could push me.

I was often met with, "Emma, have you given any more thought to your college applications? You still have time." Or she constantly reminded me, "Emma, you know I'm here if you need anything right?"

I knew that I could talk to her, I just didn't have anything to say. I'd said enough a couple of weeks ago during the group session at the detention center. After weeks of listening to Mr. E, I was considering the possibility of going to college, but I had no idea where to begin. I had decided not to tell Mrs. Lee that though. She would only take the information as an invite to smother me with suggestions and ideas. I doubted that she would respect my need to process things without her usual level of intensity. I wasn't up to handling all of that right now.

Riiiiinnnngggggg. Finally!

Maddie met me outside of Mrs. Lee's classroom with her predictable smile.

"Hey Emma Rose! I'm so hungry."

"You're always hungry Maddie."

"Well… what can I say? I do love food," she giggled.

She had been hanging around me even more at school nowadays. She would walk around with her friends during passing periods and talk to them briefly before and after school, but she was usually the first to my side during the lunch break. I didn't know if it was my birthday party that had brought us closer or the fact that she had patted my back, rubbed my hair, and hummed to me the evening Mama had brought me home from Mrs. H's house.

That night my face was so soggy that it was in danger of falling away. I could barely stand so Mama and Maddie had to help walk me up the steps.

"She's had a hard day, Maddie Lyn," Mama had whispered.

Mama was never one to overshare. She gave you just enough information to go on; never less and certainly, never more.

I could imagine Maddie's eyes dropping and her heart burdened with concern. She had never seen me so downcast. Her voice was soft as she replied, "yes ma'am." She then strengthened her grip around me and didn't ask questions. She just laid beside me in our bed and helped comfort me until I had fallen asleep.

When I had awakened the next morning, she waited to see how my mood was before leaping into action. Once she had realized that I was doing okay, she pounced.

"Soooo… what's up with you and Terry?"

"Ugh Maddie." I covered my face with a pillow. The mention of his name made me smile like a silly girl in love.

I had told her that Terry kissed me on my birthday, and she about dropped her hot chocolate she was drinking at the time.

"Don't you drop my mug!" Mama scolded as she walked by shaking her head.

"You have to tell me more, Emma." Maddie had scooted in so close that I felt the warmth coming from her drink.

"Maddie, geesh." I couldn't help but laugh at her eagerness. "There's not much to tell other than what I just said."

"Oh no ma'am. There's always more to tell." Her eyes were unrelenting with anticipation.

"I don't know, Maddie. We talked about how I was stupid for being mean to him. I told him I hated seeing him with Rochelle."

"Oh yeah! Rochelle! Emma, he already has a girlfriend."

"No, actually he doesn't. They're just figuring it out." I rolled my eyes.

"What? What does that even mean?"

"I know right?! I guess they don't want to be a couple since school is almost over and they will be going to different colleges."

"Orrrr… because he doesn't feel the same way about her as he does about you." Maddie waggled her eyebrows as she smiled. "I do recall someone mentioning this to you before—"

I had thrown a pillow at her before she could finish her sentence. She then tackled me in retaliation before taking the pillow and tossing it back at me. We had giggled for a few moments before laying on our backs and looking up at the ceiling.

"So seriously, Emma, what are you gonna do?"

"I don't know, Maddie. We haven't talked about it."

"Well, it seems like you probably should, huh?"

"Yeah, I guess you're right," I had agreed.

Maddie nudged me in the side, taking me away from my thoughts. "Here he comes," she said in a high whisper.

I watched as Terry approached us, attempting not to stare at him, but I couldn't help it. Our eyes tended to maintain contact no matter where we were located within a room.

"Hey! Ya'll look like you're up to no good."

Maddie snickered; no doubt still overtaken by the fact that we had kissed. She was such a hopeless romantic.

"Oookay." Terry turned to me, choosing to ignore the girly feelings that Madison had become lost in.

"What are we eating?"

"That is the question, isn't it," I joked.

They both knew I was terrible at making food choices. I wished they would learn that if left up to me, five minutes later we would be back in the same spot, asking the same question.

"Umm, here comes your girl." Maddie failed to accomplish a hushed whisper once more.

Terry and I turned to see Rochelle bouncing over. She had a genuine smile spread about her face and seemed unconcerned that Terry and I's friendship (or whatever it was) had been restored. I wondered if he had told we kissed. Maybe that wasn't a requirement in their "relationship." I was too scared to ask him though. I had just gotten used to having him back around and didn't want to force an argument that could cause me to lose him again.

We hadn't talked about the kiss anyhow. I had deliberated whether he thought he might have made a mistake. And if so, maybe he figured if we didn't discuss it, it would simply go away. Personally, if the guy I liked had told me that he kissed another girl, his "best friend," I'd disappear but here Rochelle was acting as if nothing had changed between her and Terry.

She reached out and touched him on the shoulder, "Hey everyone!"

He stepped away uncomfortably. "Hey Rochelle! What's up?"

"Ya'll wanna go to lunch?"

Maddie and I shifted around, unsure of what to say. Lunch would be awkward with Rochelle there. Also, I didn't think I could manage to keep silent if she continued making goo-goo eyes at him.

"I was thinking we could head over to—"

"We are gonna head out on our own right now, but Rochelle let's talk later." Terry looked at her with a matter-of-fact expression I'd never witnessed before. It was a cross between perturbed and sensitivity, as if he didn't want to come off rude but wanted to be clear in his stance.

"Whatever." She spun on her heels and stomped off.

Terry didn't wait for Maddie or me to say anything. Instead, he grabbed me by the hand and headed towards the front door. Maddie followed quickly trying to keep up.

"Umm, where are we going?" I asked.

"To eat." I ignored his terseness.

"Yeah, but where?"

"I don't know, but we're going."

Maddie laughed, "Calm down there, tiger. Let's get a plan together before we begin walking circles in the cold."

His face remained stressed yet his grip on my hand was relaxed. Weird. *What was with the tenseness?*

"Terry?"

It was as if he was snatched out of his thoughts when he heard my voice. He looked over at me calmly, "yeah?"

I watched as his face recovered, returning to a settled cool expression. Tension began to fall from his face while he simultaneously repositioned my hand into a more supportive hold. I marveled at the fact that I too had a soothing impact on him. It was he who typically centered me but in this moment my heart beamed as his uneasiness melted away as he looked back at me.

Suddenly feeling inspired, I blurted out, "Let's go to Taco Bell."

Terry and Maddie stopped walking abruptly and gawked at each other with amusement.

"Did that just happen?"

"Yes, it did Maddie. We have just witnessed a miracle."

"I know. I feel so special."

They both hollered in laughter. For once in our high school life, I had been the one to choose a restaurant.

Chapter Seventeen

"I love this time of year," Maddie twirled along the sidewalk on the way home from our bus stop. She looked like a little girl whose mother had just freed her to play outside. Her eyes were full of wonder as she spread her fingers, combing through the air. It always amazed me how genuinely happy she was with the simplicity of her everyday surroundings.

I could not remember a time in which she wasn't able to find some sort of a silver lining. Even though we didn't grow up having a wealth of things, she was always content. I laughed as I recalled how she would make up fake lives for the sticks and rocks outside. She would spend hours with "Mister and Miss Rock" or "Sammy the Stick." The girl was just able to find bliss in whatever was in front of her.

She continued to hold her hands out, daring the wind to push against her palms with the same dopey smile lingering on her face.

"Emma." Her beautiful face turned towards mine. Her big grin peered through sheened lips as she spoke.

"The outdoors is just so pretty, don't you think? Like, how can you feel the wind, or see the clouds moving and not feel something special happening around you?"

"Oh my gosh, Maddie," I laughed.

"You look like those women in movies that randomly spin around fields except you're not singing or holding on to some old lady skirt like them." I couldn't control my laughter because it was so true. She reminded me of the leading ladies in multiple films that had aired on TV throughout our childhood.

Maddie, pleased with the comparison, began vocalizing off pitch as she began overembellishing her twirls.

"Hey lovelies!" Mrs. Hennagen waved to us from her porch.

She was headed back indoors and looked as if she had come out briefly to grab her mail. She carried a couple of pieces of post into the house as she stepped into her door frame.

She was beginning to find a place within my heart. I recalled our first encounters and how I would not have lost any sleep if our paths never crossed again. I thought of how she had miffed and frustrated me so easily, especially when she had refused to call me by my name. Now I knew her to be a kind, understanding and a non-judgmental woman that I could depend on. I caught myself smiling and shook my head. *Who in the world was I becoming?*

"Emma Rose, are you listening?" Maddie repeated my name until I responded.

"Yes, what?"

"I think you should just kiss him instead of waiting on him to kiss you again."

"Wait, what?" Leave it to Maddie to have moved from the beauty of the outdoors to planning my next romantic encounter within a manner of minutes.

"Girls, come on!" Mama's voice called out as the Buick began to slow down near us.

"Get in. Hurry up!" Her voice sounded panicked. She was all but screaming and the creases in her eyebrows looked as if they'd never be able to be straightened.

Although we had plenty, we didn't ask questions. We threw our bookbags in the car and flew in after one another. Maddie hopped into the front seat while I gladly occupied the backseat. There was no way I'd be able to remain calm while sitting next to Mama right now in her current state. She was stern. She was firm. She could give you a look that made you fix your behavior quickly. But Mama was not typically frantic and didn't usually raise her voice in the way she had just done.

What was happening?

My heart began racing as I thought of the day she had told me about Daddy passing away. She wasn't hysterical but she did begin hyperventilating until she could no longer speak aloud. And then she slept. She slept for the remainder of the day and the next day she was back in the kitchen cooking breakfast and brewing tea.

The days following Daddy's death, Mama was like a stone, only a very fragile one. If I had touched her, asked her how she was doing, or even mentioned his name, she would have crumbled. Not in front of me and Maddie of course, but she would retreat into her room and surely collapse.

"Breathe, Emma. Breathe." I attempted to remind myself that those events were in the past. In this moment, I needed to try and stay calm.

"Aunt Ruthie?" Maddie hesitantly called.

A tear rolled down Mama's face as she accelerated onto the highway. She didn't wipe it away but continued to stare straight ahead. Her face remained tense and she did not respond to Maddie. Something was up, and my anxiety magnified. I stared out of the window and tried to focus on my breathing once more.

Breathe, Emma.

I couldn't tell if Mama was okay, and it was beginning to really frighten me. *Just breathe.*

"I love you, Aunt Ruthie." Maddie touched Mama's shoulder quickly, making sure to not rest her hand there too long.

Maddie was never comfortable leaving something in a negative way. If she could bring some sort of joy or peace into a situation, she would give her all to do so.

Mama pulled the car over on the next exit and began bawling. Maddie stroked her back in support as I sat frozen in the backseat.

After a few moments, Mama began crying out, "Oh Lord Jesus! Lord Jesus."

She repeated those words over and over until she rested her head on the steering wheel and let out a long breath.

"Maddie… Give me strength Jesus…" Mama attempted to look at Madison but quickly averted her eyes.

Maddie waited patiently, staring back at Mama like an innocent child looking up into his or her mother's eyes.

"Baby, your mother is sick. She's in the ICU on life support."

Her breath quickened as she rushed the last sentence. She looked over at Maddie who was now the second frozen person in the car.

"Life support?" Maddie said, barely moving her lips.

"Baby, it means some machines are keeping her alive. She would be dead without them."

Maddie remained fixed.

Hearing Mama's words caused my limbs to feel numb and impossibly heavy. I couldn't even make out if tears were falling down my face or not.

Maddie sat back in the passenger seat, but her eyes remained glued on Mama's.

"I have been looking for your mother for months. Something didn't feel right in my spirit, so I hired a private investigator to help me find her. I was hoping we could locate her in time for your graduation."

Still no motion from Maddie. I thought I saw her blink and take one breath though. I leaned in closer to make sure—okay, yes, she was breathing.

"But baby, it was worse than I thought. Your mom has been sick for a while and there's no fixing it. I've prayed and prayed but the doctors and nurses are certain that there's nothing else that can be done for her."

Maddie turned and stared out the passenger window as a statement that she didn't want to continue the conversation. Mama, taking the hint, wiped her eyes and pulled back onto the road.

"We're going to the hospital now, baby, so begin praying."

Maddie had shut her eyes, protesting reality. I looked at her profile, suddenly missing that spunky, happy-go-lucky cousin of mine that so often annoyed me with her positivity. Instead, a near listless young lady sat before me as if the last bit of energy and will had been drained from her body. I didn't know what to say so I just stared, protective of her breath. If I couldn't control anything else, I'd keep track of her respirations in time. I'd breathe for her if I could.

And right on cue, like every sappy romantic or overly dramatic movie I'd watched before, rain drops began to slap the windshield. They began softly at a slow manageable rate, allowing Mama to maintain her sight without the use of the wipers. But as we entered the hospital parking lot, the rain had begun pelting the windows and the Buick's wiper blades were at max capacity.

Maddie's tears flooded her cheeks in sync with the rain. Ironically, she had always welcomed the rain and now, it was as if the rain showered in support of her, showing up when she needed it the most.

While I did enjoy sitting on Missums and watching when rain would fall, Maddie loved it even more. She would sit on the edge of the porch and let her feet dangle in the rain drops with a whimsical smile on her face. She would lean back and tell me, "Emma Rose, doesn't it just smell like love outside?" I never understood how she equated the rain drops with love but in this moment as we were entering the hospital, maybe the rain was somehow sending her a reminder that love was still near. Maybe it was God sprinkling her with affection in such a hard hour.

Parking the car and finding the nearest entrance, Mama looked at the directory ahead of her and led us to the elevator. As the doors closed, I glanced at Maddie one more time. Her tears were gone, replaced with a blank and expressionless countenance.

Her face had lost some of its coloring, and she appeared tranced. When she didn't move once the elevator doors opened, Mama took her by the hand and led her onto the unit. MEDICAL ICU-2ND FLOOR, the sign attached to the ceiling read.

My heart skipped a beat and my legs felt weak. *Hold it together, Emma.* I could hear Terry's voice calming me. *They both need you to hold it together right now. You can do this.* I *could* do this.

One step at a time. One breath at a time.

"Hello, we are here to see Joleen Harrison." Mama spoke to the young woman at the nurse's station.

For some reason, I imagined all nurses to be old and dressed in white. The woman before me was no more than forty years old with a gorgeous almond complexion and dark wavy hair pulled back into a ponytail. Her eyes were dazzling. She wore a plum-colored lipstick and greeted Mama warmly with a smile.

"Yes ma'am, I believe the doctor has been expecting you all." Her accent was slight. "I'll let him know you have arrived. Do you mind letting me know your relation to the patient please?"

"I'm her sister, Ruthie, and this is her daughter, Madison." Mama motioned at a still numb Maddie.

I wasn't sure if she had forgotten to introduce me or if she didn't find it necessary but either way, I was thankful she hadn't.

I was never close to Aunt Joleen and didn't prefer to be associated with let alone identified as a relative of hers. She was the sort of woman who knew she was gorgeous. Her light skin tone, medium-sized lips and perfect facial features were undeniably appealing.

She was not the quiet type. If she was in the room, she made sure that everyone knew. She would laugh loudly and always had an opinion on whatever topic was being discussed. And she believed that children should not be in the same room as adults for long periods of time. She would dismiss Maddie and I to go play if she noticed us. If we were quiet or she was involved in a drawn-out conversation with someone, particularly a man, she would sometimes forget we were there.

I once heard one of Mama's cousins mutter, after Aunt Joleen told Maddie to "go play," likely forgetting I was still in the vicinity. "It's a shame that she can't put that same attention she puts into men into her own daughter."

"I know that's right," Mama's other cousin had chimed in.

Well, they were right because Aunt Joleen discarded Maddie onto Mama like it was no big deal. She didn't call. She didn't write. She *just* didn't.

I tried to push the anger away but there were no pleasant memories that could be mustered of Aunt Joleen.

"Hi folks." An older white man with baggy scrubs and a white coat approached us.

His voice was sensitive. He had bags underneath his eyes and scratched his head as he took a seat in front of us. The nurse had us sit in the waiting area because she thought it would be best if we did not speak with the doctor in Aunt Joleen's room. She thought it better to meet with him in the waiting area.

"I'm Dr. Kent. I have been taking care of Ms. Harrison for about a week and a half now. I understand you are her sister, and you are her daughter. Who are you, young lady?"

He looked over at me awaiting my response.

"I'm Emma, her niece." *Not by choice.*

"Well, I wish I could have met you under better circumstances, but it is a pleasure to meet you all."

We all looked back at him hoping that he'd jump straight to the point. Although I did appreciate his compassion, the apprehension within me was mounting. I needed him to just spit out the words at this point. Obviously, the news was bad since the nurse decided the best place for us within the waiting room was an isolated area in the back conveniently stocked with Kleenex, a Bible, and artwork on hope and love.

"This is not going to be easy to hear and I apologize. Madison, you are eighteen. Is that correct?"

"Yes sir," Maddie whispered.

Dr. Kent turned towards Mama. "Since she is eighteen, we recognize her as her mother's next of kin since Ms. Harrison is unmarried."

"Next of kin?" Maddie questioned softly.

"Yes. It means that whatever decisions need to be made regarding your mother's healthcare will be ultimately up to you."

Maddie turned quickly to Mama, angst coated on her face. Mama reached over and placed her arm around Maddie and looked sternly at the doctor.

"Ms. Harrison—"

"Mrs. Griggs," Mama corrected him.

"Sorry about that. Mrs. Griggs, I want you to know that we in no way expect that you will allow her to make such difficult decisions on her own. We know that you will be here to support her and that you will offer wise counsel for her. It would be remiss of me to not bring the information to you up front, however."

"I do understand that sir." Mama's tone did not warm.

"Can you all tell me what you know about Ms. Harrison's condition?"

"Not much. Only that she is not doing well and y'all feel like there's nothing else to be done for her."

Maddie cried as Mama continued speaking with the doctor.

There was no way she was hearing anything he or Mama was saying at this point. She was a wreck.

I readjusted my body next to hers and rubbed her back as Mama and Dr. Kent continued speaking for another five minutes or so.

What I gathered from their conversation was that Aunt Joleen was rushed to the hospital by ambulance after her friend was unable to wake her. She had not been conscious since and machines were keeping her alive. The doctor felt like the machines were no longer safe for her body to remain on.

"You all can go in to see her whenever you are ready." Dr. Kent motioned to the hallway where Aunt Joleen's room was located.

He walked away and said something to the nurse before she looked our way with sympathetic eyes.

"Maddie honey, let's go see your mama."

Maddie's tears became audible sobs. "No, Aunt Ruthie, please don't make me."

"Come on now, baby, we have to go see her."

"No, please no." She sat up pleading with Mama.

"Baby, the Lord is ready to take your mother home, whether we go see her or not. I think you would regret if you didn't go in and see her."

Maddie turned toward me as if I held leverage that would change Mama's mind. My heart sank knowing I didn't.

Her face was swollen and distraught. Her eyes begged me to not let Mama take her. Her breath was now so rapid that I thought she would pass out. I pulled her head onto my shoulder and began humming.

Breathe, Maddie, breathe.

I held her and continued to hum. Mama watched, understanding that if she forced Maddie into that room, she would be pushing her beyond her capacity. She would fracture her more than she was already broken.

Mama touched Maddie's back softly, took a slow deep breath and rose to walk unaccompanied to Aunt Joleen's room, leaving me to protect and console my cousin.

Chapter Eighteen

Terry swayed back and forth with me on Missums. The last time we were on the swing together was the night we had kissed. I thought of how warm and comforting his lips were the evening of my birthday party. They were soft, delicate, and distinctively sweet.

I wasn't sure how a boy's mouth could taste sweet since they were typically running around acting like wild animals and smelling similarly to them. Not Terry though. He always had a pleasant scent and I was pretty sure he was one of the few boys that willingly bathed. The kiss we had shared that night made me appreciate his cleanliness even more, being so close to him that I took in every bit of his aroma.

Today was different, however. Even though I loved the idea of kissing him again, my heart was consumed by the sorrow flooding our home. Mama had only been out of her room for work, church, and repeat. She had even been eating in her room. And Maddie… Maddie was much worse. She would come downstairs to eat, but any time she caught a glimpse of my eyes, hers watered unforgivingly. Her pain radiated within the room and her torment was palpable.

"Emma, why me? Why now?" She had tried to work through her hurt.

"She left me before and now she wants to leave me for good… but…" Maddie was one word away from weeping.

"But… but now she wants me to *make* her leave me. Was it not enough that she chose to leave me here all those years ago? No! She couldn't even take care of herself so that I wouldn't have to be the one to do something so terrible. Selfish! Just selfish. I won't do it, Emma, I won't."

Maddie had collapsed onto the bed underneath the covers and didn't reappear until almost ten o'clock that night.

What was I supposed to say? *Yeah, Maddie, your mom sucks. Sucked*— does someone being kept alive by breathing machines count as dead or alive? *Ugh!* This is why I kept my words and my thoughts to myself most of the time. Aunt Joleen was indeed selfish, but I'd never mutter that aloud. Those kinds of words were Maddie's alone. Maddie had the right to feel and spew such harsh yet true verbiage but not me.

"Emma." Terry rubbed my shoulder as he spoke my name as a sentence.

His saying my name in a hushed supportive tone said enough on its own. His being there spoke volumes. He was my woobie. Daddy and I had sat and watched the movie *Mr. Mom* a few times when it aired on the television. He'd murmur: "Ain't that the truth" at the TV every time the little boy clutched his little worn-out security blanket as his dad explained to him that one day his woobie wouldn't be able to save him from adult problems.

I loved Terry's ability to just *be* with me, not having to say or force anything. I held his hand and leaned over to kiss his cheek. My face got stuck next to his neck, however, as I inhaled the familiar fragrance he wore.

"Emma—"

I scooted myself up so I could get a better angle of his mouth before diving in for a real kiss. So much for my heart being too worn to give in to Terry's presence. His lips were calling me in so they could console me. As I cocked my head to the side, pressing into his lips a bit more, he softly held my back returning my affection. Snuggling into his touch made me feel harnessed and secure. Before I knew it, tears began flowing down my face cutting our romance short.

"I'm sorry, Emma. I thought you wanted the kiss."

He withdrew to the edge of Missums and looked at me as though he had just pushed me off the swings.

"I did," the tears continued. "I don't know what's happening."

"Me neither." His face sat in a confused state.

I headed to the edge of the porch to see if I could catch a touch of the wind while a befuddled Terry sat motionless on the swing.

I let out a nervous laugh. He wasn't the only one confused right now.

"Emma?"

"Terry, I don't know whether it's worse to experience the pain of someone you love dying *or* to watch as someone you love endures the same."

His hug enveloped me as the tears returned. "I don't know either, Emma. I don't know." His eyes focused on mine with understanding.

I had been sitting by feeling helpless as Mama and Maddie tried to cope with Aunt Joleen and today, I realized that Terry was doing the same with me just like he had done as I grieved Daddy.

I pulled away, needing to get away from the intense emotions in my chest. Terry held on to my hand as long as he could before I had fully removed mine from his, turning back towards the street, hoping the wind would deliver me.

Suddenly, an insecurity began to grow inside of me, needing to be reassured that I wasn't overthinking his affection.

"Terry, what are we doing?"

"Pretending like you don't know what we are doing."

"Ugh! Seriously, Goof-head." I spun to face his smug expression.

"Do we really need to say what we both know?"

"Yes. Yes, we do so I can make sure I'm not trippin'."

"You're not trippin', Emma."

"Terry!!"

"What do you want me to say?"

"I *need* you to say what this is. Please." I sighed, fighting to hold back more waterworks.

"This is us, Emma."

I glared at him both irritated and relieved but if looks could kill, I would have just shot him dead.

"Emma." His laughter was adding more fuel to the fire. "Emma, what is your earliest memory of us?"

"Terry this is NOT a question-and-answer type of moment. I'm being serious."

"I am too. Just answer the question please."

"I don't know! We were small, I guess. You've been there for as long as I can remember."

"We have always been attached to one another, Emma. We have always been beside each other, through both hard and fun things. You and I have been stuck together like glue. It's always been easy for us to just be together. We are *being* together."

"But—"

Terry's brown eyes were unyielding. I swear that boy had mastered the art of eye contact.

"But are we still just friends?" I dared to look up at his eyes once more.

"Emma, I don't know if we have ever *just* been friends. We have something different."

"Terry if you speak one more riddle to me, I swear—"

His laughter always came at the wrong times. I was being vulnerable, and he was chuckling. He reached his hand to me, coaxing mine into his.

"Emma, I love you. I've always loved you."

"So?"

"So what?"

"Am I your girlfriend?" My flirtatious punch landed on his chest right before I leaned into it, hoping he didn't see how nervous I was to ask the question.

Terry, knowing me well, recognized that I was hiding so he pulled me from his chest to gaze into my eyes.

"Is that what you want?"

He was going to college soon though. How would that work? Maybe it wasn't smart to label ourselves. But what if we didn't and he decided to date another girl? My heart couldn't deal with that. Why was this so hard?

"Stop thinking, Emma. Do you want us to be boyfriend and girlfriend?"

"Do you?"

"I see you're going to put this all on me, aren't you?"

"Maybe."

He was for sure going to come to his senses and realize this conversation wasn't worth it. He would start thinking that I wasn't worth all the hassle I was giving him over a dumb question and dart away.

"Okay, then maybe we will revisit the topic when you have a better grasp on what you want?"

His words were not leading but surrendered. He had put the ball in my court. It was such a Terry thing to do. He wasn't going to let me scoot out of the fire even though I was the one who had set it ablaze. I listened to his heartbeat ever so sweetly as I found my ear back onto his chest.

The wind whistled, daring me to speak up and use my words and tell him how I felt. The truth was he was more than a woobie to me. I couldn't answer the wind's challenge, not now. Instead, I focused on his chin resting on my forehead and melted further into his embrace.

Ahem. Sister Brown cleared her throat in a forced dramatic fashion.

Startled, we both faced her with matching expressions. "Emma, you think I can steal my son for a minute?"

She looked at me with a protective mama bear glance before she let a small smile spread over her face.

"Yes ma'am."

Terry walked his mother to her car. I watched as they quietly exchanged words. She used her hands a lot when she spoke, so it was easy to imagine what she was saying.

She and a handful of members from the church had come by to visit, check on Mama, and pray with us as the days had moved forward. The doctor had called Mama a couple of times to see if a decision had been made as to what to do with Aunt Joleen. She was still not making progress and they feared the worst.

I had heard Mama tell Maddie that Aunt Joleen didn't have much time and if *we* didn't make a decision, her body would make it for everyone, without a chance for a final goodbye. Mama had mentioned having peace from the Lord and that it was time to let Aunt Joleen go and be with him.

Maddie never replied to Mama with words, just tears. She simply wasn't ready to have any conversation regarding Aunt Joleen let alone decide to unplug the machines that were keeping her mother's body on this earth. It was too much for an eighteen-year-old to decide. She had been dealt a raw hand that I wished I could somehow help her hold.

Sister Brown turned to look at me with another simple smile before returning her focus to Terry. He mumbled something causing her to laugh before responding. Whatever she had said caused his expression to turn from calm to embarrassment. He shyly looked in my direction and then looked at the ground before meeting his mother's eyes again.

I wondered if she was giving him a hard time for *liking* me or if she was admonishing him to "not be making her a grandma before her time." What I *did* know was that she would have every right to warn him that he could do much better. After all, his future was planned, and he was bound to be successful. He shouldn't be tied down to a girl like me who had no idea what she wanted to do with herself.

Mrs. H had described me as a "runner." She said that it was easier for me to run away from what I was feeling. It was easier for me to run from hard things instead of dealing with them. After a five-minute spiel on not letting my potential get away from me, she had attempted to embolden me to stay put and deal with the tough things and not flee from them.

My life had been a series of tough things though. No one in their right mind would want to sit still and wallow in such hard memories and intense emotion, would they? Nope, I'd take my chance with running for a little while longer. But this thing with Aunt

Joleen and my feelings for Terry would require me to stop running sooner than I'd like.

Terry hugged his mom before she got into the car to leave. I guess he was staying a while longer.

He tucked his hands in his pockets as he walked up towards me. *Uh oh!* That meant he was nervous. If he wasn't fiddling with his hands to distract himself from nerves, he'd shove them in his pants pockets to hide the fact that he was fiddling with them in the first place. I'd pick on him about it after a while unless I knew it was a calming response to something serious.

If it was a serious matter, instead of teasing, I would just move a little closer and give him a reassuring smile. There was not much that had ever made him squirm though. He normally was the brave and grounded one in our friendship so whenever he was nervous, I felt the need to step up and be the mature one in the relationship for once.

What was he going to say to me when he got back on the porch? Was he going to tell me what I already knew? That I wasn't worth pursuing… that we didn't need to have the discussion about being an item later after all. The knots in my stomach became more evident as I worked the conversation out in my head.

Emma, I care about you a lot. I really do. But we only have a few months before we are preparing to go to college. I will move away, and you will stay here. We shouldn't waste each other's time. College and adulthood will be hard enough so let's just pretend those kisses didn't happen. Let's just keep this as a friendship and not force things into something it shouldn't be.

"Emma."

"What?!" Oh boy, I was snapping at him.

"You're blocking the steps. Do you not want me to come back up?"

His hands had cleared his pockets and they were at full speed, twisting and turning around one another.

"I don't know."

"Huh?"

"I guess it depends on what you are going to say when you get up here."

"Depends on what I'm going to say?"

"You heard me."

Why was I being so rude? One moment I'm daydreaming of being held by him and the next I'm ready to bite his head off.

"Is there something I'm supposed to say?" His words were slow and questioning.

I shrugged as I cleared the steps so he could come back onto the porch.

"What did your mom say?"

Now it was me fidgeting with my hands. I looked at the porch waiting for him to respond. After a few seconds I looked up in annoyance realizing he wasn't going to answer me. Instead, his silly grin awaited me.

"I really can't stand you."

"Sure," he jested.

"I'm going to punch you." I warned him as I prepared my right arm to land a blow.

He grabbed my arms and held them down to my side, goofy smile still intact.

"I think you'd rather kiss me."

"Ugh, you're so smug—" His kiss ended my words before I could finish letting him know what I thought of him.

"You still wanna know?"

"Know what?"

I had lost my train of thought. My mind was now back on him and how he made me feel when I was with him. Nothing else mattered as much anymore. Or at least they paled in comparison to his passionate kiss.

"I guess it doesn't matter what my mom thinks about us anyways."

"Oh no, no *that* does matter." The nervousness rose within my chest again as I pushed away from him as a skittish look gripped my face.

He chuckled, clearly amused by my jumpiness. "Well, you know she has a way with her words."

I groaned, knowing that to be true. "She told you not to get serious with me, didn't she?"

"She was very short."

"What did she say?"

"You know she doesn't like to waste her words, so they tend to pack a punch."

"Terry."

"The woman should work on her tact sometimes, ya know?"

"Terry!" He dodged my sloppy punch.

"I think she may be right though, Emma."

"You think she's right? Wait, you agree with her?"

"Yes, I do Emma."

"So, you're not even going to—"

"She said, 'Well, that took long enough.'"

Terry held my chin back upright, staring deep into my eyes.

"Tuh! You got that right!" Maddie's voice intruded on the tender moment.

She had burst through the front door wrapped in her old robe, looking like death warmed over. But there was a glint of a smile in her eyes as she observed Terry and I standing on the porch unable to let go of one another.

"Maddie!" My eyes began to fill with tears. "Maddie."

She slowly came over and wrapped her arms around me and Terry. She and I were leaky faucets as we sat holding each other. Terry on the other hand was once again the grounded one, keeping us afloat as we stood there.

"Y'all, I don't know what to do." Her voice was barely audible, her face hidden in my arm.

"You don't have to know, Maddie. Just choose to go."

Terry always knew the right things to say.

"I don't know if I can, Terry."

"Sure, you can. Choose to get dressed. Choose to get in the car. Choose to walk through the doors. Each step is a decision you have made to go in the direction of your mom. There's no pressure to know it all. Just choose one thing at a time, okay?"

"Okay," Maddie let out a heavy sigh. "So, are you two an official couple now?"

Terry and I looked at one another.

"Ugh, you know, like boyfriend and girlfriend?"

Maddie's annoyance was hard to miss.

We shrugged and laughed simultaneously, "Maybe."

Chapter Nineteen

The school had been understanding and excused most of Madison's absences once Mama had explained what was happening with Aunt Joleen. The guidance counselor had checked in with me three times this week alone to see how everyone was doing. Teachers sent work home for Maddie to help her keep up with her grades while she was out.

Terry and I had been helping her "finish" her work though. Those teachers were crazy if they thought she was in a place to be able to complete homework, let alone correctly.

"Miss Emma." Mrs. Lee smiled at me as she sat across from me.

"Hi." *This couldn't be good.*

"How's your volunteer hours going?"

"Fine." I still didn't care much for the casual chit chat she liked to prelude her conversations with.

"Okay, good." She patted my hand. "Let me know if you need anything. I know this semester is barreling on. It'll be the end of the year before we know it."

Ugh! I didn't need the reminder. So much has happened since this second semester began. There wasn't enough time in the world to assist me. We were already approaching February and year-end assignments were due by the end of April so our grades and GPAs could be finalized for graduation.

By May, there would be no real education happening. The senior class already had a list of designated days such as Senior Breakfast Day, Senior Skip Day and Senior Scheme Day. Although the administration warned us to not engage in such days, I think they said it more out of obligation but were not under any false pretenses that they wouldn't actually happen.

"Oh Miss Emma, did you get through that SAT study guide I sent home with you?"

"Yes ma'am."

I had spent several evenings reviewing the sample questions to try and take my mind from my problems at home. Terry and Maddie had already taken their SAT last year. Terry scored very well, and Maddie's score was in the average and acceptable range, so neither felt the need to retake it as seniors.

I had until the second week of February to complete the dreaded test. I still couldn't believe I was going to attempt it. I even considered submitting a couple of college applications, not that I thought I would get in at such late notice but for some reason I felt as if I needed to try especially with the whole "Aunt Joleen situation" going on.

"Emma Griggs." A student peer, sent by office staff, called into the classroom.

He was holding a white office pass as he scanned the room awaiting a response.

"Is she returning?" Mrs. Lee inquired.

"Early dismissal." The kid said nonchalantly as he waited impatiently for me to gather my things.

"See you next week, Emma. Remember, let me know if you all need anything."

I stuffed everything into my backpack and followed the boy out into the hallway towards the front office where Mama was resting on the secretary's desk looking tired and worn out.

"Hi, Mama."

"Hey, baby." Her face screamed of exhaustion.

As we walked down the steps of the school, I spotted Maddie in the back seat of the car staring out the window.

This couldn't be good. There was only one possible explanation for Mama checking me out early with Maddie slumped like a sack of potatoes in the back of the car.

I slung my backpack onto the floor of the passenger seat while keeping my eyes on Maddie.

"Baby, won't you sit back there with your cousin for me."

"Yes ma'am." This was *definitely* bad.

As soon as my seatbelt clicked, Maddie rested her head in my lap and Mama began to drive along.

"Maddie, what's happening?" I chanced asking.

"I'm choosing."

****

"Take your time ladies." A different nurse ushered us into Aunt Joleen's room this time around.

Aunt Joleen lay in the hospital bed motionless. She had a tube in her throat that was connected to some huge machine that sounded like a fan on steroids. I watched her chest rise and fall each time the fan noise swooshed.

Gone was the beautiful woman I had seen as a little girl. Instead, there was a person who was almost unrecognizable. Her hair was matted, but it appeared as if someone had tried to put it into a high ponytail. There were multiple wild strands that couldn't be tamed into the rubber band, however.

Her skin was blotchy and bruised, especially along her arms where IV's and chords surrounded both sides of her. Her face was abnormally puffy along with her hands. This woman lying before us was not the carefree beauty I'd known.

"Oh Mama." Maddie had begun processing what was before her.

She leaned over the bed rails and took her mom's hands in her own. "They're so cold. Why are they so cold?"

"Her circulation isn't as good as it should be, sweetie."

The nurse remained in the doorway, not necessarily hovering but being available should we need it. I could only assume that this was not the first encounter she had with someone in this way. She knew there would be questions and that we wouldn't know what we needed so she stayed.

"Can you give her something to make it better?"

"I'm sorry, honey, but no. We have tried. Right now, we are giving her the most medicine possible to keep her heart pumping at the rate it is. If we give any more, it could make her worse off."

"Oh."

"My mother didn't always look like this, ya know." Maddie explained to the nurse.

"She was actually quite beautiful."

The nurse smiled as Maddie continued to work through what was happening.

"Did she look like this when she got here?"

"She was brought in by the ambulance. They couldn't revive her, and she wasn't breathing on her own, so they had to put that breathing tube in to help her breathe. She didn't look exactly like this when she came into our ICU, but she was close. Now she's more swollen from lying in the bed and from fluids in her body shifting around. Does that make sense?"

Maddie shook her head in response before continuing the interrogation, "The bruises?"

"We take blood quite frequently on patients as critical as this. I know it can be hard to see. I'm sorry."

"If we take all these tubes out, will she stay alive for a while?"

Maddie's eyes longed for a response that would satisfy her but no response the nurse could give would ever relieve the pain she was in. Her last memory of her mother was her being abandoned in the middle of the night. Aunt Joleen had probably told her something along the lines of "I'll come back to get you when I'm settled" or "Don't worry, baby. This is only temporary."

The fact was it wasn't temporary. Aunt Joleen had snatched away a piece of Maddie that she could never regain. And now, Maddie, years later, was having to say goodbye to the hope of her mom's return or better yet, an apology for the years lost.

Her mom would never be able to hug her and let her know how much she may have loved her. Her mom would not watch her graduate. She wouldn't be there when she was married, and she wouldn't watch her give birth to her first child.

There were a lot of things Maddie had been robbed of and now, I had to sit and watch the joyful Madison Lyn Harrison, usually full of wonder and awe, pull it all in. I had to watch her grow up instantaneously and step foot into adulthood. She had to put aside all the things Aunt Joleen chose not to do for her and make a choice for the woman who had not made the appropriate choice for her.

Maddie was right. Joleen Ann Harrison was as selfish as they came. Selfish in life and selfish in death. I hated her in this moment. It felt as if fire was coursing through my body.

"It's hard to say since we aren't God, but we think she won't live very long after the life support is removed. It would be wise to gather her loved ones to say their final goodbyes just in case, before removing her breathing tube and medications."

The nurse spoke to Mama because even she understood that this was all way too much for the young Madison to take on alone.

Tears streamed down Maddie's face as she turned towards Mama and then back to the immobile woman lying before her.

"Mama?" Maddie was full of sobs at this point.

"You left me."

Mama flew to Maddie's side, recognizing Maddie breaking. She held fast as Maddie continued to cry.

The nurse had left the room but was sitting at a nearby nurses' station with her eyes attentively upon us.

"You left me once. Now you're leaving me again." Maddie stood tall although the tears continued flowing.

She freed herself from Mama's grasp to look boldly at her mother.

"You made your choice to leave me, Mama. You made a lot of choices that I wasn't a part of. I waited for you every day. EVERY DAY!" Her voice was a scream.

"And this is how you come back?"

Maddie hit the bed rail and turned towards me, her chest moving in and out with force as both tears and mucus flowed from her face.

"I'm here, Maddie." I hugged her tightly and prayed God would give me strength to help hold my cousin up.

Through tears, I tried to look into her eyes to let her know that even though her mother had failed her, I would stay beside her. She pulled away from me and returned to the bedside once more.

"You know what, Mama, I pray your spirit is received by God. I can't forgive you at this time, but one day I pray to God I will be able to."

Mama inched closer again.

"Today, I choose to do something that you wouldn't do. I *choose* to make the hard decision. I choose to not do what's easiest for me. I choose to think of someone other than myself."

She eased herself to the hospital floor and wrapped her hands around her knees. She began rocking as Mama hovered, not daring to get on the ground with her because she would likely not be able to get back up.

Not wanting Maddie to be alone on the floor, I sat beside her and began humming.

"Aunt Ruthie, I choose to let her go. She can't stay like this."

"Baby, are you sure? No one's rushing you."

"Yes ma'am. I choose to let her go. I have to let her go, Aunt Ruthie."

Mama made her way over to the chair in the corner and sat slowly. Sorrow engulfed her as Maddie's words resonated. She too would have to say goodbye to her sister. Audible blubbers came from her as she sat with her face in her hands.

It was all too much for me to process. My chest felt as if it would burst wide open. I leaned into the hospital bed, hoping to catch a deeper breath, careful not to move too far from Maddie. I needed her to know I'd be with her through the devastation.

"Hi family."

Right on cue, Brian, our youth pastor, walked into the room. His face, although indistinct due to my weepy and puffy eyes, was tense yet soft. He wore a concerned and empathetic expression.

He had probably been on his way to or coming from the gym as he was wearing black sweatpants and a black cotton jacket with a hood. His tennis shoes were almost immaculate of course. He couldn't have made much of a salary pastoring at our small church in Byron, but his tennis shoes were always impeccable.

He still drove around his little Toyota that was handed down to him when he graduated from high school, and he never dressed flashily. However, tennis shoes were the exception. When anyone made mention to them, he would shrug, bring forth a shy grin and say, "What can I tell ya? I'm a sneakerhead!"

It was no secret. He'd tell us youth, "Look! I pay my tithes. I save a little and the rest is for you all and my tennis shoes."

No one ever questioned the "you all" part. Everyone knew who the "anonymous" donor was that sponsored so many of us to go on various youth engagements or who pitched in extra to ensure no one went without at Christmas or during a particularly hard time.

Honestly, it didn't really make much sense how he had so much to give. "You pay your tithes. Return it back to the Lord like the Bible asks of you and watch how He blesses the rest." I recounted Pastor Brian explaining finances in one of his weekly sermonettes.

Today, I missed that cheerful face of his. Instead, the hint of disheartenment met us in the hospital room.

He walked slowly towards Mama and rested his hand on her shoulder, "Mama Griggs."

I couldn't make out whatever else he whispered toward her ear. Her face remained positioned in her lap as she continued to mourn.

After addressing Mama, in true Brian fashion, he sat in the middle of the floor with Maddie and me. For the first few moments, he said nothing. I observed a few tears on his face as he shared in our heartache. It was so thick that if a stranger had entered the room, they'd be thrown into heartbreak as well.

Another thing I absolutely loved about him is that he didn't come in spewing the Bible the first chance he got. Instead, he tried to be with the person he was talking to. He could sit comfortably in silence and showed no signs of judgment.

He had been there when Daddy died too, although he wasn't a youth pastor at that time. He was still a teenager and was recognized as a "good boy." He had grown up in our church and was the prized male of the teens. I remember girls finding him attractive and wanting his attention, but he was only focused on completing school, community outreach, and spending time learning more about God. The church mothers would say things like, "Whoever marries that one, is going to be blessed for sure" or "Chile, if I was young enough, I'd snatch him right on up."

Although Brian had always been mature for his age, he was still fun to be around. He was known to be a practical joker and went to great lengths to put a smile on someone's face. He was never labeled dull; just focused on the important things in life one could say. So, it was no surprise that after high school, he went straight to Bible college and asked if he could work as a pastor at our church.

He was already an established member and knew all of us kids so the church thought he would be a great fit as a youth pastor, especially since we used to go on and on about how much we needed our own preacher. That, and I'm sure Brian worked charitably or received very small compensation coming out of school.

He was indeed a great guy. He always acknowledged you and what you were enduring. In this moment sadness loomed but Brian respected our anguish and did not try to cheer us up. Clearly this wasn't the setting for that. He was wise enough to be mindful of where we were. He just sat nearby.

He did, however, finally get into what God's Word had to say about what we were going through though. He eased into it gently while recognizing that despite having scripture there to help encourage us, it was still a difficult path to be on. He prayed over us and sat with us for a while longer before encouraging us to reach out to the church when we were ready. Then he took his leave.

Once Brian had left, only four women remained. Three of us were full of an array of emotions while the other lay in bed seemingly oblivious and likely not feeling anything at all.

Yep, Joleen Harrison, cold and unaware of those around her, sat in the result of her actions.

Chapter Twenty

There were no words that could adequately describe my dislike of funerals. Since Byron was such a small town, I had attended my fair share. Most of the people who had died were older and I didn't know them well. Sometimes people would shout and scream and even pass out. I didn't quite understand why they did that until Daddy had died. Mama didn't wail and carry on, but she looked as if she'd collapse at any moment as she leaned over his casket.

The military had assisted in his funeral which was ironic because Daddy mentioned time and time again how the military robbed him of his youth.

"Don't get me wrong, baby girl, I would serve for my country again if I had to, but any young man that goes to serve will never come back the same. There are things you see that steals your innocence right away. It hardens you. You just can't unsee certain things." He'd carry on for a while recounting his troubled times in the service.

Daddy was too young to die. Aunt Joleen was too young to die. Yet, they did and alas, here we were again. Of course, Aunt Joleen had not left behind any funding for her demise so expenses were on Mama and whatever boyfriend she had picked to galivant off with when she left Maddie behind was nowhere to be found. It was just those she had chosen to leave behind that was left responsible for caring for her final arrangements.

Mama couldn't afford day to day necessities, let alone an end-of-life expense. Thankfully, she was able to strike a deal with the owners of the funeral home to have Aunt Joleen cremated. They had lent us a casket so that Aunt Joleen could have a normal funeral service with the understanding that there would be no graveside procession. Mama and a couple of the church mothers had worked on Aunt Joleen's hair and clothed her so she'd be presentable at her homegoing but after the funeral, her body would be taken to be cremated immediately.

I felt as if I was thrown into knowing way too much about a woman I disliked so deeply. But every time I looked at Maddie and Mama's faces, my heart softened, and I tried to remember how much they had loved her. I guess my face couldn't hide my disdain of Aunt Joleen because Mama looked at me one night and said, "No one's perfect Emma. We all make mistakes."

"Yes ma'am," was all I could manage.

I mean, I knew no one was perfect but leaving your child behind was a pretty big offense. How was that even possible as a mother? *And* never checking in on her; I felt like that was worse than the original transgression. *No one's perfect. Tuh! Perfection was most definitely not the target with Aunt Joleen. She was not even average in my book. I'd never grow up and create a child and then toss him or her to the wolves. Nope, perfection did not belong in the same sentence or thought as Aunt Joleen.*

"Emma, honey, we are praying with you all." Sister Brown interrupted my thoughts as she gave me an awkward hug, trying to stoop down and reach her arms around me.

The weird hugs…yes, I hated those more than I hated the actual funeral. People who you hardly knew you would come up and hug you. They'd say things that weren't helpful even though I'm sure they meant well. Sister Brown, I knew but still I'd love to pass on the odd interactions right now.

I glanced over at Maddie who was seated to my right. Her head was down, avoiding eye contact with anyone. Mama, dressed in all black with one of her church hats positioned flawlessly on her head, kept a straight face as she held Maddie's shoulders. No one was perfect. Mama was right about that but her hats, now those always seemed to be perfect.

"Emma." Terry squatted so he could see my eyes.

He said nothing else but that was enough. He then walked over to Maddie and whispered something in her ear, something awkward and unhelpful, I'm sure. Next, he nodded at Mama and touched her hand before he took his seat.

There weren't many people in the room apart from church members. Aunt Joleen had grown up in Byron with Mama, so she was known by the church and the neighbors. It was hard to not be known in Byron; it was so small.

Mama and Aunt Joleen had essentially grown up peach farming. Mama said she never really cared for farming, but it was just a part of life. She explained how she and Aunt Joleen had chores that began at dawn and would sometimes end at dusk. I imagined Aunt Joleen didn't tend to do much of the grunt work. She was probably preoccupied with her looks or chasing some neighborhood boy. Then again, Mama would reiterate how strict her father was growing up. Her face would sour anytime she mentioned her dad, which wasn't very often. As a matter of fact, all I knew was that she had a dad, he was strict, and he lived in the same house as Mama. Anything beyond that was a mystery.

She had made mention of how much Byron had grown over the last decade, but I still looked around and saw a small town with almost no outlet. When she had married Daddy, they moved into his family home away from farming. I believe the farm was sold because Mama never really brought it up again.

She had gotten a local job and didn't return to the rural life while Aunt Joleen, on the other hand, was "always itching to leave." Mama said she wasn't meant for small-town living. "Her eyes were too big."

Now that part, I resonated with. I didn't love the idea of staying in Byron, but I wasn't quite sure how to escape it just yet. Thankfully, the county had voted to begin public transportation to help get people over to the nearest city where there were more things such as the detention center and popular stores.

"At this time, we would like to give you a moment to read Sister Joleen's life account."

Everyone looked down at the flimsy paper with a picture of the then-pretty Joleen Harrison, smiling brightly. Her eyes were dancing, and it appeared that whatever was happening in that second was the best experience of her life.

Joleen Ann Harrison
Sunrise: 7/15/1955
Sunset: 2/1/1993

Joleen Ann Harrison was born to the late Joe and Erma Harrison. As a little girl, she enjoyed being with her family and working hard on their farm. She attended church every Sunday and had a joyful spirit. Joleen graduated from high school with ambitions of becoming an actress, but the Lord had different plans for her, and she was blessed with a beautiful baby girl in the year 1974. Joleen's smile lit up every room she entered, and her light never grew dim.
The Heavenly Father saw fit to call Joleen's bright light home on the evening of 2/1/1993. She is preceded to heaven by her parents Joe and Erma Harrison, her brother Joe Harrison Jr. and she leaves behind her precious daughter Madison Lyn Harrison, sister Ruthie Eleanor Griggs, niece Emma Rose Griggs, aunts and cousins and host of friends for there was never a stranger she had met in her lifetime.

The program was short and sweet. It made me wonder if when I passed on to heaven one day, my obituary would be longer. Aunt Joleen's seemed to lack particulars and was full of generalizations.

"We would like to open up the floor for remarks and any comforting words for the family." The service continued right along.

The church's secretary read the standard announcement and words of encouragement aloud and returned to her seat, followed by a couple of our church members. Everyone seemed to say the same things. They used different words but essentially it was all the same. Of course, they had to give honor to God the Father and the church pastor and so on first. That part was pretty much identical and the expectation of any person that attended a southern church.

"I'd like to share about Joleen." A petite and stunning woman stood in front of the church.

She wore a sequined black dress with long silk gloves. Her earrings sparkled and her deep-colored lipstick was the focal point of her face. She had a good face. It was wrinkle free, and her skin was well moisturized. The shape of her eyes was in a slight slant. Their hazel color was accentuated by a set of full lashes. Her smile was large, and when she talked her eyes reinforced her words, along with her one free hand. The other held the microphone in place.

"Joleen was a good friend of mine. We met a few years ago."

A few years ago.

Good of Aunt Joleen to be out there making friends while her daughter was stuck in torment wondering how she was doing. So glad she could find the time to establish new "friendships." I found myself rolling my eyes before quickly catching myself.

"It's true, ya know? She really did light up the room when she entered it." She looked over at Maddie with a soft smile.

"My first time meeting Jolie, she had come into the store where I worked. She was bubbly and asked me about the town attractions."

Yep, that part sounded right but who the heck was "Jolie"?

"I offered to show her around and we hit it off right away. Soon, she began working at the same store I did, and she would encourage me to never give up hope.

"You see I had dreams of wanting to become a teacher, but I needed to straighten up some things in my life first."

She cleared her throat before continuing.

"'Lynn, no one's perfect.'" She'd tell me that over and over when I would get down on myself."

I'm guessing Lynn was her. It had to be, or her story wouldn't make much sense. I really did wish she'd get to her point though. She was just rambling at this point.

"Well one day, I got into a bad accident and Jolie never left my side. She was at the hospital with me day and night until I was released home. She helped take care of me and nursed me right back to health."

Lynn took a slow breath, looked at the faded church carpet and then looked back up with a weak smile.

"I didn't have anyone but Jolie. My parents— let's just say that I left their house as soon as I could and never looked back."

Her head dropped for a second before she lifted it again.

This story was not what I expected. No one ever shared their personal memoirs during a funeral. I hoped wherever she was going with this story would lead to some sort of encouragement because the whole point of congregational remarks was to uplift our family not throw us further into despair. We weren't interested in Lynn's life drama. We had enough of our own.

"Yeah, as I was lying in that hospital bed depressed, she told me about this 'girl' she knew."

Lynn looked over at Maddie once more. This time with tears in her eyes.

"She knew there were some things that I just couldn't forgive my parents for." Another pause.

"'Lynn, you must forgive them. Sometimes people are just people, and they cause hurt without meaning to. And sometimes they do mean to, or they just don't care if they do, but in the end if you don't forgive them, you will carry an anchor around your neck forever. You'll be a slave to their actions because you refuse to forgive.'"

This story was getting uncomfortable. *Who was Aunt Joleen to be teaching someone about forgiveness? What'd she know about it?*

I looked over at Maddie to make sure she was still intact. She was.

"She told me, 'Lynn, I knew this girl who thought she knew it all. She knew that if she escaped her living situations, she would find peace and happiness. She fell in love with some boy who could care less about her. God gave her a baby out of it though. She initially resented that baby but grew to love it with her full heart. She just didn't know how to show the baby love, but she tried her best.'"

Lynn's eyes were now locked into Maddie's. Maddie returned the gaze with a pool of tears welling in her eyes.

"'That young woman grew up feeling depressed inside. Every day was a fight to smile. Every day she would have to push past the hurt. And one day that young woman met another man who she thought would help change her world. They were in love for a little while or so she thought. Then that man began beating on her and the young woman began spiraling.

"'Lynn, that baby was no longer a baby. She couldn't hide the pain from her any longer. She was so scared that the child would be the victim of her boyfriend's next attack so she had to do the hardest thing she could ever think of.'"

Don't you say it, Lynn. You better not say it.

Lynn and Maddie were full-on crying at this point. Mama was on full alert, sitting tall, as close to Maddie as she could possibly be, and I didn't quite know what to feel.

"'That young woman left her baby. She left her baby.' She kept saying that over and over to me and that's when I realized she wasn't speaking about a woman she knew, but of herself. She had left behind a child."

At this point it was so quiet, we could hear a pin drop, and the floor had carpet.

"Jolie lit up a room for sure, but she always carried a hint of sadness because a piece of her wasn't with her. I begged Jolie to take the advice she had given me about forgiveness, but she would tell me, 'Lynn some things will never deserve forgiveness.' But that's not true.

"I want you to know that Jolie encouraged me so much that I was able to forgive my parents and finish my schooling. And now I am a theater teacher. I feel like I owe it all to her. No one's perfect but she was an angel that God sent to me. I pray that your family experiences God's comfort in this time and that He gives you all space to forgive. Thank you."

Thank you? Were we supposed to say you're welcome? It wasn't happening.

Lynn offered one more smile and then returned to her seat. Maddie, Mama and I sat frozen in our seats full of shock and a new wave of feelings.

"Do we have any other—"

A loud shriek came from Maddie, catching the preacher by surprise.

Maddie doubled over and wailed for a while. It was unbearable to watch, to hear. I didn't know what to do other than lean over and embrace her.

Mama covered both of us and continued to whisper, "Lord help us" as we held onto Maddie, willing her to not fall apart before us.

All I could think about was the story of *Humpty Dumpty*. Nothing and no one would be able to put her together again if she became completely dismantled. I couldn't hold the broken pieces inside her together, but I'd be darned if I'd let anything on the outside spill over.

Chapter Twenty-one

"You really aren't all that, you know?" Raymond tried to remind me that my last few Uno wins didn't amount to much.

"Sure." I smirked. "It's hard being a winner, ya know."

He and I had become sort of like peas in a pod since my unraveling within the group when I shared about my dad.

He didn't really know what to say at first and offered a couple of awkward, "Hope you're okay" and "I guess you didn't run away after all" comments to try and make nice.

I appreciated his attempts, so I'd follow up with a "Yeah, I'm fine" or "What? And miss all the fun with you guys?"

He hadn't quite figured it out with his grandparents yet but he openly shared that he was trying very hard not to disappoint them.

Mr. E jumped right on that statement of course. "Raymond, I'm sure that it's not about disappointing your grandparents but much more about them wanting what's best for you."

"Potential." A few of us said in unison before laughing.

That was the theme nowadays. *Potential.* I wondered if there were secret meetings held by adults that discussed the topic of helping their kids unlock their potential or something along those lines. *Seriously guys, it was time to switch it up.*

"Yeah yeah." Mr. E had attempted to bring the group back into a serious tone.

Gathering that his attempt was futile, he had decided to give up and join in our silliness.

"What ya gonna do when you graduate?" Raymond played a red reverse card.

"Aww man, not you too." I glared my eyes at him.

"What?"

"I knew you were hiding a somber middle-aged man inside of you."

"Whatever. *You* will be middle-aged way before I will."

"Never."

"Yep, you will."

It would be pointless to go back and forth with him. He'd only keep going and I'd never win so I conceded by not answering.

"Uno!"

"Wait, what?!" Raymond's eyebrows furrowed as he gave me a death stare. "You just had like five cards."

"What can I say? I'm smooth like that."

He played a yellow number four card hoping that it would deter me from going out and winning another game.

"Well done, Raymond."

He looked over me with a premature look of celebration before I slammed down my green number four card.

"Boom! Well done giving me exactly what I needed," I taunted.

"Ah man." His annoyance was well displayed as I did a little happy dance.

He threw on his headphones and chose to ignore me for the next few minutes. I didn't blame him. I could be a bit much once I got excited. I didn't know if I was more pleased that I had won again or the fact that I had broken into some sort of acquaintanceship with the boy who refused to even look at me when I first began coming. He had now allowed me a glimpse into who he really was.

Mr. E told me that most people would never show who they really were unless they felt safe. He said that's why it could be so hard on the people others felt closest to. It was those that were deemed safe, that would catch the brunt of other's negative behaviors and choices.

"Hey sweetie. How's it going?" Lisa's eyes were bright as she checked in.

"I'm doing okay."

"Remind me how much longer we have you here again?"

Oh man. I hadn't thought about that. Volunteering in the SOAR room had become a part of my day-to-day life. Other than needing to have Mr. E or Mrs. Myra sign off on my weekly hours, I often forgot that I was here as a part of a school assignment.

"I think I have until the middle of April to complete my required hours."

What would I do when my time was completed? It didn't feel right just walking out on the relationships that I had worked to build. It seemed unfair to the SOAR kids. I'd just be one more person to leave them. Wasn't that what they thought of me when I first arrived anyway?

My stomach sank.

"Well, I guess we'll just have to enjoy you while we have you, my dear."

Lisa patted my shoulder and gave me one more genuine smile before going over to check on things across the room.

I glanced over at Raymond who shook his head at me and continued to look down signifying that he was still not talking to me quite yet. I giggled at his stubbornness knowing that he'd warm up to me again before I left for the afternoon.

There was no way I could leave Raymond and the rest of the SOAR group behind. I'd just have to find a way to stick around somehow. I wondered if there was any way I could become a YD like Mr. E and Lisa.

What are you doing?

I questioned the abrupt thought that entered my mind unsolicited. Who was I to just invite myself to a future at the juvenile center?

"Aha Emma, ready for our catch up?" Mrs. Gaines popped into the room summoning me in for our weekly progress meeting.

We called it a weekly meeting, but in all actuality, if we were able to meet at least every other week, we were doing pretty good.

"Yes ma'am, I think I am. I have a question for you."

"Oh."

Mrs. Gaines gave me a tell-me-more look as she motioned for me to follow her out of the door.

****

"I don't know why you're so hard on yourself."

Terry sat beside me on the school steps. I stared at him, annoyed at the one quality of his that I could live without. The boy loved chewing sunflower seeds. He looked a bit like a talking horse.

"Seriously, Emma." He spit one of the seeds into the paper bag he had gotten from the corner store during lunch.

"What?! You are just jealous that I don't care how I look when I chew my sunflower seeds."

"Yeah, that's it," I retorted.

Everyone at school had pretty much accepted the fact that Terry and I were dating. We never had the boyfriend/girlfriend conversation we were supposed to, but also didn't deny the whispers and labels people placed on us when they began noticing us holding hands and standing unusually close to one another.

We had even gotten a stern eye from a teacher who had caught us giving a quick kiss during our passing period. The only other person who seemed to mind was Rochelle. She steered clear of us for the first few weeks until she began catching eyes for another guy at school. After that, she'd at least look in our direction and nod or wave.

Her friends weren't so forgiving, however. They'd cut mean looks my way every now and again as if I had stolen their best friend's boyfriend. I still wasn't quite sure I hadn't. Terry said they were never dating so I guess he wasn't stolen. I mean he *was* the one who kissed me after all.

"I'm not hard on myself, I'm just realistic is all. My SAT score was only 920, Terry."

"That's not bad. I think the average score is somewhere around 880-900."

"The fact that you know that is upsetting." I frowned at him.

"I am who I am," Terry popped another seed in his mouth.

"Yeah, well you got like a million on your test so you're not worried."

"It only goes up to 1600. If you do the math, you scored what—"

Terry focused as he tried to find the answer in his head. He definitely wasn't asking me. He knew better. I wasn't the mental math type of girl.

"Yep, around 56-57% I believe. That's better than half Emma. That's not bad at all."

"Yeah, well what percentage are you in?"

"That's not important." He laughed, turning away from me as I leaned in to give him a love tap.

"Hey you two!"

Maddie walked over to us. Her voice had almost returned to its normal octave.

It had taken a couple of weeks after Aunt Joleen's funeral for her to recover to a place where she would at least come downstairs and hang out for a bit. Plus, Mama wouldn't allow her to stay in the room all day. She said it was important to keep carrying on with our normal routine even if it felt forced. The rest would come in due time. So, eating meals with the two of them for those two weeks was pretty much like eating alone except the former was more uncomfortable.

Maddie had surprisingly managed to slip right back into school. She was quieter than usual but was able to grasp her assignments without difficulty. She had not worn her denim jacket since she returned though. I remember seeing her pack it up neatly and place it on the shelf in our closet. I had quickly turned my eyes away to avoid making the act more awkward for her. It was strange seeing her without that jacket though. It had become etched into her persona. Without it, something was missing like she had removed her armor and was now a vulnerable and uncertain teenager like the rest of us. Gone was her joyous cover.

"So, what's up?" Maddie sat down beside us on the steps stuffing a potato chip in her mouth.

"Oh, you know… discussing our futures," Terry said smugly.

"…as in your futures with one another?" Maddie raised her eyebrows. *So much for being subtle.*

"Uhhh…" I stared at Terry who was wearing a satisfied smile.

"Although Emma cannot imagine a future without me, we were *actually* talking about the SAT."

"Well, that's lame." Maddie threw another chip into her mouth.

Lame? Madison Lyn Harrison was big into planning for the future. She had taken her SAT early just like Terry and was all set to go to college in the fall. She had been bugging Mama and her guidance counselor nonstop about scholarships, reference letters and things she could do in advance to help her be best prepared for her freshman year. She was almost on the same level as Terry except I didn't know of any human that was as eager and psyched to attend undergraduate school as he was.

I was becoming worried that Maddie would not recover from Aunt Joleen's death anytime soon. I knew that grief was a long bumpy road, but Maddie still appeared to be railroaded and it scared me. She was doing her best with the situation, but I wished I could snap my finger or flip a switch to free her from her burdens. I'd do almost anything to see my cousin's eyes light up with genuine joy again.

"Hey, all I'm saying is I think we need all hands on deck to get Emma to understand that she is definitely college material."

"You know Terry, everybody doesn't have to go to college to be successful." It was true. I'd seen it in several movies.

"True, but you forget that I know you and I *know* that you belong in college, Emma." He kissed me on my forehead, his goofy smile had faded.

"Yeah, that's actually true Emma," Maddie chimed in without looking in my direction. She was staring out, looking into the distance.

"Maddie. Terry. Let it go."

"Nope." Maddie pushed back, still caught up with whatever she had her eyes locked on.

"Not a chance." Terry was still looking at me with a semi-serious, semi-concerned look.

He felt as if he had to be my protector and the one who looked out for me since Daddy was gone. He was very vocal about wanting what was best for me. He wasn't overbearing nor did he ever push his position on me, but he was not afraid to make his stance known when he was worried about me. He was my personal lighthouse, consistent and unwavering.

"Look, if you're so sure that no colleges will accept you, why don't you just apply to one or two? 'It couldn't hurt anything. I could help if you want."

"Terry! You're driving me crazy. I don't see what the big deal is."

"Emma, the big deal is—

Oh boy! Here we go. A long spiel on me selling myself short that I didn't want to hear.

"You know what, fine. Fine, I'll apply just so you two can get off my back."

"Really?" Maddie's eyes looked as if someone had just lit a fire within them.

Her excitement made me laugh.

"Yes, really Maddie. You two are driving me crazy."

I covered my ears as her high-pitched girly squeal assailed them.

"So how about you apply to CGTC, and we can go together?" Maddie's squeal had stopped but her persistence remained.

"Why don't you just go to Georgia State, Madison?"

Terry had overshared on the differences between CGTC and Georgia State, riling Maddie up one day. She had her mind set on going to CGTC although she had been accepted by both places. She didn't want to go to a larger campus such as Georgia State, meanwhile Terry thought it was a waste of time and "resources" to attend a school to only graduate with an associate degree. He had gone down a long list of pros and cons as to why it was more practical and beneficial to attend a four-year university.

"Are we seriously doing this again Terry?" Maddie's eyes narrowed at him.

"Fine. If you apply to CGTC then it's only fair that you apply to Clemson as well." Terry turned his attention to me.

"Clemson?!"

"Yeah, what's wrong with Clemson? You saw the campus. It was amazing right?"

"Yeah, that's one word for it."

Clemson was huge and I felt out of place there. My stomach knotted as my mind replayed the trip vividly. The only thing that made me feel welcomed there was his smiles and the occasional nod I received from other students who looked as clueless as I did. I suppose one inexperienced person could spot another.

"Come on Emma, you gotta give things a chance or you'll never know if you like or dislike them. Plus, I'll be there."

"Hey! That's a foul!" Maddie threw her empty potato chip bag at Terry.

"Well, I *am* her new favorite, Madison." The smug smile returned.

He was so darn cute, but he wouldn't be for long if he kept poking the bear.

"Whatever. Let's go to the counselor so we can get our girl set up with some applications." Maddie hopped up on the steps and did a small jig.

She was sincerely excited, meanwhile I was dying on the inside. I couldn't believe I had given in to them. Terry was right, it wouldn't hurt anything to try but I felt certain that I would not be getting into any school this late. March 15th was the extended deadline to submit applications and here we were, only two weeks away. I could just conveniently not fill them out in time but there was no way Terry and Maddie would let me get away with that plan.

"Quit dragging your feet. Let's go, missy." Maddie marched along, heading towards the student entrance.

Terry grabbed my hand and smiled reassuringly.

Clemson? Did he really want me there with him? We had not discussed going our separate ways in the next few months. Maybe if I got into school with him, we wouldn't have to have that conversation at all. It was much easier to avoid hard talks than to deal with the elephant in the room.

I squeezed his hand as I imagined lying on the grass studying with him on campus. If anyone could make a move away from home easier, it would be him. I'd follow him to the end of the earth and still feel secure.

Wait!! What was I saying? I loved Terry for sure, but I would *not* be making my decision based on following *any* guy anywhere. Daddy had taught me a lot better than that. Plus, I'd watched plenty of movies to know that the girl ultimately ends up heartbroken while chasing some guy and then she is left feeling stuck and alone while he moves on carefree with his life. Nope! No way! I refused to be that girl. Cute or not, I was not following him anywhere. It would be *my* decision.

"After you." Terry held the door open for me so I could pass.

I couldn't clear the door however, before he swept me into its shadow underneath a small breezeway. His soft lips had returned to mine, his hands resting on the small of my back. I felt a tingle shoot up my spine, bringing about a simultaneous hushed gasp. I leaned into his body with an insatiable desire for more as he repositioned himself back a step. My hands, not ready to release him, began framing his face as the kiss began to slow until he gently pulled away.

"Emma, I love you so much. You are smart enough to make your own decisions, but I'll always want what's best for you. Go wherever you want to go but know that you will have my heart waiting for you at Clemson."

Seriously was this an eighteen-year-old boy or was this some thirty-year-old man from a scripted love scene?

"Excuse me, can you two detach your faces so we can catch the counselor before the bell rings?" Maddie was irked we had left her hanging for a quick kiss session.

Terry laughed and held the door open for me once more, this time allowing me to pass through it. Our eyes lingered as I entered the door, longing to be alone with him for a few more minutes. I wished I could hear those words come out of his mouth once more… *"you will have my heart waiting for you at Clemson."*

I mean Clemson *did* have great academics. It couldn't hurt to apply. I wouldn't be following Terry per se.

Maddie cut her eyes at him, knowing that he held the winning hand thus far. She knew I was mesmerized by the romance that only he could give me out of the two of them.

"That's just great." She rolled her eyes and shoved the counselor door open.

Terry laughed, "What?!"

Chapter Twenty-two

"I'm so very proud of you."

Mrs. H sat at her dining table sipping tea. I'd learned to just accept a cup when she offered. I appreciated hot tea occasionally but the fact that she preferred herbal teas that were not always dressed with honey, lemon and sugar like Mama prepared hers made them less enjoyable.

"It's not easy taking the difficult road." She blew her tea without taking her eyes from me.

"When I was young, I knew that all too well, especially being married so young and to a pastor at that."

"That sounds like something I'd never want to do." The words came out before I could catch them.

"Oh yes, it's not for the faint of heart." She laughed quietly. "There are some really good times but Darling, let me tell ya, there are also some *really* tough ones."

"I bet."

"You know, when Alfred asked me to marry him, he didn't have much to offer, except that charm of his."

She leaned back into her chair and smiled as she drew her cup near. She never actually took a sip though. The cup lingered by her mouth as I saw the wheels in her mind turning. Her face was filled with bliss. Her eyes, satisfied and jubilant.

"Yeah, that charm. He was a smart man, and I knew he would be able to accomplish anything he set his mind to. I had no idea he would end up being a pastor but when God has plans for your life, you can't outrun them."

It was things like that last sentence that made me question so many things. What were God's plans for me? And if I couldn't "outrun" them, was there a point in trying? It was very confusing.

"When Alfred took over the church, we had no idea what we were doing, and we sure didn't know what we were up against. Even if God is working for you, there will be so many people and things that try to work against you, Darling."

"Well how do you deal with that?"

"You must choose to believe that what God is doing is more important and worth more than the things you're up against. It's all about your mindset, Darling. That's why the Bible continually talks about the way we think. You must set your mind on God and what He wants from you. Nothing else really matters once you have your mind focused on what truly does."

"It just seems hard." I sat my drink down. It was beginning to cool. Besides, I could hardly take the taste while it was hot, let alone lukewarm.

"Oh, it *is* hard Darling. But life is hard baby."

"Did you and Pastor H both want to have kids?" I figured I'd already blurted out a few insensitive things so may as well continue.

Her eyebrows wrinkled as she sat her cup down on the table. Surely, she had blown all the heat away by now.

"Well Darling, we did want children, but they didn't quite make it into the cards we were dealt." Her eyes flickered with loss as she looked beyond me.

"Darling, it's important to remember that everyone has their own stuff they're dealing with. Choose to be kind because you never know what a person has going on that you don't know about. You never know what kind of baggage they are carrying around with them."

"Yes ma'am."

"Alfred and I tried to have babies. We lost a few and after that we just couldn't get pregnant anymore. It was one of the only things that I wrestled with God about. I had always wanted to be a mother. As a girl I didn't know much about what I wanted out of life, but being a mother, that's one thing I was sure of."

She had picked her tea back up but never took her eyes from whatever it was she had them fixated upon.

"I'm sorry." I didn't know what else to say.

"Darling, hear me now, okay? There are things in your life that you can't control. Sometimes you get dealt a bad hand. But there's nothing you can do about the things that happen to you that you can't change.

"You have to figure out a way to make peace with it and move on. If you don't, it will weigh you down like a boat anchor. You have too much life to live to be stuck because of one or two things that happen, you hear me?"

"Yes ma'am."

"I could have allowed myself to stay in a well of self-pity or even to choose to be angry with the world. It would have been easy to be jealous of any other woman who was blessed with a child but that's no way to live the life we've been given. Besides, there is always someone else who's got it worse than you do.

"Instead, I chose to trust that there was a reason I didn't have my own children and decided to love on everyone else's kids. You see God always makes room for what you feel you're lacking in your life. He gives you extra space that you didn't know you had within you and is willing to fill it with something good if you allow him to do so."

I thought of how supportive Mrs. H had always been of the youth of our church. She was one of our biggest advocates. At one time, she oversaw the children's programs and made sure there was an angel tree and food bank available for every child within our congregation.

I was a recipient of those things many times but had never given it much thought until right now. After all, it was the Church's duty to care for people in need, right? People within the neighborhood, whether they attended our church or not, would come sign up for the annual angel tree and monthly food bank.

Mrs. H had since passed the responsibilities to other deaconesses within the church but now that I really thought about it, she was always the crucial piece.

"You ready to accept why you were born on Christmas Day, Emma?"

I wasn't fit to be born on Christmas and she knew how much the topic bothered me. Christmas and I were a stark contrast. I wasn't ready to accept her or Mama's rationale, but I had no doubt she would spend the next few minutes trying to persuade me to.

"Hmm." She smiled sweetly, her eyes restored to mine, refusing to let my silence end the conversation.

"Well, hopefully God will spend your lifetime revealing that to you but what I will remind you of little Miss Emma is that you *are* a gift."

Here we go again with this metaphor. Me, a gift? Nah. I was just an ordinary girl from Byron, Georgia.

"Yes, Darling, you are a gift. I see so many things that you have to offer the world if you continue to push through. You've already made such a big impact at the detention center. Myra has mentioned it to me multiple times when she's called. She thinks… well her thoughts are her own to share, but know that we see you, little missy. We see you pushing through."

"Honestly, Mrs. H, people talk so much about convoluted things such as potential, purpose, *gifts*." Now, I was the one using my hands as I spoke which I'm sure conveyed annoyance.

"I think no one knows anything for certain and they just use those words to encourage one another that somehow it will all work out in the end."

Amidst her gentle laughter, she said, "Well, you may be right about that to a certain point but those of us who have earned our white hair know a thing or two about it. It may take a while to discover it, but it's stored within you. You just have to be courageous and patient enough to let it emerge. And you, my dear, are *pushing through*."

I'd just have to agree to disagree with Mrs. H for now. Maybe one day I'd discover that her words were true but, today, my skepticism remained. It was just best to change the topic.

"Terry and Maddie made me apply to college last week."

"Did they really?" She took a sip of her tea, humor hinted within her eyes.

"Yes, they did," I laughed. "They are tenacious, Mrs. H."

"Uh huh." The humor remained. Her brief word choice was oozing with it.

"Mrs. H, not you too?"

"Not going to say a word."

"What?! Tell me."

"No need to tell you what you already know."

"Ugh!"

"I will say this though. I've been noticing you and a certain little handsome young man getting quite close; closer than you normally are with one another."

I didn't respond aloud but my cheeks filled with heat. I never quite knew how to handle the questions and comments about Terry and my relationship.

Mama hadn't said much, which was odd. Her and Sister Brown would sit and talk while looking at us from the other side of the church. Maybe they both had always known that a relationship between Terry and I would happen at some point. Either way, I was thankful they didn't make a big deal out of it.

"Young love. I remember it well." Mrs. H's smile grew. "Enjoy it, Darling. Just make sure you don't lose yourself in it, okay?"

"Yes ma'am."

Speaking of losing myself in it, Terry had begun mentioning prom. It was over a month away but with all the things piling up at once, we'd probably need twice that amount of time to plan for it. Plus, I didn't even want to go. I didn't want to tell him no though. He seemed so giddy whenever the topic came up.

Maddie had been asked to prom by at least three boys so far, but she had turned them all down.

"Do you think if I did something because Terry asked me to do it, but I didn't really want to, that would count as losing myself?"

The cup she was holding made its way quickly to the table as Mrs. H sat up tall. Her face turned serious and she was all ears.

"How do you mean?"

"I just mean that some things Terry wants, I don't, but I wonder if I should do them for him because I care about him and I know he'd do it for me."

"Listen to me, Darling. You are your own person and very special. You don't have to compromise yourself for anyone. And if a person loves you, they won't ask you too."

By this point, her face displayed zero humor.

"I know. I think he's asking me because he loves me is all."

"Well love or not, he better not be pressuring you."

Pressuring?

"You know there's a reason God asks us to wait until marriage, right?"

"Wait until marriage to do things that we may not want to?"

"Well, sacrifice is a part of marriage, but a God-led, love-filled marriage is meant to protect you and your spouse. Once you two become one with another, you can never get that back. And it's not something anyone should try to force or guilt you into before you're ready."

Wait?! Sex?! Oh no.

We were definitely having two separate conversations right now.

"Um—"

There was no doubt that I had begun to enjoy conversations with Mrs. H and had begun spending way more time at her house than I usually would, but we were not at the level to be having the "sex talk."

"Your body is a temple, and the key word is its *yours*."

Her elbows were now resting on the table and she was fervently leaning in towards me. If her face got any more twisted, the creases in her skin would splinter.

"Um—"

"If you need me to handle this for you, you just let me know because that little boy is clearly not thinking with his head but—"

"Um, Mrs. H."

The sternness in her face had reached its peak but she stopped mid-sentence to acknowledge what I was trying to say.

"Mrs. H—"

"I know this is a hard topic and I'm glad you brought it up to me because what he's asking of you is unacceptable."

"It's prom, Mrs. H." I blurted out, interrupting her. I couldn't risk the conversation getting any deeper.

There was no telling what she would say next and some things my ears just couldn't unhear.

"Prom?!" She slapped the table and gave me an indescribable look.

"Child, you're talking about prom?" The loudness of her voice hadn't quite returned to normal.

"Yes ma'am."

We looked at each other for a few seconds before she burst into laughter. I had never seen her laugh so hard in all our times with one another. Tears began rolling out of her eyes.

Sex was not a topic I was ready to visit with Terry, let alone an 87-year-old woman. Mrs. H let her hand rest upon mine as her laughter slowed.

"Oh Darling, let an old lady slide, would you?"

Hearing the amusement and embarrassment through her words caused laughter to rile up within me. I had to admit, the situation was quite funny.

"Yes, Mrs. H. Yes, I'll let you slide this once."

Chapter Twenty-three

"You look beautiful, Emma Rose."

Mama stood staring at me in awe as I modeled the long black, sequined dress. "So beautiful."

It was highly likely that she was on the verge of tears but I was hoping to avoid any more mushiness. Her and Maddie had finally begun engaging in conversations and eating meals with humor and I didn't want to go backwards.

Although I knew they both missed Aunt Joleen dearly, I was thankful they were no longer in the beginning phase of shock and grief. Maddie was actually smiling nowadays and had finally accepted a prom proposal.

I had eventually given into Terry's perpetual hints: *"I wish I had someone to go to prom with. If only my girlfriend would let me take her to prom. I knew this girl once who finally said yes to going to prom."*

One day I just caved. His persistence was exasperating and often came in the most awkward times like when other people were nearby. Plus, I wouldn't let Rochelle be the only girl Terry had ever taken to a high school dance.

"You are quite the catch." Maddie chimed in with Mama.

She had already secured her prom dress. It matched her personality. It was flowy and bright. After buying it, she had threatened her date that he had better find a suit to coordinate because if she had to keep her prom picture forever, it would at least be a good one. As if Maddie ever had to worry about how she would look in anything. Every picture we had of her around the house looked like it was purchased with the frame. She was breathtaking, even when she wasn't trying to be.

"You don't think it's too tight around my booty?" I twisted toward the mirror so I could get a better view.

"Well, the dress can't hide what you have, Emma." Maddie raised her eyebrows.

"I know, I just don't want it to be too tight."

"Turn around." Mama twirled her finger in the air.

I turned slowly, careful not to overextend my butt.

"Looks fine to me."

"Me too."

Maddie gave me a suggestive smile while Mama looked for something in her purse.

"Terry's going to love you in that dress," she whispered.

"Shut up, Maddie."

The sex question had come up a few times from Maddie. She wasn't convinced that Terry and I had only just kissed. She would give me a look of unbelief and just sarcastically say, *"Uh huh."*

First off, where in the world would we ever be alone to pull something like that off, and secondly, the thought of sex was scary. Even Terry and I had avoided the topic altogether. I had taken a liking to Mrs. H's view on sex. Waiting for marriage sounded like the best plan. Plus, who was Maddie to talk? Maddie had never even kissed a boy.

She was unimpressed with the boys that surrounded her. Although they always worked hard to get her attention, she could care less. She said she just wasn't interested anytime I'd ask her about any possible attractions. She had her head on straight, but I wondered if she thought I was weak somehow and would be the one to give in to some sort of teenage sex drama.

"I'm just saying is all," Maddie continued.

"I'll be right back. I need to go to the bathroom." Mama headed towards the far side of the store, unaware of our conversation.

"You know it's okay for him to think you're attractive, right?"

"Maddie! Yes, I know that, but can you get off it please."

"Get off what?"

"The fact that you think I'm just going to be the cliché girl who goes to prom and has sex with some boy, only to regret it later."

"What?! That's not at all what I said."

"Maddie, seriously if you bring up or hint at me having sex with Terry one more time, I'm going to lose it."

"Kind of like you are now? Plus, I don't know about Terry being some random boy. You two have known each other forever and have a storybook kind of love, don't you think?"

"I do love Terry, but that doesn't mean I want to have sex with him, Maddie."

"Fine. I'm not saying you have to. I just know that you two love each other and it would kill me if you kept that kind of a secret from me. I tell you everything."

Maddie anxiously fidgeted with some loose hangers left behind in the fitting area.

She really didn't have much *to* tell. She was a good girl who had simple interests. She wasn't sneaking into corners with boys or stealing kisses. She was too busy making sure the room sparkle with her dazzling personality and cheerfulness.

"Maddie, look, if there was something to tell, I would tell you. But right now, Terry and I are both new at this. We are trying to get our heads around the fact that we are in a relationship and what that means. We can't afford to complicate it with anything else, especially not sex."

I ensured my voice was at a whisper, but my face remained firm.

"Okay! Sheesh and you call me the sensitive one." Her eyes looked relieved.

She had been worried that she was missing out on a piece of me. I bet it was hard to watch her best friend become romantically involved with someone, whether it was someone they had both known for forever or not. That made more sense. She just wanted to make sure our connection wasn't being lost. There was no way it could ever be broken though. We had been through too much together. We were practically sisters at this point.

"So maybe he won't like you in that dress then," Maddie teased.

I shot a quick sideways glance her way before yielding to a smirk. "Are you excited about your prom date?"

"I mean, he's cute and is nice but I don't think we'll have a love connection. I'm only going because prom is a must. I don't want to look back someday and regret not going."

"We should totally double date on the way there and back though, huh?"

"Absolutely! Was that not always the plan?" Maddie's face was concerned.

"Honestly, I've been letting Terry work out all of the details because you know I'm terrible with this kind of stuff."

"It's hard to believe we are related some days… letting Terry plan prom…" Maddie mumbled as she continued organizing the hangers in the room.

"We all weren't born like you, ya know?"

"What? Perfect?" Maddie jested.

It was one of the only times I had heard her mention herself with a compliment even if she was just being funny.

The thought provoked a smile.

"Yes, Maddie. Perfect, like you."

"Are you two about done? Emma, girl we can't pay for the dress if you're still wearing it." Mama had returned quicker than I expected.

"Oh yeah." I scrambled into the fitting room to get changed.

"I can't believe my baby girl is going to prom," I heard Mama say to Maddie as they waited for me to return.

"I know, Aunt Ruthie. It's kind of crazy, huh?"

"And she's going with Terry. I thought those two would never figure it out."

"Yeah, that's true." Maddie's voice was faint. "I think they will get married one day for sure."

"That's what your uncle always thought too."

It was hard to continue changing when I heard those words. Daddy thought Terry and I would be together?

Mama continued, "He would always say, 'there goes the future' when those two would head out to play. He'd smile and laugh as they spent hours on end with one another. It surprised me because I thought he would lose his mind once Emma began dating you know? But for some reason he always felt good about Terry. He said that there were some things inside the boy that he could trust.

"Hmm."

"Yeah, ever since Terry was a little boy, he'd hold the door open for Emma. He would do things like stop her when her shoes were untied, and he'd stoop down and tie them for her."

"Wow, Sister Brown raised that boy right!" I imagined Maddie leaning in eagerly to Mama as she talked.

"Yes, she did. He would make sure she never came out without a jacket if it was too cool. One day your uncle gave her permission to go play. Emma came back in with her arms crossed and a frown on her face. He had asked her what was wrong, and she went on and on about how Terry was bossing her around about her needing a jacket. Child, she was so mad. Your uncle just laughed which made her madder. You know Emma was a stubborn child."

"Was?!"

"Then in comes Terry staring your uncle straight in the eyes as if he was disappointed he had let her come out without a jacket in the first place. Your uncle just laughed and laughed and finally told Emma she needed to grab a jacket before heading back out.

"She was so furious that she didn't even want to come back downstairs. As a matter of fact, she stayed indoors and refused to go back out and play. Your uncle sat in the living room and talked with Terry for a while that night while they waited to see if she'd change her mind. She didn't. I sensed they were having a man-to-man type of conversation."

"Oh boy," Maddie giggled.

"He'd be proud of her. He would rest well knowing that our baby girl ended up with someone he knew would take care of her and protect her."

"Well Aunt Ruthie, I said one day. Not today." Maddie giggled some more. "Let's not go marrying her off right away now."

"Yeah, you're right child. But you know back in my day we would be as good as married by eighteen or nineteen-years-old."

"Well, good thing it isn't back in your day anymore," Maddie joked.

Ahh Thank you Maddie! There was no way I was getting married within the next year. Was Mama crazy? Whether Daddy loved him or not, I would not be engaged or married before I was good and ready.

"Emma, are you almost done?"

"Almost, Mama."

I leaned down to tie my shoe but was still focused on Mama's words. Did Daddy really say those things? And if so, how come she was telling Maddie about them but not me? She hardly spoke about Daddy and here she was sharing his memories with Maddie, not me. So typical of our relationship that lacked heart-to-heart qualities. In her defense though, the last time she had tried being sappy at my birthday party, I had ruined it notoriously.

Now the jacket incident Mama was referring to, that I remembered. I couldn't help but laugh to myself as I recalled how upset I was. Both Terry and Daddy had ganged up on me. They knew something I didn't know. I wondered if Terry remembered that night too. Better yet, did he remember that "man-to-man" conversation Mama had brought up?

"Emma—"

"Yeah, yeah, I'm coming."

"Finally!" Maddie huffed.

"You know, you two can't whisper worth nothing." I shot my eyes at them both.

"What?! At least I'm trying to keep your mama from marrying you off tomorrow."

"Well, I had no intention of whispering in the first place." Mama looked at me with an unrecognizable quality in her eyes.

It was endearing. It was soft. Was it love?

Chapter Twenty-four

"You know you can always just come work for us?" Mrs. Gaines tried convincing me that my help would be beneficial at the detention center in the future.

"I just might." I said, attempting to be nice.

Everyone was watching as I stood in the front of the room being acknowledged by her, Mr. E and Lisa. They didn't want to make it a big deal but also said they couldn't just allow me to leave without mentioning how much they appreciated my hard work. Some of the kids poked fun at me as I stood there fully embarrassed. My talk with Mr. E about not liking the spotlight was not heeded.

"Emma, you will be missed. I agree with Mrs. Gaines though. We could always use you around here so don't forget about us."

I wanted to continue my community service hours there until the end of the school year but apparently there was no official volunteer capacity in which I could be allowed to stay on the premises once my time had been completed. I was bummed about it but there was nothing that could be done about the rules that were in place.

I didn't want to say goodbye to the team, especially not Raymond, who sat in the corner, intermittently making eye contact with me. I wondered if he was mad at me. Surely, he knew I would have to leave at some point. Mr. E had mentioned it more than enough these last few weeks hoping to prepare the kids for the upcoming shift.

"Mad at me?" Raymond avoided looking in my direction for a few seconds.

"Nah, but it sucks though."

"Yeah, I know. I'm going to miss you, Raymond."

"Well, I am a *missable* person, so I get it."

"Haha! I bet you are. Wanna get a round of Uno in? You may as well let me beat you one last time."

"Nah, I'm good. I don't feel like it today."

"Oh, okay."

"Emma, I think they're right, you know?"

"About?"

"About you going off to school and then coming back to work here at the detention center."

"Going off to school? Who says I am going off to school?"

"You'd be dumb not to."

"Excuse me?"

"You heard me. You'd be dumb not to. What's the point of sitting around here doing nothing when you can go learn how to help people. Honestly, you've helped me a lot and I didn't even think that was possible."

Do not cry. Do not cry. Maddie was right, maybe I was turning into a sensitive individual.

After clearing my throat, I pulled together the clearest quality of voice I could. "How have I helped you?"

"By showing up. By being real. By caring. And by not pretending you had it all together. I can't tell you how many people come through here just to say they did. They come in here like they're better off than us. They're not here to help us. They just show up to make themselves feel good. People like Mr. E and you though, y'all are real. Y'all aren't scared to show us that you have struggles too. Y'all take what we are willing to give and don't force anything on us."

"Honestly, Raymond, I never really thought of it that way. I've never been good at pretending. My cousin and I joke around about 'being on' from time to time, but that's just putting our good face forward around other people to get by. No one wants to be around a miserable person all day long. And I've learned that only a handful of people care so it's easier to just try to be pleasant and move along."

"Well, I don't like the sound of that. That doesn't seem like you at all. Whatever 'being on' is for you, you've never done it here. You've been kind of a dumpster fire ever since you got here."

"Gee thanks, guy."

Surely, I wasn't that bad, was I? Well, maybe.

"I'm kidding, sort of." His poker face was terrible.

"All I'm saying is, maybe everyone doesn't deserve the right to know the true you, but the you that I know is too incredible to play second fiddle to some made up piece of you."

"Raymond Banks!" He moved back from me as I squeaked his name loud enough to make everyone turn their heads.

"Sorry. No, No I'm not sorry," I continued.

"What?!"

"I'm not the only one who has been hiding pieces of themselves."

He looked over at me understanding exactly what I meant. This teenage boy was no ineloquent, undereducated individual. His word choice just now proved him to be more than I expected. *Everyone has a story.* I could hear Mrs. H's words in my mind as I looked over at Raymond who was now frowning at me.

"I have never heard you talk like that before."

"You have barely heard me talk at all." He smirked.

"Hmm, I thought you were just quiet. Nope. Nope, you are a smart cookie, and you don't want everyone to know it."

I brought my voice to a whisper helping to protect his secret.

"I bet you're listening to Mozart or some other great composer in those earphones of yours. Here I was thinking that you were probably listening to some hooligan music."

"Hooligan?" Raymond erupted into laughter. "Seriously?"

I sat back in my chair, pleased with my joke. "I'm just saying."

"Yeah well, only certain people deserve to know the real you remember?"

"Uh huh. Uh huh. You're just full of surprises aren't you sir?"

"Well, just know that I let you win in Uno all those times too."

"Okay now you're pushing it. You may be smart, but you are not ready for me guy."

Raymond flashed me a boyish smile and I was reminded that I was sitting across from a fifteen-year-old boy who could turn almost any remark into something naughty.

"Oh brother!" I exaggerated an eye roll and narrowed my eyes at him.

"Don't worry. I know you have a boyfriend."

"How do you know that?"

"I just do. Plus, you're not my type so—"

"Um, what is that supposed to mean? What exactly is your type, sir? Someone mediocre?" I pretended to fluff up my hair as I vogued.

"You're too old. I don't date geriatrics."

"Okay, okay, you have loads of jokes, I see."

"Maybe."

"Well, I'll make a deal with you, Mr. Banks." *Oh no, I was beginning to sound like Mr. E.*

"And what is that?"

"If you decide to show people more of the real Raymond, I'll do the same. I'll try to stop 'being on.' Fair?"

"I'll consider it. Let's add you going to college to that offer though."

"So, if I go to college, you'll go?"

"There's no question about that. I'm going to college, Emma. I've made some bad decisions, but I told you, I hate disappointing my grandparents. They've done so much for me, and I know that the least I can do is go to college, get a good job and be able to take care of them one day. They don't have anyone else. I owe them that much."

"Oh. Well, what college do you want to go to some day? It sounds like you have it all figured out."

"Well, it sounds like you keep avoiding the topic as it pertains to yourself, *Miss Emma.*"

Okay now he was just mocking me and showing off at the same time. I seriously couldn't believe I was talking to the same boy who refused to speak two words when I first set foot in the SOAR room. This was the same boy who carried around a tattered teddy bear for goodness sake.

"I did apply to two schools. Clemson and CGTC."

"And?"

"CGTC accepted me pretty much immediately. Clemson's Dean of Admissions told me they were reviewing my application and would let me know within the next week or so. But no one knows that so keep that quiet, okay?"

"Fine. Who am I going to tell? Which school is your boyfriend going to?"

Seriously, how did he know I had a boyfriend and how did he know that Terry would be going to one of the schools?

"Clemson. But how did you —"

"Emma, come on now. You said yourself. I'm a smart guy. Plus, it doesn't take a rocket scientist to figure out why you would apply to one local college and one college out of state."

"You're about to get on my nerves, you know that?"

"Yeah, it serves you right since you're leaving."

"So, what do you think?" I was still whispering for some reason.

"About what?"

"Do you think you could see me at a school like Clemson?"

"I think that you've already decided where you want to be, but you have to be brave enough to go. Quit making excuses and quit asking for everyone else's opinions. Just go where you want to go. Plus, if your boyfriend is a good guy, he'll understand whatever decision you make because he will want what's best for you. And if he doesn't, he's lame."

Lame. There goes that word again. It was beginning to catch on, but I personally couldn't stand it.

"Well thanks for the life advice, guy."

"You're welcome. And don't forget to come back and work here too, okay?"

"Maybe."

"Okay good, now go away, I need to listen to some of my 'hooligan' music. Talking to you has been exhausting."

He faked a yawn, placed his headphones on his head and walked away from me in what seemed like a singular motion.

Who would have known that would be the kind of conversation I'd be having with him today. I expected it from Mr. E and Mrs. Gaines, but never in a million years did I think a fifteen-year-old boy would have me questioning my goals in life.

****

"Sounds like he likes you to me." Terry was now convinced that Raymond had some sort of crush on me. Their way of teasing was similar except Terry was unrelenting. At least Raymond backed off after a little while.

"Yeah, true Emma. Look at you with two boys fighting over you." Maddie couldn't help joining in.

"Guys, seriously enough! This is why I don't share things with people."

"Oh, come on Emma, one day you'll have to face the fact that you're hot stuff."

"I think so." Terry's smile faded fast when he saw Mama's eyes cutting him.

Had he forgotten she was sitting at the same table. The food surely wasn't that good.

"Baby, I'm very proud of you. I'm proud of all of you." Mama chose not to comment on his remark.

When I had gotten home Friday evening, Mama couldn't wait to hand me the envelope from Clemson. She looked like she was going to explode from excitement as Maddie and I walked through the door. We were both just happy we had some time off from school for Spring Break but when I saw Mama's face the happiness heightened. I couldn't remember seeing her beam with that much pride before.

"Baby, just know that whatever this letter says, I'm so proud of you."

She had pulled me to her chest tightly before I could respond. Usually, I would want to pull away, but I allowed my head to settle into her bosom without a fight. I wasn't sure if it was from the anticipation of the letter or the loving words Mama had just bestowed upon me, but tears began crawling down my cheeks.

Mama didn't say a word, probably out of fear that the moment would be ruined. Her embrace strengthened as she granted me permission to rest on her as a near-weaned child. We stood there holding one another for a while before a weepy Maddie took hold of us as well. There was no doubt that we looked like a leaking blob, the floor receiving our tears, entrusting them into its memories.

"Aunt Ruthie, what will you do when we are all gone?" Maddie cut into my thoughts, per usual.

"Child please, y'all will be still bugging me no matter how far away you are. And you will practically be down the street, so I'll probably get tired of seeing your face."

"Aunt Ruthie!" Maddie faked an offended gasp.

"I'm ready to have some 'me time.'"

There was no way Mama would be okay with some "me" time. She'd probably fill her extra time with activities at the church or maybe she'd hang out with Sister Brown more. They had already begun spending more time together since Terry and I had become an official item, as if they were plotting something.

"Or some 'Joe time.'"

Terry and I fired our eyes over at Maddie. She was feeling quite brave to insinuate that Mama would be interested in entertaining Joe. We joked around about it privately but would never dare say it to her face.

Mama continued to be conveniently available whenever Joe would cut our yard. She would suddenly need to check the mail or have a cup of tea out on Missums. It was like clockwork. Joe would start up the lawnmower and Mama would head out front. If she was wearing her house dress or didn't feel presentable, she'd just sit in the front area with the window or front door open so she could get some "sun."

I wouldn't be upset if she chose to date. It had been a while since Daddy had passed and I didn't want her to be lonely. I told her I couldn't promise that I'd be as close as Maddie at CGTC, but I'd make certain to check in with her as much as possible if I did decide to go to Clemson now that I had an official admission letter. She had responded by reminding me how I needed to decide quickly and quit dragging my feet and told me that either way, she would be fine.

"Hush child!" Mama didn't refute the idea of having "Joe time."

Terry and I exchanged looks of disbelief, surprised at Mama's restraint. Now if it had been me that made the little smart aleck comment about Joe, she would have put me in my place real fast. I hoped Maddie knew how close she had come to seeing Jesus after her little statement.

"Joe's a good man but I don't know about anything other than that."

"Well, I *know* he sure enjoys cutting our grass."

"Girl, hush! Don't nobody just like cutting grass."

"Joe does."

Maddie begun laughing while Mama became nervously flustered. "I'm just saying, Aunt Ruthie. Where do you think Emma gets it from?"

Mama decided to check out of the conversation by going to rinse a dish in the sink that could have waited.

"What are you doing?" I mouthed to Maddie. "Are you crazy?"

She shrugged her shoulders before giving me an annoying wink.

"Love you, Aunt Ruthie." She sashayed over to Mama and gave her a hug and kiss from behind before looking inside the refrigerator.

"When do you leave again?" Mama quipped right before we heard a knock at the door.

"Oh, that's probably my mom." Terry got up to open the front door.

It wasn't customary for a visitor to answer someone else's door or answer their phone, but since Terry practically grew up in our house, it was permissible.

"Hey hey!"

Sister Brown bounced into the room with her usual contagious energy. "Something smells good."

"Mama made meatloaf, but we ate it all."

"Why thanks. Surely my son thought of his mama and saved her a plate?"

Terry looked away towards the far wall to avoid eye contact. He had helped himself to seconds but did not mention putting any food aside for Sister Brown.

"You know I put you a plate in the microwave. Want me to heat it up for you?"

That was just like Mama. She wasn't going to let anyone go hungry. I couldn't remember her fixing that extra plate though. I was probably caught up in dialogue with Maddie and Terry.

Most of our conversations had included prom and college. Maddie had been badgering Terry about prom details and he'd listen intently, careful to take note of the things that he had better not leave out. I was easy to please when it came to stuff like prom, so he was more so shooting to not disappoint Maddie as opposed to me. Either that, or he feared the wrath he would receive from her if she thought he had let me down in any way.

Sister Brown offered to let us use her car while she hung out with Mama at the house until we returned. They'd probably just watch some movies, play cards or do a little bit of both.

"So, I have a surprise for you, Emma."

Sister Brown had gotten her coveted plate and had a scheme in her eyes. What was she up to?

"Actually, it's a bit of a surprise for all three of you."

We were all ears, attuned to whatever she was about to say next.

Mama sat down with her eyes locked, anticipating our reactions. She had to be in on whatever was about to happen.

I looked over at Terry, expecting to see some satisfied look on his face but he was full of anticipation just like Maddie and me.

"Any guesses?"

Sister Brown was met with silence, but her laughter broke it. She was quite proud that she had managed to draw three teens in which was no easy feat these days.

"Okay fine, I'll tell you. Well actually, I'll give you a hint. Your surprise includes driving in the car for about six hours."

"Mom!" Terry exclaimed, clearly solving it before Maddie and I had.

He looked over at me waiting for me to catch on.

"Are we going to Clemson?" Maddie was now looking over in my direction as well.

Wait! Were we? I turned to look at Sister Brown who was dang near bursting.

Mama's face matched her excitement.

"Let's go check it out again, Emma. This time, for you. See if it's somewhere you could see yourself."

I didn't know what to say. Sister Brown and Mama had been in cahoots planning a trip for me to Clemson. I was flattered but uncomfortable with the idea of being the center of attention.

"When are we going?" were the only words I managed to get out.

My arms were weak and my breath felt as if it weighed a ton. Why was I so nervous?

Terry sensed my emotional gears shift and scooted closer to me, placing his hand upon mine.

"Tomorrow morning, bright and early."

Oh man! They knew me well. If they'd given me enough time to think about it, I would have come up with some convincing reason as to why the trip wasn't necessary.

"This is going to be sooo fun!" Maddie was at a full squeal. "Emma Rose, let's go pick out our outfits."

Outfits were the last thing on my mind.

Terry, sensing what Maddie obviously didn't, gave my hand another gentle squeeze to reassure me.

Mama and Sister Brown had maternal smiles fixed upon their faces. I couldn't tell if they were enthralled with Terry's attentiveness or if they were just pleased with themselves.

"I can't wait to go back there with you," he whispered to me.

Well, that part I could handle.

Being able to go back to Clemson with Terry once more would be fun. And plus, Mama and Maddie would be there too.

This trip could actually be fun if I allowed it to be. My favorite people would be together for possibly one of the scariest adventures in my life.

What was the worst that could happen?

"Okay, yeah. Let's do it!"

Chapter Twenty-five

Riding in the car, sandwiched between Terry and Maddie, would have probably been more uncomfortable if I didn't permit myself to lean a little further left than necessary onto Terry. I was careful not to become too laxed with my positioning since Mama and Sister Brown were within arm's reach. Although, there were no plans of crossing into a promiscuous territory, I didn't want either of them to misconstrue my posture.

My arm found itself nestled against Terry's leg time and time again while my shoulder pressed into his with the slightest bump or jerk of the car. It was obvious to anyone who was actively observing us, especially Maddie. Terry didn't seem to mind the additional physical contact. He'd shoot a smile in my direction every now and again or move closer to enhance the interaction. Maddie appeared unbothered though. She spent most of her time looking out the window and enjoying the scenery as we drove along.

Mama and Sister Brown were occupied singing to their favorite tunes. If they weren't singing, they were engaged in random conversational topics during the radio commercials. Every now and again I'd catch sight of either of their eyes in the rearview mirror before they were distracted by one another or a familiar song once more.

The ride was quite peaceful. It was peaceful enough for Terry and Maddie to fall asleep, leaving me with my thoughts and Mama and Sister Brown's singing.

Maddie was a quiet sleeper which made sharing a room with her a plus. Terry, on the other hand, gave off a light snoring hum as he slept with his arm curled up next to his carefree and tranquil face. I wanted to kiss his cheek badly but decided against it, knowing I'd never sneak it in without our moms noticing.

The fact that they were okay with us dating didn't mean that they'd tolerate excessive public displays of affection. They didn't need to tell us that they expected us to be respectful to one another and them by being modest in our relationship. We both just knew.

I examined his serene face, wondering if he was dreaming. The radiance of the sky, plastered with shifting clouds drew my attention from his profile, however. I bent slightly toward the door to get a better look out the window, tranced by the beauty before me. The splendor of the scenery, accompanied with Terry's light snores must have lulled me into a nap because the next voice I heard was Mama's.

"Wake up now." Her voice was mild.

Terry and Maddie were now both wide awake, leaning through the windows as they took in the vast campus. Neither one of them flinched as I overextended my arms into a large stretch, taking notice of a light crick in my neck from leaning onto Terry as I slept.

As I began rubbing my neck with a couple of quick massages, I was enveloped by Maddie's arms while her familiar squeal assailed my ears.

"Sheesh, Maddie." I groaned, hoping she would take the hint that my excitement didn't currently match hers.

Meanwhile, Terry looked as if he would erupt into a bout of glee at any given moment. His dopey, captivated face was rather amusing. This truly was where he was meant to be.

Sister Brown found parking at the visitor center and led us over towards the main building. Despite it being spring break, dozens of college students lounged around the massive outdoor grassy courtyard. Some students were engulfed in what I assumed was schoolwork while others tossed frisbees or balls to one another.

Then there was the group of friends who just sat near one another, not necessarily needing communication but just enjoying each other's company and peering around. It was an interesting picture. I was drawn to the fact that these students resembled kids my age, some a bit older than myself, but the majority appeared as young as I was.

I wondered what reasons they had for staying behind as opposed to going home or traveling with friends. Some likely couldn't afford to travel, and some may have just not wanted to.

"Heads up!" A medium-built boy shouted to warn the others that a ball had flown away wildly.

"Would you look at that?" Sister Brown continued to lead us toward the building pointing out a huge clock tower. It was situated near the top of the brick building.

"It gets me every time. It's just so beautiful." We stopped to take notice and admire its artistry.

"That *is* something." Mama peered up at the clock, careful to shield her eyes from the sun.

She had never gone very far from Byron. I couldn't make out if she had no desire to do so, if she felt like her sticking close to home was the responsible thing to do, or if it was just plain fear of the unknown that kept her in Byron.

"Sure, makes me wanna consider coming to Clemson now." Maddie nudged me jokingly.

There was no way she would enroll at a large university such as Clemson. She was not Aunt Joleen, who wanted to go out and capture the world. Maddie was content and enjoyed smaller settings. Although her good looks extended far past the "girl next door," on the inside, she was a small-town girl that possessed a certain charm and allurement built for quaintness. She was indeed picture perfect for it.

"It's not too late," Terry began. "Well, actually yeah it might be too late."

"You're annoying." Maddie stuck her tongue out, not amused by him.

"Okay here we are," Sister Brown pushed open the doors and guided us toward the help desk, determined to keep us on track.

"Hello, we have an appointment with—"

Her voice trailed off as I turned in a slow circle to take in the building. The walls extended very high, the ceilings were grandiose, and the windows were scattered around like Monopoly houses. I felt like I was standing amid a greatness that I couldn't grasp. An exclusive type of history was built within the corridors and memories lingered within the foundation. The concreteness of the building escaped me as I allowed my senses to be overtaken by what felt like someone else's nostalgia. It was palpable on a level that I didn't know existed.

The hairs on my arm responded to the coolness of the room, reminding me that I was present. Rubbing my arms to warm them, my gaze affixed upon a mocha-skinned boy settled into an orange and brown chair across the room. He had his headphones in place and appeared to be in a zone until he stopped and flipped over his cassette tape. After pushing the buttons down to press play, his eyes found mine.

Even though staring was customarily acknowledged as being impolite, I couldn't take my eyes from his. His youth was emphasized as I fixated on his large round eyes and his patchy facial hair. His mustache and beard hadn't quite made a connection. His demeanor was reserved but inviting and his facial expression all but welcomed me to come over.

"Emma, stop staring." Maddie whispered roughly into my ear; no doubt embarrassed by me at this point.

Terry had taken notice of my inordinately lingering peer with the random boy as well, coming over to place his arm in mine.

After shifting his t-shirt around his abdomen, I guess the boy decided the eye lock was more of a nuisance than anything worthwhile. He grabbed his belongings but instead of walking away, he headed over towards us.

Uh oh! I looked over to see if Mama or Sister Brown had noticed but Sister Brown was still carrying on in discussion with the girl at the desk who couldn't seem to find the "appointment" that Sister Brown was insistent she made.

"Great." Maddie said through clenched teeth as the boy did not veer away from us but continued straight in our direction.

I wondered if he was going to come over and explain to me the rules I already knew about how staring was rude. Or if he was coming over to let us know that this was his territory, and we'd better watch out.

No, that thought was stupid. We weren't in some random neighborhood, Emma.

His walk was casual and his posture was non-threatening as he stopped a few feet away from us. He wore his headphones around his neck at this point, the wire hanging loosely toward his pocket. I could make out his facial features much better at this mark. His beard and mustache had no relationship with one another other than the fact that they were both situated on the same face. He had mild acne scarring, mostly prominent around his cheeks. His eyelashes were full, and his round eyes were more appealing up close.

The previous rearrangement of his t-shirt became more apparent as well. He could have done well with a size up. His current shirt was fitted around his toned stomach and his muscular arms held his sleeves captive.

"Hi!" He smiled at us, showing his near-perfect white teeth and revealing double-sided dimples.

Maddie drew in closer to me, covertly grabbing the back of my shirt, while Terry stuck close to my other side. He was unmistakably handsome and all three of us knew it.

"Hey!" I waved as if he was still across the room.

Awkward!

"I think you all may be looking for me?"

He looked towards Sister Brown who was refusing to retreat at this point, now going on about how long our drive was.

"Excuse me, Lindsay."

Maddie grabbed my shirt even tighter, bunching it as she looked over the young man who was attempting to gather the girl at the desk's attention in an attempt to rescue her from what was now turning into the wrath of Sister Brown. If Maddie got any closer to me, we'd be wearing the same clothes.

I patted her hand to try to calm her down. I'd never seen her this worked up about any boy before. Granted, he was older and carried himself as more mature than any boy at Peachtree, but still, I'd never seen a near reaction to the one she currently had as she continued looking him up and down.

"Okay, it's becoming noticeable." I whispered as softly as I could.

He had moved closer to the help desk to try and get between Sister Brown and "Lindsay."

Maddie ignored me and carried on admiring the boy from behind. Her cheeks had become red-tinged as she entered full blush mode.

"Maddie!" I gasped as I tried to contain my amusement.

"What?" She whispered back to me, not shifting her eyes from him.

Terry had released his hand from mine, realizing that Maddie was the one who was enamored with the boy and not myself. He was easy on the eyes, but Terry was the only one I truly cared for. Besides, I was trying to figure out what the whole staring fit was about in the first place. I was not normally easily impressed, but it wasn't that I was mesmerized by this guy. It was something else that I couldn't determine.

I looked over at the guy once more trying to understand. I noticed his baby-oiled skin and watched as he repositioned his headphones from falling too far to one side.

Aha, Raymond!

He looked nothing like Raymond but the baby oil tint and earphones reminded me of him.

No, it was more than that. What was it?

I scrutinized "Mister Fitted-shirt" a bit more. It was as if this guy was a foreshadowing of where Raymond could be headed one day. Raymond belonged at an institution for higher education, not a detention center. This should be his future. It didn't have to be

Clemson, but the idea suited him. I wanted to see him take advantage of every opportunity he could.

Oh wait! Who am I? I sound like….

"Emma." Terry cleared his throat and nudged me away from my thoughts and apparently another long staring daze at whatever his name was.

"Huh?"

"You're staring, again." His voice was now irritated but the emphasis on the word "again" made me smile.

"I was staring?"

Of course, I was staring but I was tempted to see what sort of response I'd get from Terry if I acted unaware.

"Seriously?!" He didn't find me funny.

"I didn't mean to. This place is just a lot to take in. And he reminds me of Raymond."

It probably wasn't the best idea to bring up another boy who may or may not have liked me when Terry was already showing signs of jealousy.

"It's fine. I've decided you can't come here now. You have to go to school with Maddie."

He was back to his teasing nature, a full smile spread across his lips.

"Now that we have that straightened out, I'm so glad you all made the trip over. Clemson is a great school. Not only does the university offer high-quality academia, but it's laid back and I'm sure you all would have a good time here."

The boy, who we now knew was named Johnny, turned out to be our tour guide and advisor for the day. Apparently, the appointment was "off books" because no tours were typically scheduled during breaks, but Sister Brown knew someone who made it happen anyway. She knew how to pull strings.

The girl's face at the desk had now switched over from nervousness to relief and Sister Brown's to satisfaction. Sister Brown could be a lot to take in especially if she had her mind set on something. She was the walking epitome of the term "Strong Black Woman."

Although she was married, her independence could be sensed across any room. She was quiet and always in a state of observation unless she didn't agree with something or felt as if a point could be built upon. It was then she would open her mouth with an articulation that forced every eye upon her. She had a way of handling things tactfully, but one should never expect her to back down if she perceived something as erroneous or amoral. I looked up to her in so many ways.

As we followed Johnny, we learned that he was in his junior year and was a student advisor, currently in need of extra hours for his spring semester, so he volunteered to show us around and answer as many questions as we could think of. Maddie didn't have many because she was so captivated by him as a physical specimen while Sister Brown and Mama threw them out as fast as he could handle them.

Of course, Mama was concerned about safety and questioned the busy highway that ran next to the campus and if security was readily available due to the distance students had to walk in the dark. The registrar had already updated me and Mama that if I enrolled at Clemson, I'd have to stay in a shoebox dorm that was at least fifteen minutes from Terry's on the east side of campus. I had originally imagined we would be almost inseparable apart from classes and library time.

The library itself was amazing to witness. It had the most beautiful windows with a view of a gorgeous fountain. Johnny guaranteed us that we would be spending a lot of time at the library in between classes. The dining hall and scattered food stations would also be frequented by us he assured.

Sister Brown inquired about the amounts of parties on campus. Not wanting to speak too much on that topic, Johnny gave a soft chuckle and said, "Well, yeah there's that, but you don't have to attend them."

Sister Brown, of course, shot Terry a look while Mama simultaneously gave me an identical one.

I tried to imagine Johnny in a party atmosphere. He seemed as if he was all about his studies and didn't waste any time on nightlife.

But that smile and chuckle was knowing. Maybe he was the student that was able to juggle both books and social life.

"Are all of you thinking of coming here?" Johnny looked at Terry, Maddie and I but was really focused more so on Maddie than me and Terry.

Yep, he was a healthy human male, I giggled on the inside.

I knew he would eventually take an interest in her. I hadn't met a boy who hadn't been attracted to her.

"I'll be here." Terry responded passionately.

"Possibly."

"Possibly?" Johnny raised his eyebrow at me.

"I'm still trying to decide between here and Central Georgia Tech."

"Is there really a decision to be made there? I mean its Clemson."

Oh yeah, definitely a healthy, testosterone-loaded human boy.

His chest stuck out with beaming pride and those dimples were drawing me in a bit more than they should have.

Mister Johnny, you're trouble.

"That's what I've been saying too." Maddie and I both looked at Terry as his masculinity piped up with Johnny's.

"I mean you're right. It's Clemson." They both laughed, thrilled with themselves.

"Hey! CGTC is a great school too." Maddie interjected, quickly catching Johnny's attention.

His smile loosened and he was suddenly all ears. Maddie had a way of doing that to guys. They'd lose their train of thoughts or change their opinions if it meant getting into her good graces. Although, she was never impressed by such things. She merely wanted to express her views.

"I'm sure it is a good school. But it's no Clemson is all I'm saying." The dimples were back.

Lord help me!

"Of course, it's not Clemson. It's CGTC. And that's what I like about it." Maddie stood strong daring Johnny to hold the gaze longer.

A strand of her hair had fallen from her ponytail and outlined her gorgeous face. She had chosen a pink sparkle lip gloss to wear today that flattered her natural lip color. It glistened as she held her face in flirtatious opposition to Johnny.

Her eyes possessed a longing for him to say more but I knew she wouldn't budge on her position. She would, however, welcome any extra time conversing with him.

Madison Lyn! Go girl!

"Hmmm. Okay." Johnny conceded but not without a lingering smile and elongated look before breaking eye contact.

At this point the interest between the two was quite tangible, causing Sister Brown to sternly nudge Johnny into moving forward with the tour.

Mama looked at Maddie with the "don't wear your heart on your sleeves" expression. She had frequently quoted that to us as we'd gotten older. "Never show him all of your cards," she would say. Boys liked a chase and were created for it. "Don't make it easy for them."

"Yes ma'am." Maddie said quietly, not denying the accusation.

She looked over at me hoping for some sort of input.

I smiled at her and shook my head in full agreement with Johnny's attractiveness.

She let out a small giggle before tucking the wild strand of hair back into her ponytail and grabbing me by the arm as we followed the group across the campus.

Chapter Twenty-six

"Emma Rose?"

"Yeah?"

Maddie and I were lying in the bed attempting to fall asleep since we had to return to school the next day. Spring break had officially ended, much to our regret. We had enjoyed our time off so much and hated to see it end.

Besides the Clemson trip, we had spent a couple days at the lake and attended a brief youth conference in Atlanta. Brian supervised the trip with a few chaperones from the church. Since it was a two-day conference, we stayed overnight in a cheaper hotel, with four to five of us sharing a room.

I had even interacted with Annette and Shyla since they shared a room with Maddie and me. I could see why she liked them. They were easy to be around and were not the boy-crazed girls that I expected them to be. Ironically, despite my prejudgments, I was the only one of us four who even had a boyfriend.

Thankfully we weren't in the same room as Chelsea. She had made it clear that she wasn't thrilled about Terry and my relationship since she had already made up her mind that she was supposed to be the mother of his babies. We purposely avoided her for most of the conference.

"I know you and Terry have never considered having sex, but do you think about it?" Maddie's words were low and curious.

"Well, yeah. I've thought about it but it still kind of scares me you know?"

"Yeah."

"Why? Are you thinking about having sex with your prom date or something?"

That seemed to be popular these days. A few girls had mentioned going "all the way" with their boyfriends after prom like it was some rite of passage.

"Ugh no!" Maddie quickly dismissed the idea. "I've just never felt that way before you know?"

"Oh okay."

"I mean when I saw Johnny and heard him talk, I felt something I'd never felt before."

Ahhhhh! This was about Johnny. The boy was kind of unforgettable.

He had a body that could make a girl wonder. He was older too, so he probably knew the different things that guys took a while to learn as it related to wooing and hooking girls. He most definitely was the sort of guy that drew females in. His mischievous smile and sly responses told me that they lined up to spend time with him. Maddie's feelings were justified.

"My stomach felt all crazy, you know? I couldn't stop staring at him."

"That's fair."

"But Emma, I felt weird down *there*."

I shook my head in acknowledgement, remembering the times in which I, too, was particularly drawn to Terry.

My body had longed for something unfamiliar if we kissed for an extended amount of time or if he held me against his chest for a while. There was an invisible steaminess that exuded between us. Terry, no doubt, had felt the same, often repositioning himself in those moments. We never talked about it but we both recognized what was happening.

"Yep, I know what you mean."

"That's normal right? I mean, I'm not bad for having those kinds of feelings, am I?"

"No way!"

"I mean God created attraction to the opposite sex, yes?" Maddie was attempting to work through her thoughts aloud. "As long as I don't go out there acting on it all the time, right?"

"All the time?"

"Well, you know… I mean, as long as I'm not actually having sex, the feelings are okay, right?"

"Yeah, Maddie. We long for closeness with a person that is safe for us. I think if we don't let those urges control us, we should be okay. They must be healthy, after all God created us this way. I think it's when we act on those impulses just because they are there that the problem comes in."

"You get them with Terry?"

I wasn't one to be open about such private things. I was still trying to figure them out myself, but this was not one of those times that I should shell up. I didn't need to "be on." I needed to just be honest with Maddie. She was brave enough to ask, so I needed to be brave enough to have the conversation with her.

"Yes, I do."

"What do you do when it happens? I mean it felt strong just looking at Johnny. I bet it's even stronger when you and Terry kiss."

"Well, we just kind of move over or change what we are doing."

"How?"

"Well, Terry has gotten up or walked away a few times. He would say he needed to stretch his legs or move around or some other excuse, but I know it's because of hormones kicking in."

"Oh."

"You know how he likes to make jokes, so sometimes he will just crack a random joke to break up the tension that's building."

"So, you guys never—"

I waited patiently for Maddie to finish her sentence, knowing what question would follow.

"You never touch or anything like that?"

"No, we don't." I attempted saying it as softly and understanding as I could.

"Maddie, when I say I'm terrified about sex, I really am. Don't get me wrong, I'm curious. I would love to know what it's all about, but I'm just scared of what may happen, especially after you know?"

"Yeah, that makes sense."

"I have wanted to touch and I'm sure Terry has too, but I don't know if either one of us would be strong enough to stop after that. Besides God created it for marriage for a reason, right?"

"Yeah. That's true."

We sat in silence for a few minutes, neither one of us ready to fall asleep. We were both certainly thinking about our conversation and imagining things.

"So, what do we do about it?" Maddie couldn't let it go.

I didn't have a good answer for her though.

"Well, maybe ask Sister Brown."

Maddie erupted in laughter at the thought of approaching Terry's mom with the dilemma. "No way!"

"Can you imagine?"

I joined in the laughter knowing that there was no way either one of us would ask for help with this particular topic. Not now at least. It was something we would have to figure out on our own or in time. It was best to not ask our peers about it either. I presumed the answers would range from dismissiveness to outlandish guesses. There was no way any other teenager had this thing figured out either. Absolutely no way.

I closed my eyes, finally ready to give in to sleep before hearing Maddie chime in once more in that familiar soft and hesitant tone, "Emma?"

"Huh?"

"I think you should go to Clemson with Terry."

Her words caused me to sit up and face her. It took a while for my eyes to adjust to the darkness of the room and even still they could only make out her silhouette.

She was lying on her back and looking up at the ceiling. Her covers were up toward her chin, but her hands could be noticed bunching them from the bottom to hold them in place where she wanted them to stay.

I didn't know what to say but allowed my posture to speak for me. I was shocked because besides Mama and Terry, Maddie was the most overprotective of me. She was a bit more so than Terry, and that's saying something. That boy would be ready to jump out in front of a moving bullet for me.

As I considered that thought, gratitude flooded my heart. I was blessed with people who truly cared for me. Even if I doubted how special I was, they never did.

"Emma, I don't think you should go *because* of Terry but I think you should go *with* him."

I remained quiet, not sure it was even appropriate for me to respond. Maddie was working through her thoughts once more. She wasn't talking to me, but she was talking about me. This conversation was hers alone, I was simply the topic.

"You were made to be someone special, Emma. It makes me sad when you doubt yourself because you are so smart, witty, and beautiful. Any person who gets to know the real you would find themselves blessed. It would be selfish of me to want to hog you to myself. I've had years of knowing you. Plus, it's time for you to begin to know *you*. You'll never know you if you stay here. You have to go out there and learn what you like and don't like. You must learn to know what it's like to not be able to run to Missums and to withdraw within yourself when things are hard.

"You gotta go out there and see how other people are in the world, outside of your comfort zone. I don't think you'll find out how great you are until you see how much you can impact other people who don't know you. Plus, with Terry being there, he will always bring out the best in you. He always has. Even when I cannot get through to you, he can. He's your safe person and if you have your safe person near you, you will be more likely to test the waters. Emma, you *have* to go."

Maddie's hand emerged from beneath the cover and I watched in the dimness as it wiped at her face. I couldn't make out her tears, but I knew they were there, matching my own.

My heart was stilled, and I couldn't bring myself to wipe the tears from my face. I was fastened in on Maddie and wrapped up in her words. The hush in the room was so loud that it was unearthing.

The feelings of being some lackluster thing born into this world was no longer large enough to match Maddie's perception of me. A rising determination was fighting within my chest. My mind, as always, attempted to correct me and remind me that I was simply a girl from a small town, being raised by a single mother. But Maddie's words! It was as if they had declared residency within the room, ready to combat anything that dared speak against them. Courage swelled and swirled with anxiety as I attempted to imagine that her words were true.

She reached her hand to mine and the truth of her words became etched and gridlocked within my being. Tears flew down my cheek rapidly, unforgiving. As the tears dropped, each negative thought of myself fell with them.

Emma Rose Griggs, the gift God sent on Christmas to Ruthie Elanor Griggs. Emma Rose, the girl whose father committed suicide, leaving her way too early in life. Emma Rose Griggs, the girl who has been in a fight with herself for far too long. Emma Rose, the girl whose life was far from perfect but full of everything she needed.

I contemplated the unacknowledged love that had encompassed me my entire life. Daddy showered me with his time although he warred within himself every day. His words, laced in praise and preparation of my becoming a young woman one day.

Maddie who was exuberant and relentless in her affection and admiration of me. The girl who was motherless but found contentment and joy with God's provision of an aunt who adored and sacrificed time and time again for her. The girl who had planted her feet within a journey of healing and exploration in dealing with loss and unanswered questions. The girl who despite it all, found happiness and never failed to encourage others.

Then there was Terry. His unwavering friendship through insecure and unwarranted attacks from myself. The boy who had grown into a young man and lavished a different level of love that only God could help explain in time. The boy who had a secret conversation with my daddy when I was young and had undeniably fulfilled whatever promises were exchanged in that room that night.

And then there was Mama. The woman who I thought would prefer Maddie as a daughter to the one she gave birth to. The woman whose love I could never connect with. But Mama's love was found in her consistent actions, not the words she spoke. Her hint of care was found in between the lines: When she asked about my poor performances, unsatisfactory days, what time I was coming home, or if I was hungry. One thing I could never accuse her of was not taking care of me. She was overprotective, but I'd take that over her abandoning me on a doorstep any day.

Maybe Maddie needed that extra nurturing that I perceived as a special connection. Perhaps it was to instill worth into the abandoned girl despite her being left behind. Maybe Mama thought that I'd never doubt her love for me because of how she took care of me day in and day out. Maybe she didn't say it aloud often enough because she thought her actions were loud enough. Maybe she was an imperfect human just like me and she was dealing with not just her own demons but also those of people around her, such as Daddy's, Aunt Joleen's, Maddie's… and mine. Mama's love, it was unquestionable.

The saturation of my face was apparent as I lay there, no longer welcoming sleep but instead entering a new surrender of who I could discover myself to be. A kindness and forgiveness swept through my body as I realized the anger and harshness in which I had treated myself. A veil of sorts was being removed in the shadows of the night.

My Darling.

I heard the words within my head ever so faintly. Mrs. Hennagen, the woman who annoyed me from day one. The woman who could see me as a prize even though she didn't know me. She could see beneath the callousness and the sharp tongue. She called me names that spoke to the young woman I had not encountered and recognized yet. She patiently welcomed me believing that one day I would find that young woman and I'd receive her too. The cups of tea she made for me even though she knew I would waste most of them. Her stories she would tell and her hard truths that I'd come to long for met me in the blackness.

Darling, her expression of affection and love.

Maddie's breathing resounded within the room, and I imagined her heartbeat as she slept peacefully. I leaned in closely to her and tried to match her breath. My mind slowed accepting of the shifting course within it.

A sliver of light entered the room as the door opened and Mama's head slowly appeared.

There it was. Mama's love, sensing my needing her and being there. Always being there.

"I love you, Mama," I whispered, my eyes heavy but my heart fully awakened.

"I love you too, baby." She closed the door and the darkness swept back over the room, unable to stifle the light that I had just found.

Maddie repositioned to face me, sleep still overtaking her. Her breathing, still rhythmic and soothing.

I turned to face her and snuggled into her once more.

My eyes fought to stay open, reveling within the enlightenment of the night but soon they could fight no longer. The fight within me had quieted. There was no longer room for warring.

No, instead I allowed sleep to wash over me as I entered the most peaceful slumber I'd ever known.

Many things had changed in my life, but hating funerals was not one of them. I looked around at all the people who had turned out to Mrs. Hennagan's homegoing. It was a beautiful spring day, and an assortment of azaleas were everywhere. The wooden casket that was being lowered into the ground held a purple arrangement, coupled with the many flowers that people had laid atop it as they stated their final goodbyes.

I had placed a lone purple hydrangea from Mama's garden on the casket. Although I knew azaleas were her favorite, I wanted to be sure to bring a flower that she knew would be from me and maybe it would speak to her in the same way she used to speak to her own flowers. Maybe my flower would help her stand taller wherever she was at this moment.

It was strange, this funeral. Every funeral I had attended before made me want to run home, replace whatever clothing I was wearing and sit outside to debrief. This one though, I wanted to sit with Mrs. H for as long as I could.

I felt her smile in the breeze and could hear her voice in my head as I remembered our times with one another. I was happy for her, that she'd be reunited with the love of her life.

It was remarkable seeing the different people who were there. Her legacy was felt as people shared how she had impacted them and how they admired who she was. None of them had the quiet moments that I had though. I was special to Mrs. H.

She had been so proud that I had chosen to go to Clemson and "spread my wings." She had come to my high school graduation and watched as I read my community service essay aloud. It was hand selected by the principal to be read at graduation after Mrs. Lee passed it along.

Typically, essays weren't read at the graduation apart from the Valedictorian and Salutatorian addresses, but apparently my paper included some very relevant and inspiring material that the administration staff wanted to share. Mama was beaming with pride from her seat and Mrs. H, although her energy had decreased, sat peacefully, content with her influence on my life. I had never thought I'd be on a stage speaking to my peers and adults.

My visits to Mrs. H's house had increased as she became feebler and less mobile. Maddie and I would go and bring her food. We'd sit with her and chat with her even though she would fall asleep during our conversations quite often. She would arouse embarrassed, but Maddie and I would carry on like we hadn't noticed.

Mama and the deaconesses at the church set a rotation of helping her around the house and with things such as getting bathed and dressed. They had all agreed they would not allow her to land in a nursing home.

Last week before midterms, Mama had called to let me know that Mrs. H had passed to be with the Lord and wondered if I could come home. Terry offered to bring me home immediately. He was one of the few lucky freshmen to be able to have a car on campus and didn't think twice about driving us back home.

While at Clemson, we couldn't see each other as much as we had thought we would. College courses turned out to be a lot more difficult than expected. We talked on the phone as often as we could and tried to carve out time for an off-campus date once a month.

Johnny had been right. The library and dining hall were our best friends so we met there as often as we could.

Turns out, I was right as well. When I had seen Johnny around the campus once or twice, he had given me a head nod. He was in fact one of the students that could juggle school and his social life. He was quite popular with the girls as I imagined, having a few different ones with him the times I'd seen him, and random students always acknowledged him as he passed.

My mind returned to the present as Terry squeezed my hand as I stared at the casket in its final resting place.

The ushers dismissed us from the grounds, and we headed toward the cars where Maddie had already retreated.

Memories of Aunt Joleen flooded back when she received the news of Mrs. H's passing. She had called me right away from her dorm crying. We had sat on the phone all night, although I had an assignment that I needed to complete. Maddie was more important than the assignment and I knew I could finish it later. Plus, we needed to cry together because we both held a special connection to Mrs. H and only I could recognize the stirring of loss it would bring within Maddie.

Her prom date, now boyfriend, approached her at the car, giving her an extended hug. I still couldn't believe she was dating. The only boy she'd ever mentioned feeling anything for was Johnny and that was more hormonal than anything else. It was short-lived and anytime I'd see Johnny on campus I was thankful Maddie wasn't there too.

My gut told me that he was trouble and not good for her. He wore a fraternity jacket one time I saw him, and his particular frat was known for some of the craziest parties and hazing tactics around.

Her boyfriend took her by the hand as we approached.

 I gave her a hug, causing their grip to fall. "You okay?"

"Yeah." Maddie smiled and I could tell she was at peace, which was all that mattered to me.

****

Mama had offered to hold the repass at our home. People had been bringing casseroles and desserts over since last night. I could smell the buffet of food as I approached the front porch to the house.

I looked through the screen and saw the amount of people milling around. I caught a glimpse of Mama who saw me watching and motioned for me to come inside. I smiled and put up one finger letting her know I'd be in soon.

Joe placed his arm around Mama's back and kissed her forehead. She had finally given him a chance once Maddie and I had moved into our dorms. When she told us they were dating, she waited for some sort of reaction but neither one of us were shocked. We had known it all along and expressed our happiness for her. She was a great judge of character so if she thought Joe was respectable and worth pursuing a relationship with, we trusted it.

"Ready to go in?" Terry held the door open for me.

He had really filled out over the semester. There was a free gym on campus that allowed him to work out after hours. He was so worried that he'd put on an increased amount of weight from the late-night eating and studying that he decided to begin working out to counter the possible effects. Lifting weights had become a part of his routine so he was no longer thin.

Sometimes, I would catch him shirtless in his dorm and admire his build. His pectorals were formed, and his stomach had a defined six pack. The feelings "down there" that Maddie had mentioned was more palpable than ever.

He had caught me ogling him once and gave me a proud smile. "Checking me out?" He had asked.

I didn't deny it but continued to eyeball him. He had quickly put on a shirt and gave me a sensitive kiss. I'd accepted the smooch but pulled him in closer, giving in to the growing urges.

I remembered kissing him with such eagerness. His roommates weren't there, and I craved him so badly. His body landed on top of mine, and we carried on for a few seconds more before he leapt off me.

"Emma, no." His words were short but sweet.

He paced to the other side of the room and squeezed his face in his hands. It was obvious that he wanted the same thing I yearned for in that moment, but his self-control was more developed than mine.

"Let's go." He opened the room door and waited outside of it, letting me know that he was not returning.

I followed him out the door frustrated but once we had sat outside near the surrounding lake for some time, he whispered to me how much he loved me and planned to marry me someday, causing my irritation to retreat.

He went on about not wanting to overwhelm me with the thoughts of it, but that he'd known since he was a boy that he would marry me.

"Your dad asked me that when I was younger. You remember that day you got mad at me for saying you needed a sweater or jacket? That was the day your dad asked me because he knew too."

I sat quietly, now aware of what he and Daddy had spoken about.

"Emma, you're worth the wait. I want to wait to have that part of you. I want it to be special. I want to give you all of me, but not before you're Mrs. Emma Brown."

That was the day that I knew that whenever he did ask me to marry him, I would say yes. I'd be willing to be Mrs. Brown any day of the week if it meant spending forever with him.

I found myself imagining a future with Terry, amazed by how much I loved him already.

"Emma?" Terry awaited my answer on going inside to the repass.

"No, I want to stay out here for a little while longer, but I'll come in soon."

"Okay."

He smiled and went into the house, understanding my need to be alone for a few moments.

I turned to look at Missums who was moving softly in the wind, aware of the traffic of people who had walked past her.

She awaited me and I longed to be alone with her too.

"Well, ole girl, I'm back. I've got so much to tell you." I sat down, released my scrunchie, and let my hair go free.

Marquita Antoine, is a Texas native, who currently resides in Florida with her husband and three children. She holds a Bachelor of Science in Nursing and a Master's Degree in Ministry, with an emphasis on Counseling and Family.
She prides herself on being an active part of her church community and ministering to, loving and being a mentor to women and young people in her life. A passion for experiencing the freedom of God and joy of the Lord is her utmost desire for those she meets. She hopes to identify, inspire and encourage others through her writings.